PRAISE FOR ALISA LYNN VALDÉS

The Dirty Girls Social Club

"The feel of a night out with the girls . . . charming . . . undeniably fun."

—*Miami Herald*

"This lively debut novel . . . reads like the Hispanic version of *Waiting to Exhale*."

—*New York*

"As a guilty pleasure it ranks somewhere between Valrhona chocolate and Jimmy Choo shoes—I simply could not put it down."
—Whitney Otto, author of *How to Make an American Quilt*

"The summer's must-have beach book."

—*Latina*

"A fresh spin on the best-of-friends novel that's funny, touching, and exhilarating. A winner!"
—*New York Times* bestselling author Jennifer Crusie

"The Latina community has a rich new voice, and Valdés-Rodriguez is it."

—Jeffrey Kluger, coauthor of *Lost Moon: The Perilous Voyage of* Apollo 13

"*Dirty Girls* sets out to prove Latina can mean anything—Black, white, rich, poor, Spanish speaking, not Spanish speaking."

—*Miami Herald*

"Valdés-Rodriguez has written an incredible first novel, told in six distinct voices and points of view."

—Library Journal

"In the end, it's the complex, finely drawn characters who make the book work."

—Rocky Mountain News

"A heartfelt, fast-moving, and often funny page-turner."

—Booklist

"This season's most scrumptious book . . . a summer must."

—Advocate

"Those who liked *The Joy Luck Club* or *The Divine Secrets of the Ya-Ya Sisterhood* will enjoy *The Dirty Girls Social Club* . . . It is heartfelt, fast moving, and often funny."

—Oklahoman

"An affecting debut that takes a long, hard, and funny look at life in the US for Latina women . . . an upscale telenovela with well-drawn, charmingly flawed characters from an author who explodes some myths."

—Kirkus Reviews

"Marked by fast-paced dialogue and a pop-culture sensibility, this engaging novel, each section of which is written from a different woman's perspective, carries an unmistakable message."

—Book

"The writing is strong, fluid, and sometimes laugh-out-loud funny."

—Pioneer Press

"Valdés-Rodriguez's compelling characters are enhanced by their racial identities but not at all inaccessible to the non-Hispanic . . . an enjoyable read."

—*San Antonio Express-News*

"Valdés-Rodriguez's novel delivers on the promise of its sexy title with a diverse group of women that defies stereotypes. The book addresses serious questions—prejudice, the difficulty of winning respect from Latino men—but balances them with enough romances . . . to satisfy any chick lit fan. This is a fun, irresistible debut."

—*Publishers Weekly*

Dirty Girls on Top

"The perfect chaser to the *Sex and the City* movie."

—*People*

"Valdés-Rodriguez's follow-up to her 2003 debut, *The Dirty Girls Social Club*, has *Sex and the City* written all over it—in sassy Spanglish. The six sucias return with hilarious and raunchy tales of Latina-tinged love, marriage, and sex told from each character's point of view. A–"

—*Entertainment Weekly*

"A fast-paced, sexy tale."

—*Los Angeles Times*

"*Caliente* is the best word to describe this steamy sequel to *The Dirty Girls Social Club* . . . a madcap, full-of-heart adventure."

—*Redbook*

"If the *Sex and the City* flick leaves you longing for more girl-bonding, then *Dirty Girls on Top* is the olive in the martini . . . this summer's juiciest beach read."

—*Latina*

"*The Dirty Girls Social Club* always demanded a sequel, and here it is."

—*New York Daily News*

"Valdés-Rodriguez . . . has once again written an extraordinary and impressive book. Told in six unique voices, from six unique points of view, her follow-up has a universality about it that makes it, like her first book about the sucias, an important addition to the fields of friendship novels and Latina literature and an excellent choice for fiction collections of all sizes."

—*Library Journal*

"The sequel to *The Dirty Girls Social Club*, about a posse of Latina friends still trying five years later to figure out their careers and love lives—Carrie and friends, but with café con leche."

—*Saint Petersburg Times*

"Passionate and provocative . . . the prose is fast and casual, and the plot moves at a fast clip."

—*Publishers Weekly*

HOLLOW
BEASTS

ALSO BY ALISA LYNN VALDÉS

The Feminist and the Cowboy

The Three Kings

The Husband Habit

Dirty Girls on Top

The Dirty Girls Social Club

Playing with Boys

Make Him Look Good

Haters

HOLLOW BEASTS

ALISA LYNN VALDÉS

THOMAS & MERCER

Published by Thomas & Mercer, Seattle

www.apub.com

Amazon, the Amazon logo, and Thomas & Mercer are trademarks of Amazon.com, Inc., or its affiliates.

ISBN-13: 9781662507175 (hardcover)
ISBN-13: 9781662507168 (paperback)
ISBN-13: 9781662507182 (digital)

Cover design by Ploy Siripant
Cover image: © Matilda Delves / ArcAngel; © CreativeHQ / Shutterstock;
© Kilroy79 / Shutterstock; © Olga_i / Shutterstock;
© Rebeccakarenza / Shutterstock; © robbin lee / Shutterstock

Printed in the United States of America
First edition

HOLLOW
BEASTS

PROLOGUE

Natalia had no paper and no pen. No pencil. Nothing, really. Just her rasping breath and her asthma. Just this hole in the ground where the men kept her. She and the other two. Paola, the taller one with the high cheekbones, who kept talking about how her dad was going to rescue them all. And Celia, who was short and chubby and spoke with an accent and who hugged Natalia and told her everything was going to be fine. Celia, who promised to remember the letter Natalia was writing, here in their strange prison, without paper, pen, pencil. Between gasping coughs, she wrote the letter to her parents in her head and recited it to herself over and over—and, by default, to Paola and Celia too—so that she would not forget a word. She did not speak the story exactly the same way every time, but close enough. Sitting in the dark, on the cold, damp, deep, earthen floor, humid with the stench of their bodily functions—which they kept confined to one part of the hole but which stank up the entire thing nonetheless—Natalia hugged her knees to her chest. She was still wearing only her tangerine-colored swimming suit, a modest one-piece, and the white terry cloth cover-up. Or at least it used to be white. Now it was caked with dirt and mud and blood and sweat and tears and everything else. All the animal things. She rocked a little. Somewhere, she heard something tapping, up above them. A woodpecker, Celia told them. Focus on that sound, of the woodpecker; think of how free it is, that bird. We will be like that again.

Tap, tap, tap.

They were in the woods somewhere, far from civilization. Far from help. Far from home. Natalia rocked and rocked and tried not to scream. Rocked the way crazy people rock in movies about crazy people, she thought. So this is why they do it: because the feelings are so terrible and so huge that you have to move somehow or else they will engulf you, drown you forever. She spoke the words through chattering teeth, and her eyes just stared at the nothingness of the dirt that formed the walls of this dungeon. Nothing to see here but a hole, as though she were already in a coffin and buried. The girl in the well, she thought. That's a thing, isn't it? A meme. A joke. Until they threw you in. Then it wasn't so funny anymore. There was nothing funny about this. Natalia wondered if she would ever laugh again. The two others just watched and listened. She begged them to remember the words to this letter, to tell her parents if she couldn't.

"Tell them I'm sorry. Tell them I love them."

"Don't talk like that," said Celia. "You'll tell them yourself."

"Yeah," said Paola. "We have to stay positive. I'm telling you, my dad's coming."

"Dear Mom and Dad," said Natalia, ignoring them both, coping in the way she was able. "I'm sorry to disappoint you. I didn't mean to."

"Not this again," said Paola, banging her head backward against the dirt.

"Don't," said Celia, placing her hand between Paola's head and the wall.

"Dear Mom and Dad, I'm sorry to disappoint you. I didn't mean to. I was swimming with Christopher, in the pool with the waterslides, and I know you told me to keep an eye on him, but I had to go to the bathroom so bad, and you were both in one of your discussions where you both look angry, and you had those umbrella drinks going, so I didn't want to bother you; plus, Chris is twelve now, not three, and he's a good swimmer now, probably better than me, and he was in the shallow end anyway, and there were, like, a million lifeguards. It was just

2

number one, so I thought I'd be quick. So I just ran to the bathroom real quick, because no one likes you if you're a pool pee-er. There's no excuse to pee in the pool unless you're, like, a baby. Which I'm not.

"I didn't see him there. In the hallway outside the girls' bathrooms. Not when I went in. But he was there when I came out. Standing over by the soda machine. He looked sort of normal, but ugly, and told me one of the Coke bottles was stuck, and he needed my help. He called out to me, to get my attention. 'Hey, kid.' That's what he said. 'Hey, kid, do you speak English?' It was a weird question. I said I did, and he said, 'These days you never know,' like it made him angry. He asked if I could help him by banging on the machine while he tilted it, and I was, like, to myself I thought, I know about stranger danger, but there are people around. So I said, 'I can give you a dollar or whatever for another soda, if you need money.' I held out a dollar bill I'd taken from the pocket of my cover-up. It was from that wad of money Dad won at the casino the day before and split with me and Chris, when he told us not to spend it all in one place. That made the rat man so angry, for me to offer him money. All, like, insulted. He looked around, and when he didn't see anyone, he grabbed me by the hair, and when I tried to scream, he told me he had a gun and that if I made any noise, he would kill me and then he would go and kill my little brother. Christopher. He knew Chris's name. That's what made me think he was serious."

Natalia paused to cough. She was not crying anymore. The other million times she'd told the story, she'd broken down at this part. Now, she was growing numb. Physically numb but also emotionally numb. Nothing made sense. Tap, tap, tap.

"My dad will look for me," said Paola. Natalia noticed she sounded like someone from reality television, with that same kind of spoiled-rich-girl intonation to her speech. "He's the tribal president, and he has a lot of power. A lot. He has his own police force. It's going to be okay."

Natalia held a hand up—not to be rude but to try to keep focused on her letter. It was getting harder to think. She was so thirsty.

"Dear Mom and Dad," Natalia began, again.

"Ugh, don't keep starting over," said Paola.

"Stop saying that to her," Celia told Paola. "She's just scared." Celia touched Natalia's arm and said, "Tell us about them. Your mom and dad."

"My mom is a school principal. My dad sells cars, but he's the manager. Toyotas. He used to be a teacher. That's how they met. But they needed more money than he was making when my brother came along, and so he went into sales."

"I'm sure they're looking for you," said Celia. "It's going to be okay. All right? I promise."

"Unless you drive me crazy, reciting that letter over and over," said Paola. "Then it won't be okay, for me. Until my dad gets here. I know he's coming. I feel it."

"Let her say her letter," said Celia. "What's wrong with you?"

"Fine. Just—does she have to keep starting over? She never finishes it."

Natalia didn't want them to hate her. She'd need them. So she tried to remember where she was. "Okay," she said. "I'll pick up where I left off. Okay?

"I think about it now, and it's obvious I should have screamed and kicked him or whatever, even if he shot me. That gunshot would have gotten everyone's attention, and then he wouldn't have been able to shoot anyone else, maybe. I don't know. I was stupid, and when he told me to go with him, I went with him, because when people poke the end of a gun into your back, you almost always do whatever they say. I hope the resort has video. I hope you're looking for me. I hope the police know.

"He is so ugly, Mom. And Dad. Not just on the outside, where he looks like a skinny drowned rat, but on the inside. He smelled bad, like he never brushes his teeth, and his car smelled bad, like the cages at an animal shelter. He had it parked right outside the back of the restaurant.

He made me walk across the hotel lobby with him, and people looked at us like they knew something was weird, because how many freaky rat men do you think should be walking around with a sixteen-year-old girl in a bathing suit? But nobody said anything or did anything. I think about it now, and I'm, like, so pissed at myself. I could have just yelled that I was being taken against my will, but that gun. All poking in my back. I didn't want him shooting anyone else. I was in a daze, like. I couldn't think. I didn't understand anything that was happening. He said he knew where my parents lived and that he would kill you guys if I tried to get away. I don't know how he could know that, because we were there on vacation; I see that now. Like, how would that guy ever in a million years know where we lived, all the way up in Reno, when we were just down in Las Vegas for a family vacation? It's stupid. So I'm sorry. I was stupid. I was not thinking straight."

"Don't say that," said Celia. "You did what anyone would have done. Same as me. Same as Paola."

Natalia rocked and coughed, and up above, they heard the sounds of the men's boots as they gathered around the opening of the hole. Someone moved one of the branches away, and Natalia heard the men muttering about taking one of them out. Deciding which one.

"Dear Mom and Dad," Natalia began, again.

"Here we go again," said Paola.

"Stop it," said Celia.

"The young one," yelled the rat man, and the others laughed. "She coughs like a seventy-year-old smoker. Maybe Travis can finally catch one. She's slow."

Natalia rocked and tried to remember where she was in the story. The part where he'd pushed her up against the car with his body, like they were boyfriend and girlfriend or something, and pulled zip ties tight around her wrists, binding her hands together? Or was it when he'd told her to sit in the passenger seat like a good girl, "like we're the best of friends," or else he'd open the door when the car was moving and

5

throw her "happy ass" out into moving traffic? Or the rest area, in the middle of the night, when he'd said he was sick of hearing her cry and let her have some of his warm Mountain Dew before he'd forced her into the trunk, with the cans of oil and the spare tire? How she almost suffocated back there, how she focused her mind and went over the dance-team moves she'd learned last year, tried to remember all of them, imagined herself at the football games again, remembered the way Mom and Dad beamed at her from the stands with their faces painted blue and white and gold to show their support for her high school.

The rest of the branches were removed, and Natalia and Celia blinked against the brightness of the midday sun. Nothing but forest all around them. Natalia did not even know what state they were in, only that the rat man had driven for, like, three days to get here.

"Dear Mom and Dad," she said, only now it wasn't just her teeth that chattered. It was her whole body.

"You," said the ringleader, pointing at Natalia with his pistol. He was tall and powerful, clean cut, and the others called him General Zeb. He reminded her of the youth minister at her church, one of those conservative guys who tries to look hip. "Climb up."

He unfurled a rope ladder into the hole. Natalia rocked and hugged and coughed.

"Dear Mom and Dad," she said.

"Get her up here," shouted General Zeb, "or I shoot you all, and we start over."

"Come on," said Celia. She shook Natalia. "You should go."

Natalia snapped out of it. She looked at Celia. "What do they want?"

"I don't know. But you have a better chance of running and hiding up there than down here. If you see a chance, use it. Run, Natalia."

"Remember my letter," the girl said, and Celia squeezed her hand.

"I will. I'll remember it. I'll tell them. Except I won't need to. You'll get away. You're going home."

"Okay," said Natalia. She unfolded her aching, frozen body and went to the ladder. Lack of food and water had made her weak. With her heart hammering faster than a hummingbird's, she climbed, one rung at a time, until her head was out of the hole. When he'd brought her here, it was the middle of the night. She had not seen much then, just a fire and some tents. It had smelled like beer and barbecue. They'd cut the zip ties, looked her over, three men, given her a sip or two of water from a canteen; and then she had been thrown in the hole, down maybe fifteen or twenty feet, into the dark.

Now she saw the camp in the light of day. Towering pine trees, a thick forest in every direction, mountains on every side. The men were all dressed in camouflage, with their faces painted green and black, and wore bright-orange vests. Hunting vests, she thought. Her own dad liked to take her and Christopher fishing in the Truckee watershed. She knew enough to recognize that these men were dressed to kill something. A dirty white truck, parked in the woods. The middle of nowhere. She also saw guns, lots of guns. There was a Mexican flag nailed to the trunk of a tree, with many bullet holes in it. She also saw a long plastic folding table set up, with electrical components and wires on it. They were building something. Then, behind her, she saw the small, sad, dead deer, hung by its back feet, head down, swinging ever so slightly from a branch as blood dripped from a hole that had been punctured in its neck. The blood was dripping into a white plastic bucket. Tap, tap, tap. So this was where the sound was coming from.

She began to cry, a low, terrified whimpering.

"You like that?" asked General Zeb as he and the rat man pulled her up and out of the hole. He gestured toward the deer.

"No," said Natalia.

"Deer are delicious," said the rat man.

"Shut up," the third man, a bald man, told the rat man.

"I want to go home," said Natalia.

"Well," said General Zeb, with a grin, "so long as you're faster than that deer was, you might have a chance."

1

The thing about severed heads was, they never smelled good—not even when they were fresh, which this one *wasn't*, and especially not on a warm Friday afternoon in June, which this *was*. Nothing else around could mask its stench either. Not the astringent breeze washing through the boughs of countless ponderosa pines. Not the petrichor of the dark summer thunderstorm moving toward this mountain. Not even, it turned out, New Mexico game warden Eloy Atencio's famously excessive Old Spice cologne.

A macho and mustachioed seventy-five, the sweet-smelling conservation officer, five foot three in his boots, had once been stout and strong as a bull rider. These days he strained the seams of his gray-and-black uniform the way a cooked sausage strained its skin. There was a good chance he would rather have been home with a bowl of his wife Marta's red chile posole than prying the rotting head from the bed of a rusted white pickup on an old logging road in the San Isidro National Forest, but he didn't complain. With the strength of a much younger man, he just swung that head up and out like it was a pailful of wet adobe and, holding it by one antler, lugged it toward his own New Mexico Fish and Wildlife Department truck—a black four-door Chevy Silverado 2500, with the department's silver star-inside-a-circle emblem stamped across the front doors. All this commotion worried the flies. They fizzed up out of the buck's dead eyes, orbited a bit, then burrowed in again to snack.

Standing nearby were two other people. The first was a tall bald man whose neck was wider than his pointy head, as though the whole combination were a large white bullet jabbed through the neck of his shirt and jacket. He wore an aggressive overkill of mismatched tactical camo gear, was maybe thirty-five years old, six three or four, impatient and blustery. The second person, the one watching this first man like a mother crow watches a hawk near her nest, was Jodi Luna, a game warden in training. She was a full foot shorter than he was but more than ready to pull her state-issued Glock .40-caliber pistol out of its holster if he tried to get cute. At forty-five, through sheer force of willpower and in defiance of an arthritic knee, Jodi was mostly muscle and still weighed what she'd weighed twenty years ago: 124 pounds. Her long hair, dark with a few silver strands, was gathered into a thick, straight ponytail she'd pulled through the opening in the back of her gray uniform's ball cap. Six months earlier, she had passed every physical and mental test with flying colors to become the oldest recruit ever named a conservation officer in the state of New Mexico. It was a shocking midlife career change for the former poetry professor but surprised no one who actually knew her.

Jodi was fiercely protective of Officer Atencio, not only because he was her mentor, and elderly, on his last day of work before retirement, but also because he was one of the thirteen uncles and aunts Jodi had grown up with here in Rio Truchas County in central Northern New Mexico. Her mother's oldest brother, Atencio was one of the more well-read and freethinking people in that generation of the family, which wasn't saying much, considering the rest of them were content with just one book, read mostly on Sundays. Atencio's relative worldliness was all the more remarkable for the fact that he almost never left Rio Truchas County at all, other than his weekly trips south to the big public library in downtown Santa Fe.

Atencio had mentored Jodi through her field training for the past six months without once asking her why she'd left her seemingly totally unrelated life as a celebrated poet and academic in Boston to move back to this vast but sparsely populated county she'd sworn at eighteen she never wanted to see again. He'd been the one to teach her to hunt and fish when she was a little girl, and he knew her talent and aptitude for all things outdoors. He knew her passion for protecting the wilderness. He'd been worried the department might find some outsider to take his place once he retired, which was why he was doing it ten years too late. Even though Jodi wasn't his ideal choice, she was family, and local, and she cared. It was she who was slated to take over his job as the only game warden for this vast five-thousand-square-mile territory, after today.

"This used to be a free country, you know," griped the poacher.

Jodi jutted her delicate chin toward the Confederate flag decal that took up at least half the rear window of his truck, narrowed her intelligent, dark-brown eyes, and said, "Your flag there clearly indicates otherwise."

Atencio grunted a bit more as he chucked the trophy head into the bed of his truck, a feat he managed to accomplish by spinning himself around like a shot put Olympian a few times first.

"Pues, ticktock, ticktock," he grumbled to Jodi as he tapped the face of his wristwatch. "Dale un ticket al maldito gringo ese, ya, sobrina."

This translated roughly to, *Give the damn gringo a ticket already, niece.*

The poacher scoffed at the words he could not understand and bucked his head as though someone had just told him a joke he found offensive.

"This is America," he said. "Speak English."

"I am pleased you know where you are," Jodi replied. "Because here in America, it is against the law in every language to hunt trophy bucks in June."

"Just trying to feed my family," he said.

"Planning to feed them that mount-worthy trophy head, were you?"

"We seen the rest of the animal discarded up the hill," chimed in Atencio. "Save your lies for your mama, boy."

"Don't you talk about my mama," said the poacher.

"I agree. Let's change the subject," said Jodi. "Let's talk about how I need to see your driver's license."

"It's in the glove box," he said.

"Well then, you better get it out," said Jodi.

"But go slow, and keep your hands where we can see them," said Atencio, unlocking and unholstering his own sidearm now.

Jodi tried not to think about the statistics. Being a game warden was the most dangerous job in American law enforcement, because game wardens (also called conservation officers) worked alone, other than when they were training their replacements. They worked in the remote wilderness, often in places without radio or cell phone service, at the mercy of sometimes unreliable satellite phones. Their suspects tended to be armed poachers who lacked respect for life and the law and whose general credo was "no witness, no crime." It wasn't that big a leap for guys like that to want to level up by bagging them a game warden. It happened more than people realized. At the last count, game wardens were seven times more likely to be stabbed or shot by an assailant than city cops. Not a lot of people knew that, of course. Then again, not a lot of people knew game wardens even existed, and they tended to confuse them with forest rangers. Only about 5 percent of Americans older than sixteen hunted anymore, and just 15 percent went fishing—and most of them only once.

The poacher came out with a blue nylon wallet. Jodi saw that there was an emblem hand drawn on the side of the wallet in what appeared to be gold glitter pen. It was a pyramid with an eye in it, like you might find on a dollar bill.

"Here you go." The poacher just glared at her with eyes the unsteady blue of gas flames, dangling the license between his pointer and middle fingers.

Jodi took the license with her left hand, keeping her right hand next to her pistol.

"Travis Eugene Lee," she read aloud. "From Mesa, Arizona. Wait right here, Travis."

Atencio nodded to let Jodi know he'd keep an eye on the poacher, and she went back to their truck to run his license and write out the citations. This patch of forest had only spotty radio, cell, and internet, however. And she found herself unable to run much of anything. Guess it was his lucky day.

She tore the citations from the pad, returned to the white truck, and passed them to Lee, along with his license. He crumpled them up and tossed them into the greasy cab of his truck, along with all the fast-food bags and Coca-Cola cans.

"No pude realizar la verificación de antecedentes de él porque no había internet," Jodi said to Atencio, letting him know she was unable to run the background check.

"No estoy sorprendido," he replied: *I am not surprised.*

"What's with the Mexicans?" asked Lee, mostly to himself, as he got back in his driver's seat. "Everyone else simulates. Not them. They never simulate."

He was about to close his door, but Jodi put her hand out to stop it from shutting. "What did you say?"

He was not about to back down. He grinned and centered himself toward her, proud. "I said, Why the hell can't you Mexicans simulate like everybody else? You want to speak Spanish, go back to Mexico."

"Vamos," Atencio said to Jodi, wheeling his hand to tell her to stop messing around. "Hemos terminado aquí, ya. Vamos. Él no vale la pena. Tengo hambre." *We're done here, already. Let's go. He's not worth it. I'm hungry.*

"The word you're looking for is 'assimilate,' Travis," said Jodi, staring him down with equal and greater anger than he had. "Some people might find it ironic that a man who cannot master the English language is lecturing a fully bilingual woman, with several published books in that language, about how she is supposed to speak English."

"Well, good for you." The poacher was caught off guard by this and responded with childish petulance.

"One more thing before you go, Travis, as I can only assume your understanding of United States history and the law is as shaky as your mastery of the English language. There is no official language in the United States. What's more, you're not in Arizona anymore. You're in New Mexico now. The 1848 Treaty of Guadalupe Hidalgo, signed when Mexico ceded California, Arizona, New Mexico, Nevada, Utah, Texas, and Colorado as territories to the United States, after the Mexican-American War, guaranteed our right to speak Spanish in all seven of those places. Six of the seven names of those states are Spanish words, Travis—and the seventh isn't English. It was Ute. The city where you live? Mesa, Arizona? These are both Spanish words. So if you are really going to take this whole 'speak English' crusade seriously, you are going to either have to move to New York City or lobby the state legislature to change the names of almost all the places in Arizona."

Lee tried again to close his door, and again, Jodi stopped him.

"I'm not done yet. Here in New Mexico, Travis, we Hispanos are the majority. Our state constitution has not one, not two, but three different provisions that protect our right to speak Spanish. There are a lot of little towns up here where everyone still speaks mostly Spanish, including most of my own extended family. Not a one of us has *ever* crossed any United States border. That border, in 1912, was dragged over us, like a too-tight shirt."

Lee looked Jodi up and down like she was for sale and sucked his teeth to dismiss everything she had just said. "You done now, honey?"

Jodi took her pistol out of the holster and, keeping it pointed down at the ground, stepped ever so slightly closer to Lee. Part of her knew that this was reckless, that her temper was getting the better of her, again.

"Sobrina, no," said Atencio. "Vamos."

She ignored her uncle, many years of pent-up rage from the classier versions of this same ignorance she'd faced in college and, later, academia, fueling her. She put her face up close to Lee's, then smiled in a cold and controlled way she could see finally scared him.

"Despite my sweet disposition and appreciation for the important ecological role of bees, Travis, my name is not *honey*." She locked eyes with him and let him hear the click of her releasing the safety on her pistol. "It's Jodi. But only to my friends. For future reference, you can just call me Officer Luna, ma'am, or, as long as you're in *my* state, Agente Luna, Señora."

Jodi took a couple of steps back, and Lee slammed the door of his pickup. He opened his window and glowered at her.

"You will be sorry you ever met me," he said.

"Already am," she replied.

Travis blasted some death metal now, gunned his engine, then peeled out in a cloud of dust. Jodi and Atencio stood side by side and watched him road-rage away. Atencio sighed as he placed a hand upon her shoulder.

"I admire your convictions, and your passion," he said. "Hell, I used to drink tequila with Reies Lopez Tijerina, sabes. But all this?" He gestured to the forest, and their uniforms, and the truck. "This isn't some slam poem contest, Jodi. This here is real life."

"You think I don't know that?" she asked, shrugging out of his grip. "You smell like deer guts. Get away."

"Ay, tú, all sensitive to deer guts. And she thinks she wants to be a game warden." Atencio took the sunglasses out of his shirt pocket and put them on as he took a few sore, mincing steps back to the driver's door.

They both got inside and sat in the silence of the cab for a moment before Atencio said, "I think you better learn to control that temper of yours, or it is going to get you into a hell of a lot of trouble."

"I'm fine," said Jodi. She'd heard this same kind of thing all her life.

"Some of these people you meet out here, they're crazy and dangerous."

"Believe it or not, there were plenty of dangerous and crazy people in academia too."

Atencio laughed as he started the truck's engine. "You have told me. But the people you meet out here, they don't want to deny you tenure. They want to leave you in the leaves for coyote food. Your best weapon ain't your gun, m'ija. It's good manners, that pretty smile of yours, and charm."

"Yeah, yeah, I get it." Jodi fastened the seat belt as she rode shotgun, quietly pleased that come Monday, her uncle would go back to 1972 or wherever it was he lived, and she could fight all the battles if she wanted to.

Come Monday, she'd be the one driving this truck.

2

The following Sunday, Ivan and Yvonne—both pronounced "eee-VON," both from Scarsdale, New York, both twenty years old, and, even *they* had to admit, uncommonly good looking—left the comfort of their stylish refurbished Mercedes Sprinter van, "I, Van, the Great-ful," to hike to the beautiful natural hot springs near Lower Fresita Peak in the San Isidro National Forest in Rio Truchas County, New Mexico. These particular hot springs, super out of the way and off the proverbial beaten path, were getting increasingly popular among their competitors. Yvonne had first seen the springs in that evil bitch Taylor's posts, and as she'd told Ivan, she was not going to let that fake-ass whorebag win. The whole area had its own hashtag community now, #SecretRockies. Everyone who was anyone in van life was always scouring the planet for the most gorgeous places to take relaxed shots in, where no one else had ever been before, and Ivan and Yvonne 100 percent needed to get some pics at the Lower Fresita Hot Springs, too, and, if they could, find somewhere else new around here that no one had seen yet.

The couple were in their eighth month of van life and had amassed more than two million followers to their @I_Van_The_Great Instagram account, as well as some excellent sponsorships. It certainly didn't hurt that they looked like a boho Ken and Barbie and that the van was a picture of perfection with its neohippie chicness, all beiges and guitars and hanging plants and wood, with just the right amount of warm burnt orange thrown in. To keep the momentum up, they'd gotten strategic with the help of a professional television producer, Barry, hired by Yvonne's dad once she'd started making nearly as much money as her uglier older sister, the boring CPA, did. Barry had crunched the numbers and found that photos of otherwise willowy and pretty girl next door Yvonne's amazingly tanned bubble butt, threaded with a colorful thong, floating in some natural body of water as she, in a sun hat, gazed off into the distance at some bomb-ass view, were the ones that got the most likes and shares. It was super basic, and Ivan and Yvonne knew that, and they were not, like, stupid and shallow. They were pragmatic, though, and giving the people what they wanted meant that they could self-finance their continued super-awesome travels, without continually asking their parents for money they seemed to think would have been better spent going to college, but that was just because old people did not realize that college would not help them earn more in a year than they were earning now, and everything you wanted to learn you could totally learn on YouTube anyways. Being fit and having a nice body were just signs that you were doing a clean and ethical vegan life right, too, and a big part of their production involved showing themselves preparing beautiful meals at the cooktop in their van. If people wanted to have sex with them, well, whatever. Sex sells, people were animals, and that was absolutely not their fault.

The sun was sinking toward the faraway horizon when they finally arrived at the secluded springs around eight in the evening. Happily, there was no one there but them. Yvonne had told Ivan she would just die and then kill him if there was, like, some fat old man naked in there.

Ivan and Yvonne stared at the woods, the clearing, the flowers and view, overjoyed not so much because it was beautiful and spoke to their souls but more because the whole setup would make for some kick-ass pics. There were three separate natural hydrothermal pools, with the biggest and most photogenic one being in the center, overlooking the entire mountain and valley below. This place was perfection. It was Eden. Wild strawberries grew everywhere, and the fruits were so red and so tiny and so cute; they'd make for great photos! It was amazing how far you could see in every direction from up here, and even though it wasn't cloudy or raining where they were—thank God—they could absolutely see two massive storms in the far-off distance, throwing down lightning bolts on the horizon. With the fiery colors streaking the sky, and the stars just coming out, and the sunset, and the storms, the photo potential was off the charts. Ivan would use burst mode and video to get some of that lightning. This was going to be amazeballs, and that was all.

As Ivan, who studied photography in his free time, set up the tripod and collapsible photo reflectors, Yvonne stripped down to her tangerine bikini and yellow floppy hat with the wide brim. She fixed her makeup, which was meant to look like no makeup, and crimped her long hair a bit with her fingers. Then she eased herself into the natural hot spring, which wasn't as hot as it could have been and smelled a little bit like sulfur, truth be told, but nature didn't exactly have an on-off button for volcanic action, so. As long as it looked amazing, they were golden. Careful not to mess up her hair or makeup, she found a good spot at the far edge of the pool and floated, butt up, with her head turned away from the camera, gazing out at the storms.

"Good," said Ivan. "But, like, maybe a foot or two to the right from there. Yeah. Like that! Stay right there, babe. I'm almost done."

It was then that Ivan screamed in a way Yvonne had never heard, not even when he fell off a ladder that time in Maine. He sounded like a wounded dinosaur mixed with a murdered baby. It was bloodcurdling and extremely upsetting, and when she spun around in shock to see what the heck was happening, half of her face got wet.

"Oh my fucking God!" shrieked Ivan, who was stooped over like someone had kicked him in the chest. He had dropped the camera and the tripod. One hand was pressed against his cheek and the other pointed at the ground near his feet, where long grass and wildflowers grew.

"What's wrong?"

19

"It's a motherfucking hand!" Ivan backed away, shaking his head.

"A what?"

"A. Fucking. Hand. A human *hand*. There's a human hand right there."

"Where?"

"On the ground. Under those very lovely flowers, in the middle of those strawberries."

"Like, coming out of the ground like a zombie hand?" Yvonne paddled across the natural pool to get a closer look but still couldn't see anything.

"No. Like, totally by itself, on top of the ground. Like, somebody cut that shit off, and it's right there."

"Are you sure?"

"Yes, I'm sure. Why do you always have to question me about everything?"

"I wasn't questioning you!"

"Asking me 'Are you sure?' is literally a question that is questioning me, Yvonne."

"Sorry. But sometimes there are weird mushrooms that can look like body parts. See if it's a mushroom."

"It is not a fucking mushroom! It is wearing nail polish and a ring."

"Seriously?"

"Look at it for yourself, if you don't believe me!"

"Fine. Hand me a towel."

Yvonne toweled off and joined Ivan in the grass. She wrinkled her nose when she saw the hand, and she blinked a bunch of times in a row, like maybe that could make it go away.

"Gross," she said.

"Gross?" he asked her, looking incredulous.

"I mean, yeah. It is totally gross, and it is totally ruining our shoot."

"Is that all you have to say?" he asked.

"I mean, it's sad, I guess. And creepy as fuck."

"It's not a prop, Yvonne. It's a real hand."

"I understand that."

"How can you be so calm?" he asked her.

"Well, what do you want me to do? Scream like a little girl, like you did?"

"That was unnecessary," he said.

"I mean, it's not going to help anything if I start screaming, is it?"

"No."

"So. Now what?" asked Yvonne.

"I mean, we have to call the cops."

Yvonne shrugged, like maybe they didn't.

"Right?" Ivan asked. "We have to call the cops. We found a hand."

"Yeah, totally," she said, unconvinced. "But what about the photo shoot?"

"I mean, I don't know."

"It might not even be a real hand," she said.

"It looks real."

"But what if it's not, and we don't take the shots, and then Taylor totally wins? Again. She's at three million now. That's a whole million more than me."

"Us."

"Us. Sorry."

"I can't believe that's what you're worried about right now. Followers."

"I mean, it's our job, Ivan. It's not about my ego. It's about our paycheck. I'm not trying to be a jerk here. I am trying to balance our personal professional needs with our civic responsibilities. We came all the way here. Gas is expensive. We promised our sponsors."

"Fine. So. What do you want to do?"

"I mean, we will absolutely call the cops. After we take the shots."

"You're—I don't even know what to say," said Ivan.

"I mean, it's not like it's going anywhere." She gestured to the hand. "It's just sitting there."

Ivan sighed.

"We can be quick," she said. "It's just there's a lot of money riding on this, as you know."

"I know."

They hesitated, both of them thinking about all the planning and money it had taken them to get here, about how they had a deadline to meet or they'd piss off their sponsors, and how they did not have a plan B for this shoot.

"We have everything almost ready," she said, in full sales mode with him now.

"Yeah, and tomorrow there will probably be, like, a ton of cops up here, and we won't even get to take the pictures at all."

"And that would be no bueno."

"No bueno."

"Let's just take some pics really fast. Like, in and out. We can run back down to the van."

"We can sprint. But there's no reason to not take advantage of the storm and the sunset—I mean, look at the light!"

"We came all the way here for this. And it sucks about that hand and that girl, and we will totally do the right thing, but this is also a job for us."

"And we can't screw up our job."

Ivan resumed setting up the tripod, and Yvonne, after repairing her makeup that was meant to look like no makeup, lowered herself into the lukewarm sulfuric water, for the perfect photo of her butt.

3

On Monday morning, Jodi woke at 5:29 a.m., one minute before her phone's alarm, configured to sound off as one of her favorite Lucinda Williams songs, was scheduled to ring. Her small L-shaped house, hand built with adobe and topped with a corrugated pitched metal roof, was nestled high in the Valle Ovejitas, a narrow alpine meadow cut in two by Ovejitas Creek, which ran down its middle. Three sides of the meadow were walled in by mountains, with the third side ending in a mesa that overlooked a vast expanse of high desert.

The house had been built in 1860 by her great-great-great-grand-father, Elias Chavez San Juan de Bautista, who also planted the original surrounding apple, pear, and apricot orchards. The place had been rebuilt and maintained by subsequent generations, some better than others, up until it fell into Jodi's father's hands when she was a kid, and froze, stylistically, in 1985, as he focused most of his energy on building the much larger Rancho Atencio cattle-and-sheep ranch he'd married into and then renamed Luna Land & Cattle. Until Jodi moved in two years ago with her daughter, then twelve, the house, referred to by the family as "the old Bautista cabin," had mostly sat unused by anyone but bats and mice and was used primarily for weekend camping getaways and hunting and fishing trips. The bones of the house were strong, though, and it felt solid now that she'd put a new roof on it last year. The only other major renovations she'd had time for had been deep cleaning and repairing the gutters, replanting the house's many food and flower gardens, ripping out the orange shag carpeting to reveal the beautiful pale matte pine floors beneath, and replastering the thick adobe walls a soothing creamy white. The kitchen and bathrooms still needed updating, but everything worked, and for now, that was all that mattered. Behind the house stood a large brown barn and a circle pen, and next to those were several sheds of varying sizes, which held all the equipment needed to run a small farm. To the left of the house and barn was a metal detached garage, heated and insulated, with its own small kitchen, large enough to house several trucks and home, at the moment, to a compact utility tractor and an all-terrain vehicle.

Before the alarm had a chance to come on, Jodi dismissed it with a swipe of her phone screen and snuggled in for just five more minutes beneath the plain white goose-down comforter, enjoying the earthen scent of home. The bed was the same one she had shared with her husband, Graham Livingston, back when he was still alive and they lived in a six-bedroom white colonial house on a cul-de-sac outside Andover. With its delicate Victorian-style cherrywood posts, the bed was a stylistic mismatch for this sturdy old rustic house made of mud and straw bales, and the only thing she'd kept from her former life. When Jodi put her nose just right, in certain places on that mattress, she could still smell Graham's curly brown hair. When she lay awake at night, staring up at the posts, she could remember all those times she'd held on to them as he moved in his powerful, graceful way above her. She was not quite ready to give the bed up, yet, just as she was not able to let go of the feeling that they were still married.

Jodi reached out to tap the lamp on the bedside table and rolled onto one side to look at the framed photo she kept of Graham there. In it, Graham, tanned and windswept, paddled a bright-yellow sea kayak through the dark, agitated waters off the coast of Nantucket, minutes before storm clouds lashed through. He was like that, always teetering gleefully at the edge of some dangerous thing, needing the possibility of death or disaster to make him feel alive. She'd snapped the image on her phone, taken from her own rocking kayak, on one of their many trips to his family's summer home on Cape Cod. He'd taken a pause in his latest daredevil action to give her one of his magnetic smiles. Those perfect white teeth were what had drawn her to him the first time she saw him, in their shared freshman seminar class at Harvard. Well, the teeth and the mischievous sparkling blue eyes. And the dimple. And the cleft chin. And the fact that he'd liked her, in spite of her enormous imposter syndrome. All of it.

"I love you," she told the photo, kissing her fingertips before pressing them against the glass. "Wish me luck."

After bathing in the old claw-foot tub in the master bath, she dressed in the uniform she had ironed the night before: black pants, sports bra, undershirt, bulletproof vest, black T-shirt, slate-gray button-down, and black ball cap. Jodi then tiptoed in thick athletic socks down the hallway from the back of the house toward the front, passing her daughter's closed bedroom door and then the open guest room slash home office along the way. Jodi kept both sets of her work boots—the black cowboy boots and the black lace-up steel-toed hiking boots—next to the metal gun locker in the house's entry closet. She was careful, as she prepared a pot of strong New Mexico piñon coffee, to be quiet so that Mila could sleep in. Teenagers needed rest, and it was summer vacation.

As the pot brewed, she slipped on her cowboy boots and went out into the chilly morning to let Juana out of her enclosure, and to tend to the morning chores that came along with owning your own chickens and horses. At this altitude, mornings often hovered around freezing, even in the summer. As Jodi worked, Juana, her powerful seventy-five-pound brown-and-black Belgian Malinois, often mistaken for a German shepherd, with a K-9 police dog certification, ran around sniffing everything on the ten-acre homestead. Though the dog had plenty of water in her enclosure, she preferred her morning drink to come straight from the clear cold flow of the Ovejitas Creek, fed all year round by springs and high snowpack on the surrounding Ovejas Mountains. Jodi got the dog as a puppy, and they had both gone through their training together. People said dogs were man's best friend, but in this case, a dog, Juana, was a woman's best friend, and there were times Jodi swore, looking into the soulful creature's golden-colored eyes, that they must have known each other in some past life or something.

Juana was first to hear the minivan crunching its way up the long, rough dirt road that stretched a half mile from the state highway to the locked gate to Jodi's property, an acre away from the house. The dog began to bark, but Jodi silenced her with a hand gesture and the word *Halt*. Like most police dogs educated in the United States, Juana had been trained in German, and it just so happened that *halt* was the same in English too.

"*Hier*," Jodi commanded the dog, meaning *here*, as she headed toward the broad front porch of the house to await the arrival of the expected visitor beneath its eaves, which were hung with bright-red chile ristras and hanging pots of flowering geraniums.

The brown minivan belonged to the Our Lady of La Trappe Monastery, a secluded rural abbey nestled along the banks of the Chama River, thirty-seven miles northwest of here, a stone's throw from the Colorado border. Though the monks who lived there were dedicated to prayer and study, they were best known by the heathens in the region for their tasty craft beers. Trappists had a long and storied tradition of brewing Bockbier as a way to raise funds, and those at La Trappe did it well enough, and with enough marketing savvy, to have generated high demand for their products in the finest gourmet food shops and restaurants in the American Southwest. This explained the TIPSY MONK BEER logo that had been professionally wrapped across the van's sides, and the fact that its driver, Friar Oscar Luna, thirty-five years old, short, dark, and handsome enough to have pursued a career in acting if he had not chosen instead to be a priest, exited the vehicle wearing his chocolate-colored robe and sandals but carrying a freshly bottled six-pack of Enkel, or what Jodi referred to as the Pope's pilsner.

"I see you brought me breakfast," said Jodi.

"¡Buenos días, hermana!" Oscar smiled and held his arms out for a hug as he approached the steps up to the porch, more like a guy who'd just joined a great party than a man who had come to spend the day watching his working, widowed sister's teenage daughter.

"How are you?" she asked as they embraced.

"It's a beautiful day to be alive!" he replied, coming out of the hug to kneel down and pet Juana, who, like all animals he came across, was magnetically drawn to Oscar and had trusted him from the moment she first saw him. Jodi would never forget the first time a bird landed in his hand, just because he held it out. He was two years old. She suspected, in secret, that her brother might have been some kind of weird saint.

"¿Y tú?" he asked her. "You ready for your first day as the big boss, or what?"

"Ready as I'll ever be," she said. "Had your coffee yet?"

"Pues, sí, but I am always ready for more coffee," he said, and they went inside. Jodi poured herself a camo travel mug of simple black coffee and prepared Oscar's in a thick pottery mug, just the way he liked it, with heavy cream, two tablespoons of sugar, and a dash of cinnamon powder. Her brother refused to accept payment for helping her with Mila—which he had done as a nearly full-time job these past two years as she went back to school for her fourth college degree, this one in biology, and attended the police academy. She knew she could never have made this job switch without his support, so she tried to do whatever else she could to make his life more pleasant.

"Gracias," he said as he took the cup and sat down at the rustic pine dining table that served as the line of demarcation between the kitchen and the living area. "¿Y la princesa? Still asleep?"

"Of course," she said as she set the to-go cup on the entry table, opened the closet, and began to put on her duty belt and all its assorted accoutrements, each with its own holster—expandable baton, extra ammunition magazines, bear spray, handcuffs, Glock, and Leatherman multitool. "I know you just got here, but I want to head out a little early. Make a good impression on my first day flying sola."

"Do what you gotta do," he said.

"Call me if you need anything," she said. "Hope you two have a good day."

———

Jodi got Juana situated on her blanket on the front passenger seat, then settled herself behind the wheel. She flipped on the two police radios—one for her department's dispatch out of Santa Fe, the other for the state police dispatch for the northern part of the state. All was quiet, for the moment.

She was about to radio out a 10-8—the message letting dispatchers know that she was on duty—and had just put the truck into drive when Oscar came flying out of the house, waving his arms. He had two bottles of water, one in each hand. She pressed the button to whir her automatic window down.

"Jodi," he said, breathless in a dramatic sort of way. "I thought you might need these."

"You know I always have a case of water in the truck," she said. "What do you really want, Oscar? You act like I've never met you or something."

"Okay." He smiled sheepishly. "You caught me."

"What's on your mind?" she asked, knowing him well enough to tell he wanted to say something but didn't want her to get mad if he did.

"If you don't mind—I'd like to say a little prayer over you before you go."

Jodi tried not to roll her eyes as the engine idled and the static from the radios crackled. She'd renounced any formal religion long ago, and usually they steered clear of locking antlers about it.

"I know, I know," said Oscar. "You lost your religion. But I didn't. So, please. Do it for me?"

"Fine," she said. He came to her at the door, making the sign of the cross over himself, then over her. "Dearest Heavenly Father," he said as Juana looked on. "In your divine mercy, please grant your almighty protection to this brave woman, Officer Jodilynn Luciana Livingston Luna, today, on her first day of work as a solo game warden. Please unite her safely with her family after her duty is done. I also call on you, O Holy Archangel Michael, for your special protection of my one and only sister. In the name of the Father, the Son, and the Holy Spirit, in Jesus's name, I pray."

He bowed his head, and Jodi fought back tears. The church had given her many reasons to despise it, but it was still a powerful part of her, with her having been raised by devout Catholic parents in a devout Catholic town founded by their devout Catholic antecedents, who'd come there from Spain in the sixteenth century to show their devotion to their version of God by massacring countless Native Americans and taking away much of their land. It was hard, for Jodi, to reconcile this complicated part of her family's history in this region, and though many Native Americans had married into their lines along the way (the Spanish settlers did not bring many women with them), learning about the true history of this place had left her feeling guilty about embracing any attachment to a faith that had terrorized so many.

"Thank you, Oscar," she said, clearing her throat and slipping her polarized sunglasses on, even though she might not need them until she was on the road.

"I hope you have an uneventful day," he said.

But destiny had other plans, as it turned out. At that precise moment, the department's longtime dispatcher, Becky McCarthy, put out a call specifically for Jodi.

"Luna, you up and at 'em yet, doll?"

Jodi picked up the radio microphone and pressed the button to reply. "Yep. I'm here. Good morning, Miss Becks."

"Good morning, hon. I know I promised you one of Cata's breakfast burritos first thing this morning here at the office, but I'm afraid that's going to have to wait. I need you to swing by Lower Fresita Hot Springs on your way in."

"What's up?"

"You know the glampers that have been infesting the area lately? Well, couple of them called this morning to say they found a human hand up there."

"Please tell me they didn't touch it."

"They said they left it there."

"And where are they?"

"Still at the campgrounds halfway down Old Agate Mine Road. But impatient to get going. They apologized for not calling last night but said they were so tired when they got back down the mountain they just fell asleep."

"Fell asleep? After finding a severed hand?"

"Kids today. Desensitized, I guess."

"Yeah, well, we'll see."

"Thanks, hon. I'll keep the burritos warm for you."

"See you later."

Jodi set the radio microphone down in its holder and turned to smile at her horrified brother.

"Is it too late for you to go back to being a poetry teacher?" he asked.

"Afraid so," she said, taking one of the toothpicks from the box Atencio had left in one of the cup holders and slipping it between her lips. "Don't worry. I'll be fine."

4

With Juana's nose to help, it wasn't long before Jodi was squatting down in the tall grass, squinting through her sunglasses at a dismembered hand next to Lower Fresita Hot Springs. The hand was palm up in a strawberry patch, the fingers curled into the palm in death. Chipped pink polish still graced the broken nails, which seemed to have put up a hell of a fight. There was also a ring on the middle finger, nothing expensive, just a sterling-silver band made of little stars all stuck together. The hand was small but not a child's. A woman's hand, too discolored at this point to tell exactly what color the skin might have been. Jodi took some photos with her phone and looked around a bit more. Juana led her to some spots of blood on the leaves and grass, and to a dwarf willow about thirty yards off with a bloody handprint on it. The bark was too rough for it to have left any discernible prints.

It was still early, just past seven, but she used her cell phone to call her favorite of the region's medical examiners, Dr. Akeem Hafeez, at his home in Santa Fe. After telling him about the grisly find, she asked if he would be open to her packing up the hand and bringing it to him, rather than waiting for him to come inspect the scene personally. Hafeez was paralyzed from the waist down, an accident he'd sustained as a medic in the first Gulf War. He was in a wheelchair now and unable to hike to a spot like this. He also happened to be the best medical examiner in the state. At his request, they switched to video, and she let him check out everything she was able to see before agreeing it would be fine for her to deliver the body part as soon as she could.

"I'll go talk to the hikers who found it, after this," she said. "I'll have Becky send you their contact information if you still have questions for them after you see my report."

"Sounds good, Jodi," he said. "Maybe we can grab lunch after you drop it off."

"That sounds great," she said. "But it'll depend on what's cooking out here."

"Of course," he said.

Jodi returned the phone to her pocket before snapping on a pair of purple latex exam gloves and carefully transferring the hand from the ground to a clear plastic evidence bag. As she zipped its top, she noticed that the back of the hand had been carved up, recently, with something sharp. She couldn't be completely sure, given the decomposition, but it looked a bit like the symbol she had seen drawn in glitter pen on Travis's wallet. The realization that this severed hand might be somehow related to the severed deer head from what she'd thought had been just some run-of-the-mill poacher sent a chill down Jodi's spine. She went to a ray of morning light that filtered through the thick pines and tried to get a better look.

"Well, I'll be damned," she said, making out the circle, and one pointed corner of the triangle. "What have you been up to out here, Travis?"

After storing the hand in the cooler she'd brought from the gearbox, Jodi hiked back down to her truck, feeling watched. It wasn't till she was headed back down the road, toward the campsite—and, truth be told, not until she had fished the bottle of Dead Guy Whiskey from Rogue Spirits (her go-to brand) out from under her truck seat and taken a swig to calm her nerves—that the chill left her.

It wasn't hard for Jodi to figure out which of the three groups of campers at the Lower Fresita campground was most likely to be her van life couple. They were the only ones less than fifty years of age and not traveling in a huge traditional RV. She found them outside their fancy van, which was opened up to display the trendy insides of itself. The man, in cargo shorts and a long-sleeved T-shirt, looked too pink cheeked and young for his massive beard, which, combined with the massive bun of long hair piled on top of his head, gave him the appearance of a boy in costume for a play. The woman was generic, a pretty blonde like so many others on that app, in her flowered cotton sundress and straw hat. She was trying to look natural while displaying some kind of Hydro Flask water bottle that was either made of wood or made to look like it was. When Jodi pulled into their camping spot, they seemed strangely excited and reconfigured themselves so that the girl was now talking to the camera as the guy shot a video of Jodi parking her truck.

"You believe this shit?" Jodi asked Juana, who looked at her in complete agreement. To add a bit more authority to her visit, Jodi turned on the blue lights, but not the siren, and left the truck idling in park. She opted to leave Juana inside and walked toward the van people in as confident a way as she could muster. She was friendly with them, not at all happy that her first witness interview was being captured on video. It was their legal right to film her, however.

"Oh my God, you're so pretty," said the woman, Yvonne. "Isn't she pretty, Ivan? I would never have expected someone like her to look like her."

Jodi did not want to dignify this stupidity with a response, and she was glad when the guy shook his head, subtly, at his partner to tell her she was probably being inappropriate.

"Sorry," Yvonne said. "It's just—I don't know. I expected something different. Can I get a picture with you? Would you hold this flask in it?"

"No." Jodi pulled the notepad and pen from her side pocket and began the interview.

———

The New Mexico Fish and Wildlife District Three office in Gato Montes was a flat, beige one-story cinder block box set down on a bed of puckered asphalt and weeds. Nothing but a chain-link fence with a coil of razor wire looped across the top stood between the office and the two-lane highway that was Gato Montes's only paved road. When Jodi pulled up in her work truck, an hour after leaving Ivan and Yvonne and their van, she found a few cars and trucks clumped together in the front of the building, near the empty flagpole. Just up the road to the north was the Gato Montes School, serving kindergarten through high school. To the south was a metal warehouse where Ulysses C'de Baca used to sell hay bales but that some enterprising preacher had recently converted into a Pentecostal church. Throw in a dollar store, a post office, Goldie's Bar and Grill, and a handful of mobile homes and crumbling adobe houses, and that was about all there was to the town anymore. Well, that and some of the most spectacular mountain scenery to be found on this continent and maybe the world.

The inside of the district office was just as unremarkable as the exterior. Walls masked in wood paneling from a bygone era that wasn't yet bygone enough to be charming to anyone except maybe Yvonne and Ivan. Plastic plants collecting dust in dark corners. Uncomfortable metal chairs that rocked if you moved even a little. A break room that smelled like last month's coffee. If the intention of these offices was to inspire game wardens to hightail it to the great outdoors to conserve living things, welp, Jodi thought, mission accomplished. Though she had a desk here, she intended to do as much of her paperwork as possible in the mobile office of her truck.

Becky McCarthy was a tall, red-faced, big-boned woman about Jodi's same age. Her Irish ancestors had come to this part of the world looking for gold or building the railroads back in the 1800s. Becky was as cowgirl as they came and spoke Spanish like a native, because she was a native. Culture was not genetic, it was learned, and Becky had never lived anywhere but Northern New Mexico. That's what a lot of people back east had never understood, that in New Mexico the ways people classified themselves and grouped together was not the same as it was in the rest of the nation. Becky was culturally as Hispano as Jodi, who found her now at the largest and most centrally located desk, behind the department's front counter, wearing what she almost always wore, which is to say a pair of faded Wranglers, a T-shirt, a flannel button-down shirt, a cowboy hat, and a landline telephone receiver. This last item was always perched on her shoulder like some sort of parrot, held in place by Becky tilting her head sharply.

"She just got here, Mrs. Rodriguez," said Becky, beckoning Jodi in and rolling her eyes while making the universal hand gesture for being on the phone with someone who won't stop talking about nothing. Jodi was about to sit at her desk to check the stack of pink message slips— the office still functioned largely as it had in the decade when they'd applied the wood paneling—when Becky covered the mouth portion of the receiver and whispered, loudly, "Burritos in the kitchen."

This was music to Jodi's ears, and she took a detour down the small, dark hallway whose light bulb had needed replacing for all six months she'd been in training and stopped off in the break room. It was a small kitchen, with older appliances, a shallow sink, and cabinets with a collection of coffee mugs Becky and her wife, Catalina, collected from every state park they visited on their summer road trips. There was also a little round dining table, with four chairs, and today she found one of these occupied by a young and handsome man, engaged in the ancient and forgotten art of reading an actual newspaper. She had never seen him before and would certainly have remembered a face that chiseled.

"Good morning," the man said, cheerfully rising to greet her with an outstretched hand.

"Morning," said Jodi, stepping closer and locking into a handshake. She chided herself silently for even entertaining unsavory thoughts about this man, because he could not have been older than thirty-five. Much too young for her, anyway.

"I'm Dr. Henley Bethel," he said. When she waited for a little more information, he said, "I'm the new wildlife veterinarian for the district."

"Oh!" Jodi remembered something about this now. "You the guy who'll be heading up the new rehabilitation clinic?"

"I am."

"Nice! Pleased to meet you. And welcome. I'm Officer Jodi Luna."

"Thank you, happy to be here. I suppose we'll be working closely together."

Lord help me not to spin that in ways I shouldn't, thought Jodi. She detected a bit of a California accent to his speech. He wore ripped dark skinny jeans, Converse sneakers, and a checkered shirt over a V-neck T-shirt. He had a tapered hairdo worn a bit longer on top, in short dreads, and a light, well-groomed beard and mustache. Both his forearms were sleeved with tattoos, and his red-framed eyeglasses were intended to make a statement.

"Where'd you move from?" she asked, resuming her rummaging for burritos in the refrigerator.

"No Cal," he said, adding, "Northern California" in case she did not know what the first word meant. "Tahoe area, most recently," he said. Well, she thought, that explains why he is dressed like a guy on his way to a skate park. She wondered why he'd taken a job in New Mexico but wasn't going to ask. Not yet, anyway.

Jodi found the brown paper bag with four large carne asada breakfast burritos in a snap-ware container. Catalina, the middle and high school math teacher in town, made the best breakfast burritos this side of Texas, with red chile harvested on her cousin's small farm in Chimayo. "Oh yeah. Come to Mama," she said as she dumped two burritos onto a paper plate before throwing them into the noisy old microwave.

"Want one?" she asked Henley.

He lifted his brows in interest. "Depends on what they are."

"Catalina Martinez's world-famous carne asada breakfast burritos," she said. He looked apologetic and confused and maybe a little embarrassed. "You like spicy food?"

"I mean, I'm from Oakland. Grew up in Fruitvale, so. I thought I was all *about* hot Mexican food, till I moved here. I am telling you. New Mexico? Y'all take it to another level."

Jodi smiled and nodded in agreement. "It can be shocking to newcomers."

"Yeah, well, I had the green-chile-chicken enchiladas at Goldie's last night and thought my mouth was on fire. Y'all like it hot here."

"Yes, yes, we do," said Jodi, thinking he was hot enough to start a damn fire.

"I think I'll pass on the burritos for now. But thank you. Without going full-on TMI, I think I'll wait till my stomach settles down before I try again," he said. "I hope that isn't culturally insensitive."

"Nope, not at all. I felt the same way about clam chowder when I lived in Massachusetts. It never hasn't tasted like hot snot to me."

"Hot snot." He laughed. "Quite the description. Oh, wait. Hold up. They told me one of the game wardens was a poet. That you, by chance?"

"Yes, but don't hold it against me."

He smiled. "What? No! I am a fan of the written word. I even have a favorite poet."

Jodi poured herself what was left of the coffee in the old Mr. Coffee pot on the counter, using a mug from Carlsbad Caverns National Park. She nursed this until the microwave dinged, then took her burritos to the table, leaving a scent trail of earthy red chile, garlic, onions, stewed pork, eggs, and cheddar cheese in the air.

"And who might that be?" she asked.

"Mary TallMountain," he said.

Jodi nodded her approval. "Got a favorite poem of hers?"

"'The Last Wolf,'" he said.

"Not sure I've seen that one."

"Helluva poem," he said, and Jodi tried not to reveal her surprise. When she got up this morning, she definitely did not expect to meet a handsome new coworker with an appreciation for nature poetry.

Becky swaggered into the room now and, seeing that the coffee pot was empty, went to work getting it brewing again.

"I see you two have met," she said, shooting Jodi a knowing look that was as transparent as it was embarrassing. Becky had not been shy about telling Jodi she needed to "get back on the horse again" and start dating, but the very idea of this still felt to Jodi like she would be cheating on Graham. "I don't know which of you drank the last of the joe, and I know you're both new around here, but from now on, please remember to start a new pot if you drain the dregs."

"Sorry," said Jodi through an appreciative mouthful of burrito. "That was me. I was starving, though."

Becky rolled her eyes and changed the subject. "You two set up a time for you to show him the wolf den out at Lower Fresita?"

"Sorry?" Jodi asked.

"I'm starting surveys on the endangered species in the district," he said. "Need to do health checks. Heard those ones have some pups a couple months old?"

Jodi nodded. "They do."

"I told Dr. Bethel you'd be taking him out there sometime this week." She winked, and not at all discreetly. "Fill him in on what you and Atencio know about the pack."

"Yeah, sure, of course," said Jodi. "When would you like to do it?"

Henley considered this. "Would Thursday afternoon work? I have, like, just a big old bunch of meetings and paperwork till then. Gotta get some things unpacked in my new place too."

"You get that cabin you wanted?" Becky asked him. His face lit up.

"I did!"

"The one by the river?"

"That's the one. You and Cata and the kids should come by some-time. Once I get my furniture situated." He looked at Jodi shyly and smiled. "You're welcome to come too."

"So," Becky said to Jodi, sensing her abject discomfort and trying to steer the conversation back to more professional matters, "Dr. Bethel is free Thursday afternoon. Does that work for you, Officer Luna?"

"Works for me, unless something comes up."

"Perfect," said Henley. "I'll look forward to it."

Becky came to the table, satisfied with the exchange between Jodi and Henley, and signaled that they'd said enough by dropping a pile of printouts next to Jodi's plate. "Got a present for you."

"What's this?"

"Just ran that delayed background on your Arizona poacher, Travis E. Lee," she said. "I'd say he's been a very bad boy."

Henley, taking this turn in the conversation to be his exit, went to the sink to wash and dry his mug and put it back in the cabinet as Jodi chewed her breakfast and read through the long rap sheet.

"Okay, ladies, it's time for me to head out," he announced. "I hope you both have a great day."

"You hear that, Jodes? New guy is under the impression we are *ladies*." Becky chuckled.

"He'll learn," said Jodi, with a grin to let him know they were joking around.

"My mistake," said Henley, playing along. "Nonetheless, I do hope y'all have a good day."

"Oh, hang on a second, Dr. Bethel," said Becky. "I meant to tell you, we're having a party this Friday night, at Goldie's, for the warden who just retired, Eloy Atencio. You should come."

"You think?" he asked. "That wouldn't be weird, considering I never even met him?"

"You'll meet him at the party. And he's Jodi's uncle. They're practically the same person."

"I beg your pardon," said Jodi, mock offended.

Becky kept talking to Henley and ignored Jodi. "It'll be a good way for you to meet everybody who's anybody."

"Work on your chile-eating skills," suggested Jodi, keeping one eye on the rap sheet.

"I'll be there," he said. "But I can't guarantee I'll be ready for more chile. Talk to you later."

After he left, Becky joined Jodi at the table, planted her elbows on it, and laced her fingers beneath her chin to discuss the poacher. According to his record, Lee, who was only thirty-eight, had been arrested—and served time—for numerous crimes over the past twenty years, including kidnapping, attempted murder, robbery, and, most recently, showing up to a couple of Black Lives Matter protests in different states with a baseball bat and various anti-Semitic and racist T-shirts to threaten and fight with participants. He had no active warrants at the moment.

"A real sweetheart," said Jodi as she flipped through the pages of charges.

Becky frowned. "What do you think he's doing in our neck of the woods? Not that it's not nice out here and all, but c'mon. Plenty of deer for a skinhead to poach in Arizona, am I right?"

"Yeah," said Jodi. "There's something weird going on, and he's got something to do with it. Look at this." Jodi set her food down and took her phone out to show Becky the photo of the emblem carved into the hand.

"Ugh. How the hell can you eat and look at that thing at the same time?" asked Becky.

"I mean, I'm not eating the hand," said Jodi, matter of fact. "Anyway. That symbol?"

"What symbol?"

"If you look real close, you can see it."

"I'll take your word for it. Put that thing away."

"It's a pyramid with an eye in it. Travis had that same thing drawn on his wallet."

Becky considered this, then said, "I think I've seen it before."

"You have?"

"Yeah. Follow me." She led Jodi back to her desk and pulled up an internet browser. "Check this out."

Jodi looked over Becky's shoulder at the website for a group called the Zebulon Boys, which had the pyramid logo prominently displayed.

"Little something like that?" she asked.

"Yeah. Exactly like that. What the hell are the Zebulon Boys?" Jodi asked.

"According to this website, a patriot group protecting 'real' Americans from 'foreign' invaders," said Becky. "But according to the Southern Poverty Law Center"—she opened a new tab and typed for a bit—"they're one of the fastest-growing white supremacist groups in the United States. They have no use for the Fourteenth Amendment, but lots of use for the Second. And if you believe the FBI, white supremacist hate groups are the biggest terrorist threat of all we face in this country. Not Muslim extremists, not Mexican kids in cages or whatever the hell it is the dumb half of my family's afraid of. It's these guys. Tiki Nazis."

"Holy shit," said Jodi. "How do you know all this?"

"Let's just say there are certain members of my own family I am not entirely proud of, in Oklahoma, and I can't bring myself to unfriend them on Facebook. I see all their bullshit. Never comment on it because they seem like they'd burn my house down without a second thought. This guy General Zeb is a big deal with them. They're, like, religious about it, almost. You know? They think he's some kind of hero. These people are bad news."

"Lee said I'd be sorry I ever met him," said Jodi. "Got real pissed off when he heard me and my uncle speaking Spanish."

"I know you're always careful out there, hon," said Becky, with a look of concern creasing her brow. "But I'd suggest for now you just be extra careful."

"Yeah," said Jodi. "Thanks for breakfast, by the way. Tell your beautiful wife it was amazing, as always. I'm going to head down to Santa Fe to give Hafeez a hand now."

"Give him a hand, huh?" Becky rolled her eyes. "Please tell me you did not intend that as a pun, Professor Poetry."

"I'll let you decide," said Jodi.

"Dark," said Becky. "That's what I love about you. You look all pretty and fragile, but deep down you're a goddamned vampire."

"You laugh to keep from crying," said Jodi.

"Speaking of dark—and handsome. How about Dr. Bethel, eh?" She wiggled her eyebrows suggestively at Jodi. "I'd say he's a catch and a half."

"He's a baby," Jodi said, dropping her voice to a whisper in case he was still around.

"What?"

"He looks young."

"He's thirty-two," said Becky with a shrug.

"Thirty-two? That is way too young. I'm almost forty-six."

"Yeah, but you look thirty-five. So. You'd look good together."

"If and when I ever date again, it's going to be someone I don't feel like I'm babysitting," said Jodi.

"Men do it all the time. Plus, not that I care about this, but there is testosterone to consider. You're going to need the next guy to have that in his favor."

"Stop," said Jodi.

Becky meowed and hissed and did her hand like a claw. "You're a total cougar."

"I'll talk to you later," said Jodi, mostly because she didn't know how else to get Becky to stop talking about this. She could handle severed heads and hands and white supremacists without blinking, but the thought of dating again after having lost the love of her life was absolutely terrifying.

"One more thing," said Becky. "We just got a call from Lyle Daggett, the ranch manager out on the Sauer Brothers Ranch?"

"Cattle operation by the mouth of the Carson National Forest?" asked Jodi. "Looks like Wyatt Earp?"

"That's the one."

"Been out there a couple times with my uncle."

"Welp. He said he was grazing his cattle out on BLM land, up near the wolf den—you know that little pack? Actually kind of close to the hot springs where those kids found the hand. Anyway, he saw some illegal traps set up by there, like maybe someone is trying to poach them."

"I see." This angered Jodi. Wolves were endangered, and the ecosystem badly needed them. Humans couldn't eat them, and they posed relatively little threat to ranchers when they were left alone. Only the worst sort of person would be trying to kill a wolf, and for the worst of reasons. "How many traps?"

"Said he found three. Maybe when you're up at the den on Thursday with your new and virile much-younger boyfriend, you can have another look around."

"Okay, okay, enough," said Jodi. "I do not need you to play Cupid for me."

"I disagree. Left to your own devices, that thing is going to crust over and seal up."

"Jesus, stop."

"Says the woman who can eat while looking at corpses."

"Point taken. But please. I'm not ready. Okay?"

"Anyway. You might maybe want to swing by Daggett's place on your way back from Santa Fe. Hell. Give him a blue pill or two, he might even be worth a ride. And God knows you need a ride."

"Stop," said Jodi, though she could not help smiling as she walked toward the door.

5

Alone in the vast meadow under a relentless midday sun, watched only by a half dozen Black Angus cows, Lyle Daggett mopped his brow with the tail of the paisley wild rag worn around his neck. The Sauer Brothers Ranch's camouflage all-terrain vehicle with the cargo bed was parked nearby, because it was a more practical choice for this particular job than a horse and panniers. More comfortable, too, though he'd never admit anything like that to the other ranch managers he sometimes drank with down at Goldie's bar after a long day. He wound a stiff spool of repurposed barbed wire around a broken spot in the fence. In his youth, he could have done this kind of thing without much need of help, working alone on the range, as it were. But these days, he was feeling all fifty-two of his years, in places he hadn't even known he had.

Like other serious cowboys, he wore jeans, a neat plaid button-down, tucked in, with a belt and buckle, leather boots, and a white hat. He was always meticulously put together, even though he could go weeks without seeing another person. It was a matter of pride. Everything about Lyle's life was organized and on time. As for that white hat, he wore it because it was summer, and not, as the movies had you believe, because he was a good guy. He wasn't that good. He wasn't bad, necessarily. But he had done some things that could be seen as bad. Things he'd like to forget. This was part of the reason he preferred a quiet life in a place where he wouldn't have to talk to anybody most of the time. There were things he didn't even want to risk spilling from his mouth. Things not even his late wife, Renata, God rest her soul, had known. He'd become enamored of the lone-cowboy mystique as a boy, growing up in Philadelphia, and as soon as he could, after his time in the military in just about every Spanish- or Arabic-speaking country you could name, he'd come out to the Southwest, hoping to find what the movie cowboys had. Managing this two-hundred-thousand-acre ranch for the last remaining Sauer brother and his wealthy Texas family, who had a bunch of other homes and were almost never around, was about as close to heaven as he figured he'd ever find. The youngest Sauer son, Jonas Sauer, was scheduled to pay a visit in the next few days, with his latest trophy wife, to do some business (or so he said; Lyle didn't think the man could work his way out of a paper bag) and go fly-fishing, and Lyle wanted to make sure the ranch was in tip-top condition before he arrived.

"Come on, you son of a bitch," he said to the post and wire. The perspiration dripped down his back, under the long-sleeved shirt. Didn't use to be this hot so early in the year, but times were changing. Spring came earlier, summer was hotter, and, truth be told, Lyle was feeling just a little bit too old for this shit. He'd always worked for just about minimum wage, plus room and board, never had benefits of any kind (had to learn to commit a form of amateur dentistry upon himself as a result), and sure as hell didn't have a retirement plan. He had no idea what he'd do once he truly got old. Maybe it's time to find myself a sugar mama, he thought, only half jokingly, and chuckled to himself.

He looked up from his work when the game warden's truck came toward him, kicking up dust. He gave his face another quick wipe, set down the wire and fencing pliers, took off his leather work gloves, and prepared to greet old Eloy Atencio. But as the truck got closer and parked, Lyle saw it wasn't his longtime friend driving. It was his pretty little niece, the professor.

"Howdy," she called, waving as she walked toward him from where she'd left her truck idling. He wondered if she actually ever used that word, or if something about him being a tall white cowboy inspired her to invoke it. She smiled, and he felt a little something flutter around in his chest somewhere he'd forgotten existed. Nice mouth. And eyes. Delicate little nose. And that shiny horsetail hair of hers.

"Officer Luna," he said, taking off his hat to be polite, even though he knew his damp hair—or what was left of it, anyway—must've looked a sweaty mess. He'd never had to worry about how he looked around old Eloy.

"How are you today, Mr. Daggett?" she asked.

"Can't complain," he said.

She chinned toward the fence and said, "Looking good. I've always meant to tell you, you run a tight operation here. Grew up on a ranch myself. I have never seen such consistently beautiful fencing."

"I appreciate that," he said, returning the hat to his head.

After a bit more obligatory small talk, in which her uncle's retirement and party were mentioned, and he remembered to ask about her daughter, even remembered the kid's name, Mila, Officer Luna got to the purpose of her visit. The illegal traps. He told her he had them back at his house, and she said she'd be happy to follow him there, or give him a ride. He didn't know her well enough yet to feel comfortable riding shotgun for the twelve agonizingly silent minutes it would take them to get back to his house, so he decided to waste some gas and have her follow him.

Lyle's house was one of three double-wide mobile homes on the sprawling property. The other two were used for hunters who came to the ranch at certain times of year. The owners of the ranch, when they showed up, lived in a fourth house—a luxurious seven-thousand-square-foot ranch house that did its best to look like the biggest log cabin ever made and sat, stupidly, at the top of the hill. Like a goddamned castle. Place with weather as harsh as this, you wanted your house to be down in the valleys, out of the wind. But the ranch's owners weren't ranchers. They were oilmen, who kept ranches like toys. Some of the other ranch managers he had known over the years, who had similarly absentee employers, had helped themselves to the big cushy ranch houses when their owners were gone. Not Lyle. He had a code of honor, one that involved doing the right thing whether anyone was watching or not. He also did not have need or desire for anything fancier than a double-wide mobile home, which, with its three bedrooms and two bathrooms, was already way too much house for an empty nester and widower.

Lyle and Jodi parked in front of this house, around which Lyle had built a wide, covered porch. He did most of his living on that porch. Cooked out there on the grill, sat through sunsets with his dogs—at the moment going nuts in their pens at the sound and scent of a stranger.

"Well, the traps are just over here," he said, leading her through the front gate, across the neat lawn, and toward one end of the porch, where three traps were lined up in a row. Two were padded leghold traps, one large enough to hold an adult wolf and the other, bigger one large enough for a bear. The third was an offset leghold trap. All of them were shiny, expensive, and new. Jodi picked one up and turned it around. Sure enough, the trap lacked the name and phone number engraving required by law. She stopped cold when she saw the small insignia engraved into it instead—a pyramid with an eye in it. Lyle could tell this was significant, but she wasn't about to share why, and he wasn't dumb enough to ask.

"Might be more of 'em out there," he said. "Found these near the den where that Mexican wolf pack stays. Up near those Lower Fresita Hot Springs. You know where that is?"

"Yep."

"Trappers are the sorriest sons of bitches in the world," he said. "But trying to get a wolf in one of these things?" He shook his head and closed his mouth. He didn't want to tell an officer of the law what he might do to one of these boys if he ever caught them in the act. This fear of what he was capable of was what had driven him to confiscate the traps, but he was not about to share that information either.

47

"We certainly appreciate your help, Mr. Daggett," said Jodi.

"You're welcome. I hope you find 'em."

Lyle helped Jodi take the traps back to her truck, and after an awkward dance where she went to open her own door but he felt it his gentlemanly duty to open it for her—she was not impressed or pleased by this but seemed to tolerate him—he stood there trying not to feel like a man who had no idea how to relate to women in the modern world anymore. Especially not ones this smart and, it seemed, uninterested. He remembered Renata, on her deathbed, squeezing his hand and telling him that she was fully planning to date James Dean when she got to heaven, and she would be very angry if he didn't put himself out there and find some company once she was gone.

"I was, um, sorry to hear about your husband," he blurted out as she reached to shut the door of the truck. She stopped midslam and looked at him funny.

"Gotta love small towns," she said. "Guess word gets around."

"I apologize if I overstepped," he said, his cheeks flaming red. "It's just—I lost my wife a few years back. I know how hard it can be. That's all I was saying. Just trying to be neighborly. Meant no offense."

She closed the door but leaned out of the open window after and smiled. "I appreciate it," she said. "And I'm very sorry for your loss too."

"Cancer," he said, not wanting to ask her how her husband had died, but curious.

"Cancer sucks," she said. She sized him up, and he knew that she knew he was waiting for her to share back. She sighed. "Rock climbing accident," she said. "Graham was a bit of a daredevil."

Lyle didn't know what to say. He had about as much interest in rock climbing as he had in high tea with the queen. Didn't understand why anybody would want to tempt nature that way. "Well, if you ever want somebody to talk to," he said, feeling stupider by the minute. "Not that you don't have people to talk to. But if you want to talk to somebody who's getting through something similar, or if you just want to sit and not talk about anything with someone going through something similar, you know where to find me."

She smiled warmly at him and seemed a bit taken aback. "I'd imagine you don't have a lot of people to talk to, all alone out here," she said.

"I designed it that way," he said. "But sometimes I do miss company in the evening. And I am nowhere near as good at tending that garden as Renata was."

"It still looks pretty good," said Jodi.

"You like eggplant?" he asked.

Jodi nodded. "Sure."

"Well, good. I can't stand the stuff, but Renata liked it. Got a bunch of it ready to come off the vine. Happy to grab it for you, if you like."

"We are not supposed to take gifts from the public," she said.

"I mean, it's not a gift. Far as I'm concerned, it's trash. You'd be doing me a favor," he said.

Jodi considered the proposal and finally shrugged. "Sure, why not?"

Lyle ducked into the house to grab one of the baskets tucked away in the closet of the room where Renata used to do her sewing. He grabbed one of the flowered cloth napkins from the hall linen closet. He had no use for these things anymore; might as well start to get rid of them. He went out the side door and picked six eggplants. He added a couple of tomatoes and zucchini to the mix and tucked the napkin in over the top. This, he handed to Jodi through her window.

"Thanks," she said, looking surprised by the bounty and over-the-top presentation. I am overdoing it, he thought. No clue at all how to court a woman anymore.

"Don't let me keep you," he said. "Just know, if you ever want to have some excellent Macallan whisky and some extremely subpar company, you should stop by."

Jodi laughed at the self-deprecating remark. "Think you might be selling yourself a little short there, Mr. Daggett."

"Please, call me Lyle. And I know myself pretty well. I doubt I'd be much for stimulating conversation, but I'd do my best."

"That could be fun," she said, seeming as embarrassed and awkward as he was, now.

"With the right scotch, I have found that almost anything is fun," he said. He tipped his hat toward her and stepped back, feeling awkward and stupid and guilty as hell for taking up so much of her time with his nonsense.

"Have a good rest of your day, Mr. Daggett," she said.

6

The rest of Jodi's day was pretty standard game warden fare, at least for a few hours. She stopped by Vadito Lake, to check fishing licenses from the couple dozen individuals and families who were throwing lines there. She went out on a call near the casino at the edge of the Ts'áyyi' P'óe pueblo, about a hit-and-run involving a yearling doe who hadn't quite died yet and needed to be put out of her misery. After Jodi euthanized the suffering creature, she packed it into the back of her truck. In cases of confiscated poached animals, the carcasses were usually kept frozen as evidence until the case was resolved, but in cases like this, hit by a driver who could never be found, the animal could be taken home by the game warden as food, or donated to a food bank. Jodi was running low on venison and decided she'd be keeping this one. Maybe even save some of it to give to Lyle Daggett as a thanks for the vegetables—and not because she was interested in him but because that was the sort of thing people did up here in Northern New Mexico. Or at least that's what she told herself.

She went back to the office at the end of the workday to do a Zoom presentation with a group of summer-camp middle schoolers down in Las Cruces, to answer questions about all the different wild animals that lived in New Mexico.

She was gathering her things to leave when Hafeez called on the landline. Becky, who'd been ready to head home, too, answered the call and put it on speakerphone so they could both take notes.

"Got some prints back on that hand," said Hafeez. "Belongs to a Natalia Yanez, honor student from Reno, Nevada. Sixteen years old. Family filed a missing persons on her two weeks ago, after she disappeared from the pool at a hotel where they'd gone on vacation down in Las Vegas."

Jodi felt the floor fall out from under her heart. Somehow, she felt she could have handled this news better if the owner of the hand had been—well. Not a child. Sixteen years old, on vacation with her parents. This hit a little too close to home. She swallowed the emotions and reminded herself to behave professionally. She took down the family's contact information.

"Were you able to confirm the design of that carving on the back of the hand?" asked Jodi.

"Yeah, we took a closer look. Looks like what you theorized."

"Thanks, Doctor," said Jodi, and they ended the call.

Becky looked at Jodi, reading her face instantly. "I get it," she said. "Got three of them home for the summer. Let's get out of here and go hug our kids, Jodes."

Jodi drove west, into the lowering sun, with Juana exhausted and snoring on her blanket, even through the upbeat outlaw-country music blasting on the speakers. Her house was in an unincorporated area about twenty miles southwest of town, and Jodi needed the drive and the songs to clear her head. She didn't want to think about the horrors of the day. She also needed to keep her mind off how hungry she suddenly realized she was. It was past six, had been a very busy, very full day, and all she'd eaten were those two breakfast burritos this morning. She made a mental note to start packing herself some food and to keep some snacks in the truck. Then she cranked up the tunes and sang along. All in all, she felt pretty good about how she'd handled her first day. She'd gotten a lot done and hadn't screwed anything up too much.

It was only after Jodi had turned down the long dirt road off the high-way, through the mountains, toward her house in its meadow, only after she had already crossed the wooden bridge over the stream, only once she had gotten out of the truck to spin the code into the pad-lock on her property's far gate, still a good eighth of a mile from the house, that she saw the dented white pickup. It was following her and possibly had been for some time. She remembered the way Atencio had told her to remain alert on her commutes, because, in his words, "some of these boys will want to follow you home, and never for a good reason." The setting sun was shining brightly against the white truck's windshield, but Jodi did not need to be able to see inside to know who was driving. It was Travis Eugene Lee, the white supremacist who was linked, somehow, to the severed hand of a teenage girl. As quickly as she could, Jodi opened her gate, drove through, then got out to lock it again behind her, before gunning the truck toward the house, to make sure her daughter was safe.

7

Mila Livingston, fourteen, was in one of her favorite places in all the world—on the roof of the brown barn behind her house. Tanned, strong, and confident, she wore her rock climbing gear, including the harness. Because Mila had begun jumping off the highest things around almost as soon as she began walking—and she'd walked earlier than the norm, at just nine months of age—her dad had taught her to rock climb before she'd even started kindergarten. By the time she was twelve, they were spending most of their weekends scaling the best crags to be found in New England. He'd died during one of these expeditions, to the sea cliffs in Acadia National Park. She alone had witnessed her father falling to his death in the rocky Atlantic Ocean, and while this experience might have scared most girls out of ever climbing again, it only emboldened Mila to become the best she could be, to honor his memory. Mila had heard her parents fight about whether or not to let her do such dangerous things so young, and her dad had always understood her better than her mom on this. His reasoning had been that it would be better to teach a child so obviously drawn to danger how best to run toward it with the most protection she could have than to forbid her, because forbidding one such as Mila (or her dad) only resulted in them doing the forbidden thing in secret. He'd been right. Mila came into this world craving adventure, and nothing was going to stop her from finding it. This was why the precarious squat she was holding, on the slick and sloping side of the barn's roof, was second nature for her.

As her mother's work truck crunched up the gravel road to park next to the barn, Mila paused in expertly tying a bowline knot to secure her rappelling rope to the building's cupola and waved.

Her mom parked, then grabbed the rifle from the rack in the back of the truck before she and Juana walked over to the barn.

"Hey, kid," she called to Mila. She sounded nervous, but like she didn't want Mila to notice. This was more than the usual nervousness about Mila falling too. There was something on her mind.

"Hi! You okay?" Mila asked, moving on to tying a Munter hitch knot into her locking carabiners. She had always been tuned in to her mother's moods, even as a baby, able to discern even the slightest shift. This vigilance had gotten even more pronounced after her father's death, as Mila, faced with her mother's overwhelming grief in addition to her own, had been forced to monitor and, wherever she could, manage her mother's outsize emotions. Her mother called her "my little Graham" for a reason. Before he'd died, it had been Mila's dad's job to keep her mother from losing control. Now it was Mila's.

"I need you to come down here for a second," she said.

Mila noticed her mother watching a dented white truck that was parked just on the other side of the family's property, and she immediately figured out that this was not someone who was supposed to be there.

"Okay. Be right there," said Mila. She tested the knots with a couple of quick tugs and then, with practiced and nimble expertise, and without the slightest fear, backed up to the edge of the roof and leaped off before quickly rappelling down, graceful as a spider plunging from a ceiling on a ribbon of its own silk. She unclipped herself from the rope and hugged her mom.

"Who's the creep in the truck?" Mila asked.

"You don't miss a thing, do you?" Her mom beamed at her daughter and ruffled the girl's hair.

"I miss one thing. Dad," said Mila without missing a beat.

"You definitely have his quick wit," said her mom. "Let's get inside, and I'll tell you all about the creep."

"Okey dokey," said Mila.

"Stay close to me," said her mom. "But don't look alarmed."

"Well, I'm not alarmed, so that shouldn't be too hard."

They found Oscar in a rocking chair under some hanging red chile ristras on the side porch, with a book on his lap and his cell phone and a glass of iced tea on the little wicker table next to it. He'd planted himself there, behind the banister and wall of hollyhocks, probably to keep an eye on Mila. He was a good uncle. He protected her but did not get in her way. He also seemed almost as good as Mila at reading her mom's moods, including now.

"Hey," he said, meeting them at the front of the house as they came up the steps. "What's going on?"

"Inside," said her mom.

"Mom's got a stalker," said Mila, jutting her chin toward the truck by the gate. "With a shitty truck."

"Language," said Oscar.

"People who curse are more honest, according to science," said Mila.

"In," said her mom, holding the door for the others to pass through, then locking it once they had.

"Operation four," she told them, instantly springing to the task of locking and checking all the windows and the doors, closing the curtains and shades as she went.

"Which one is four again?" Oscar asked Mila.

"Just go to Mom's room and wait for me there," the girl said as she opened the gun locker with her own thumbprint, removed the Remington 870 twelve-gauge shotgun, and loaded it. She walked calmly to her mother's room after this, it being the rearmost room in the house, and found her uncle pacing nervously.

"Should we call the police?" he asked.

ow Beasts

"Mom *is* the police," Mila reminded him.

Oscar was uncomfortable with guns. Mila could see it in his eyes.

"It's okay," said Mila. "I know what I'm doing." Mila enjoyed target practice, and shooting was one of the three hobbies she and her mother shared—the other two being horseback riding and writing, though in Mila's case she wrote songs instead of poems.

Her mom came to the doorway of her room now, to make sure the other two were in position. "Down on the floor. Stay low."

"Can someone please tell me what's going on?" Oscar said as Mila grabbed her uncle's arm with her free hand to pull him to the wooden floor, where she was already kneeling.

"I gave a guy some tickets last week," said her mom, matter of fact. "Probably nothing. But you know the rules around here. Better safe than sorry. Guess he decided to follow me home today. I'm going to go see what he wants."

"That's not good," said Oscar.

"All in a day's work now. We knew this was part of it."

"We're fine," Mila told Oscar. "I promise."

"I'm gonna go around the side fence, pay him a little visit, see just how serious he is about fucking around with me at my own home. I need you two to hang out here while I do."

"What'd you ticket him for?" asked Mila.

"Poaching, and waste of wildlife. The usual crap."

"Sounds like a loser," said Mila.

"He is," her mother replied, adding, "lock this door behind me, sweetheart, and you know the rest of the drill."

"Except it's not a drill this time," said Mila, with an excited grin. "It's for real."

"Oh God," said Oscar.

"Be back in a bit," said her mom.

57

8

Marjorie was pretty, if you didn't look at her nose. Her own granddaddy said her nose reminded him of someone named Karl Malden. He only said this when he drank, but he drank every day. Didn't matter. She could always get her nose fixed, as her meemaw had told her, but her soul? That didn't need fixing. She was a righteous Aryan woman, and that was all that counted where Jesus was concerned. Besides, you didn't need to be beautiful to be a loan officer at a bank; you just needed to be good with numbers and have good judgment, and Marjorie was very good at both numbers and judging. This is why, even though she would have rather been going to those Godly Woman book club gatherings she liked so much, she was instead dedicating herself to curbing the numbers of illegals swarming over the open border and ruining America. Somebody had to do something about them and their raping and diseases. These politicians sure as hell weren't in any rush to stop them. She narrowed her pretty green eyes while she absently flicked the lock up and down on the passenger door of the GMC Savana van in which she perched, waiting.

"Quit," griped Levi, of her nervous flicking.

Levi was Marjorie's partner in love and war. Sometimes it was hard to tell which was which. She had her tics, and he hated them. He was a real estate agent, though, and they were pretty touchy about things being a certain way. It wasn't like she didn't hate a bunch of things about him too. For instance, she wished he'd go to the men's Bible study she'd been telling him about so that he could learn how to lead with his heart and not just his head. He'd stopped going to their church since that Arab family joined, which was understandable. But it wasn't the pastor's fault. He didn't want them there either. They claimed to be Christians but were obviously Muslim.

The van was parked next to an old tire in an empty lot near West Buckeye Road and South Thirty-Fifth Avenue in South Phoenix, where all the Mexicans lived. It made Marjorie feel dirty just being down here. Like she'd need a Lysol bath after all this mess. She wore bedazzled jeans (she'd done this herself, with a really easy kit from Hobby Lobby) and an American flag T-shirt.

Levi watched the back door of the Jack in the Box through a set of beat-up garage sale binoculars. His head was newly shaved, and with the goatee, new earring, and *100%* chest tattoo, he looked hotter than ever. At least to Marjorie. Sometimes she wondered what he saw in her. His nose was perfect. He had those ads on the bus stops in Scottsdale, and, not joking at all, girls called his office just to see if he was single. They didn't want to buy or sell a property or anything like that; they just wanted her man. He could've had anybody. But he wanted Marjorie.

"It's her. It's Rica," Levi said.

The Mexican girl worked damn near every day, because those people were like that. They were built to work, like mules, and that gave them an unfair advantage, because they didn't feel pain or get tired the same way white people did. Every day, at five on the dot, she was dragging bags of trash to the dumpsters. She was all swollen and pregnant, but she didn't slow down. They were like that. Good, Christian women were fragile; that's how you knew the difference. Like in slave times. That Mexican girl took a job that should have gone to a real American Christian man. She should have stayed where she belonged, but she didn't, and the government was just giving her handouts. It was part of a conspiracy to eliminate white people. George Soros was behind it.

Marjorie didn't know the pregnant Mexican's actual name, and it did not matter, for the same reason you did not name cockroaches.

You squashed 'em. They *called* her Rica 'cause it sounded like the only Spanish word they'd ever had to learn on purpose. *Reconquista*. It meant "reconquest" in Mexican and was what those people called their plan to take back the parts of the United States they'd lost fair and square way back when. Most people didn't realize how serious this problem was. All you had to do was look at the census. These people were taking over everything. They were always talking about "la raza," their race. They thought whites were inferior, and wasn't that the definition of racism? America was just sleeping through it. The politicians were just letting it happen. White Christian people were literally *endangered* now, an actual endangered *species*, and no one cared.

They'd learned about the reconquista and la raza from the teachings of General Zeb, online. He had these amazing podcasts and videos and newsletters. Marjorie and Levi wanted to be part of the movement to save white American Christians, to be part of General Zeb's army. That's where Rica came in. General Zeb had finally written back after months of them reaching out, and he'd given them a task to prove themselves. People waited years to get tasks, because General Zeb was very careful about who he trusted. He'd been burned before. *Bring me a Mexican woman to get rid of.* That's all he'd said. That, and a date and time, and GPS coordinates.

"Go time," said Marjorie, snubbing out her cigarette in the van's ashtray.

She felt the comforting heft of the Taurus G2 semiautomatic 9mm pistol in her manicured hand. Levi gathered up the rope and duct tape. They sped the van over and used it to block Rica from the back door of the Jack in the Box. She was so small, barely five feet tall, dumb like a monkey, and so scared and stupid she just sort of stood there staring at the gun in shock while they taped up her mouth, bound her hands and feet, and tossed her into the back of the van. No wonder Mexicans had been too weak to keep their land.

As Levi steered back out onto Buckeye, Marjorie put the coordinates in the GPS. They were supposed to meet him at some old abandoned fire lookout, in the San Isidro National Forest, over in New Mexico. You had to hand it to the General. He didn't dick around. He wasn't scared of anything. He'd picked Rio Truchas County, where eight in ten people were spics and them other two were Indians. Cockroach ground zero. That's where they were going to launch the New Gettysburg, a righteous smackdown of the reconquista—in a county with one of the highest percentages of Mexicans anywhere. He'd researched it, he told them. He'd found a place so infested with public enemy number one that you couldn't go hardly anywhere without running over one of them.

According to the phone, it would take them about nine hours to get there.

Ten, if they stopped to get some Chick-fil-A.

9

Travis was just slouching there in his truck, drinking Coca-Cola, gnawing on Doritos, and sucking on a cigarette. Dinner of champions. He was, as Jodi suspected, also watching the front of her house, and every so often he took a break in his open-mouthed breathing to snap a photo of the property with his phone. Jodi crouched in the papery cornstalks by her fence and observed him. She had sneaked up on him, on foot, because he might have fled if he'd seen the truck coming toward him. Juana obeyed Jodi's hand signal to heel and waited patiently in the shadows with her. There was work happening, and this pleased the dog, who, like all pack animals, was happiest when she had a job to do.

Once he'd drained that can of cola, tilting his head back to get every last sugary, pointless drop, Travis belched into his blotchy fist, then chucked the can out his window. He smiled to himself, like he delighted in intentionally littering so close to Jodi's house. A gem of a man. He did the same with his cigarette butt, and the chips bag. He also dumped some pieces of crumpled-up paper onto the ground. Jodi assumed these would turn out to be the citations she'd written for him.

Jodi inhaled deeply, composed herself, and prepared to confront him. She stepped out of the cornfield and walked along the fence of her property, toward the gate. It didn't take Travis long to notice her there. He smiled in a dirty kind of way, the kind of smile the mythical night hag might give you if you caught her squatting on your chest at three in the morning, stealing your soul.

"What do you want, Travis?" Jodi yelled, coming closer and feeling very on edge. He did not answer, other than to look right at her and laugh. She came up next to his open driver's door window, released the fasteners on the Glock's holster, and stared him down. "What are you doing here, Travis?"

"Minding my own business."

"Unlikely."

"Am I breaking any laws, Jodi?" He was trying to anger her by disrespecting her, a man who held a grudge.

Jodi glanced briefly at the trash he'd strewed on the road. "Yes."

"I'm on a public road. I'm not doing nothing."

"I'm actually glad you stopped by," she said, with a sarcastic smile. "I wanted to ask you about something you might have left up at Lower Fresita Hot Springs. Found it this morning. Something familiar about it."

Travis balked, and seemed surprised. The conversation had taken a turn he hadn't anticipated and didn't like or, from the looks of it, know how to handle. His transparent guilt was easy to read, even though he did not say anything. But a guilty countenance was not grounds for arrest, unfortunately.

"Wanted to ask you about your involvement with the Zebulon Boys too," she said in such a friendly way that, if you didn't know what they were discussing, you might think she was just shooting the bull with a neighbor.

"I don't know what you're talking about," he said, very obviously lying, wobbly as a guy on a bike someone had just kicked as he rode by.

"Where are you staying while you're in New Mexico?" she asked. "No sense in you having to come all the way out here again, in case I have some more questions."

"I don't have to tell you anything," he said.

"Where's the rest of that girl, Travis?"

"What girl?" He smiled at her. "I'm just a guy taking a little break on a public road."

"I don't know. Looks more like loitering and blocking a road to me."

He laughed. "Sure I am. See you later, Jodi." He winked at her in a filthy way before backing that truck up, race car fast and toddler reckless, looking over his shoulder out the back window to steer through that dumb flag of his. Once he'd gotten a couple dozen yards away, he spun the truck around and hightailed it out of there in a cloud of dust and gravel.

Jodi went back to her truck, then drove to the spot where Travis had been parked. She collected all his stupid trash in an evidence bag. Especially the items he'd put to his ugly lips. Either he was the dumbest criminal who'd ever lived, or he was brazen, because leaving his soda cans and cigarette butts for her was basically a DNA offering to the detective gods. Either he was a goddamned fool, or he wanted to be followed. Jodi was going to err on the side of caution and presume the latter, because poachers were also often trappers. They knew how to hide out and wait. They knew how to get their prey to go where they wanted. Jodi was familiar with the strategies of trappers.

For now, she was going to let him go.

He'd show up again soon enough, and when he did, she'd be ready.

———

"Coast is clear. You can come out now."

Oscar seemed shaken up, so Jodi settled him on the sofa and asked Mila to make him a cup of warm tea.

"Should we put this back first, Mom?" Mila asked of the shotgun she was still clutching.

Jodi regretted having scared them and tried to seem nonchalant now to compensate. "Oh, I don't know. I'd maybe keep it out. Stand it in the corner behind the door. Just in case."

Jodi felt Oscar's worried gaze on her as she absently sorted through the day's mail on the entry table.

"It's fine," she said, without looking up. "He won't be back tonight. I need to get back out there, to throw a deer in the game freezer in the barn; then I'll get showered and follow you so you can drive back to the abbey."

"Maybe I should just stay in the guest room tonight," said Oscar.

"Brother Gary be okay with that?" Mila asked as she put the kettle on the stove. "I thought they were getting upset you're gone so much?"

This was news to Jodi, and it concerned her. "We'll be fine. Sounds like you need to get back to your own life for a while."

"Well, at least let me help make dinner," he said. "I know it's been a long day for you."

Jodi considered this. "That would be real nice, Oscar. I already have the steaks marinating. We just need you to peel and boil the potatoes. Mila can make the salad."

"Okay," he said, obviously relieved to have something to do.

"I'll be back in a bit," Jodi said.

She scanned the property with her eyes as she walked to the truck. There, she took out the binoculars and did a more thorough assessment. Travis was nowhere to be seen. All was quiet, for now.

She got Juana settled into her pen, fed her, gave her some fresh water, then checked on the horses, gave them their dinner, and brushed them down. After that, she dragged the deer carcass into the barn, wrapped it in plastic, and settled it into her game freezer.

As she dried off from a quick shower a short time later, Jodi could hear Oscar and Mila singing as they worked in the kitchen, on the other side of the wall. The feeling of having another adult in the house, helping hold it all together, was both comforting and painful, for it brought to mind memories of her dead husband. She dressed in faded jeans, a T-shirt and a plaid cotton shirt, and comfortable woolen house clogs. Summer evenings and nights were cool and sometimes even cold this high up in the mountains. She allowed herself exactly ten seconds to entertain the fear that she might have made a huge mistake by moving back here to chase this dream. She had known the job would be dangerous, but she had never considered that Mila would be involved in her work dramas.

Oscar was just finishing up when she got back to the kitchen, whipping the garlic-mashed potatoes with olive oil instead of Jodi's usual butter, but she was not about to complain. How many celibate thirty-five-year-old men of God would happily step into their dead brothers-in-law's shoes to help raise their nieces? Just Oscar. Jodi was deeply grateful. Someone had also put the elk steaks, which had marinated in soy and ginger all day, into a cast-iron skillet, where they sizzled in their own glorious melted fat. Mila stood at the island, chopping a cucumber from their own garden, to toss into the big wooden salad bowl, along with the lettuce, arugula, and tomatoes they had also grown. The kitchen smelled as rich and inviting as the fanciest steak house, and Jodi's stomach grumbled.

Together, they all set the rustic wooden table and arranged the serving dishes, then sat down. Jodi was about to dig in when Mila gently nudged her with her foot under the table. She was holding one of Oscar's hands, head gently bowed. They were waiting for Jodi to join them.

"Right, forgot," she said. Mila was starting to show an interest in becoming Catholic, a side effect, Jodi supposed, of spending that much time with her priest uncle. Jodi and Graham had not raised their daughter with any sort of religion, though they had occasionally attended touchy-feely Unitarian Universalist services with his hippie parents. Jodi was not sure how she felt about her daughter joining the church that had brought so much misery into her life, but there were worse things a teenage girl might want to become than a Catholic. An influencer, for instance. Jodi mustered all the patience she had, took their hands, and bowed her head.

"We give thee thanks, Our Father," began Oscar, his eyes closed in concentration and reverence. "For the Holy Resurrection which thou hast manifested to us through Jesus, and for the bounty and bread upon this table, and the love of the family gathered together around it. For thine is the power and the glory, forever and ever, amen."

"Amen," Jodi said, along with Mila.

They began passing the serving dishes around, and when the platter with the steaks on it got to Mila, she took it without enthusiasm, as though maybe it had poop on it, then winced at Oscar.

"It's okay," he told her, spooning a mound of potatoes onto his plate as he gave her a supportive nod. "You can tell her."

"Tell me what?" Jodi asked.

Mila set the steak plate down in the center of the table and composed herself to face her mother, the way she had the first time she had told Jodi she wanted to date that boy Marcus Barela. Fear washed through Jodi, and she found herself silently praying—to the god of her childhood, no less—that her only child wasn't pregnant.

"Mom," said Mila, seeking encouragement from her tío's eyes, "I love you, and I respect you, and I know you're all about the hunting and fishing, and that it's your whole career and life now, but I am a little different from you, I think, and I have decided to be a vegan, for ethical reasons. Please don't kill me."

Oscar nodded discreetly to let her know she had done a good job, as though he had coached her for this very moment. Jodi was relieved Mila wasn't pregnant and, honestly, taken aback that her daughter had been so afraid to tell her something like this. Jodi had tried to raise Mila to be strong in her convictions, even if others disagreed.

"I see," said Jodi.

"Please don't be mad."

"Well." Jodi reached out to take the hand Mila had set down on the table. Mila was trembling a little with the courage she'd had to muster. Why was her child so afraid of her? Was she really this intolerant? "I appreciate you telling me, and I want you to know that I believe you are old enough now to make these kinds of choices for yourself. I respect you, and I trust you, and I think it will be good for both of us to live together in a house where we have to tolerate differences in each other."

Mila's eyes grew wide in surprise as she sought her tío's quiet support again. She used to look at Graham the same way she looked at Oscar. Jodi's heart broke a little.

"Told you she'd be cool with it," he said as he speared one of the elk steaks with the tip of his knife. "Plus, órale. Just more steak for me!"

"So you're not mad?" Mila asked.

"Why would I be mad?"

"I don't know. You're always going on and on about how humans evolved to hunt, our eyes on the front of our faces, not the sides, vitamin B twelve, the reason we have language and big brains is that we had to communicate to hunt in groups way back when we were living in caves, blah blah blah."

Jodi sat with this a moment. She did not like her worldview being reduced to "blah blah blah," but Mila was a kid. Validate her, Jodi told herself. Do not argue or get defensive. That's what your mom would have done.

"You're right," said Jodi. "I do say those things a lot. Which means I am even more proud of you for figuring out my way is not your way. That took courage."

"Wow. Who are you, and what have you done with my mother?"

"You know what? I think, in fact, that we should sit down together and work out what kinds of meals we can make that will be suitable for both of us. You can help me with the weekly shopping. I am even going to get on board with you, and we can do hashtag Meatless Mondays together."

"You shouldn't say the *hashtag* part out loud," said Mila.

"Okay."

"Also, no one really uses hashtags anymore."

"Got it. So how do Meatless Mondays sound to you?" Jodi thought about how she could always grab a burger at Goldie's for lunch, without Mila knowing.

"Like something I never thought you'd say in a million years," she said, smiling.

"Sometimes you have to give your mom a chance to surprise you," said Jodi.

After dinner, Oscar asked Jodi if he could talk to her privately. She said of course and asked Mila to clean up the kitchen on her own for a minute while she and Tío stepped outside.

"What are you going to talk about?" asked Mila.

"Grown-up stuff," said Oscar.

"Well, considering that my mom gave me a shotgun to defend the house and your life today, I think I've earned the right to be in on grown-up conversations," said Mila.

"Not this one," said Oscar. "But maybe the next one."

"Aw, man," said Mila, being a good sport despite her disappointment.

Jodi opened the side door that led to the patio in the little walled flower garden off the kitchen and held it for her brother to pass through. She shut the door behind him and motioned for him to follow her through the gate leading to her small apple orchard.

"Knowing Mila, she's got a glass up to the door to listen," said Jodi. "And I can't remember a time you asked to speak to me privately about a grown-up matter. I am guessing you're finally coming out of the closet."

"That's not funny," he said.

"It's funnier than thinking it's a sin to be gay so you join the clergy instead," she said.

Oscar rolled his eyes but only a little, then cleared his throat as he gathered his courage.

"Jodi," he began.

"Jesus, Oscar, just spit it out."

He flinched, clearly hating that she took his Lord's name in vain, and took a deep breath to compose himself. "Well, I was trying. But you interrupted me."

"Sorry," she said. "You're right. Please, continue."

"So you know how we host retreats at the abbey from time to time, right?"

Jodi nodded, feeling impatient. Oscar was the kind of guy who, if you asked for simple directions somewhere, would tell you all the details about all the places you'd see along the way.

"Well, we had the opportunity to host a group from Saint Gianna's not too long ago."

Jodi felt her breath catch in her throat, and she could almost tell what he had left to say still, just from the way he winced.

"Yeah, and?" She tried to sound nonchalant.

"And I got to talking to one of the old-timers from there. And she asked about my family. And I told her about you. She's set to retire soon and seemed like she had some things she wanted to get off her chest. Some regrets."

"And?"

"Jodi. She told me."

Jodi had spent so much of her life lying about having been sent away to Saint Gianna's School for Troubled Girls when she was fifteen that she just continued to do so now. "Told you what, Oscar? There's nothing to tell."

"She remembered you," he said. "And she remembered—"

Here, Jodi cut him off. "We should really get back inside."

Oscar put a hand on her arm to stop her. "She remembered that you wanted to keep him," he said.

Jodi was surprised by the sudden rage that welled up in her. Maybe it was the fact that he looked so forgiving, of the school, of her, of everything. But she turned on him, furious. "Yeah? Did she tell you how she didn't care? How they knocked me out so I wouldn't be conscious for the birth? How they took the baby . . ." She stopped, only now realizing Oscar had said *him*. "Wait, she told you it was a boy?"

Oscar nodded.

"They never even gave me that," she said. "They never even told me if I'd had a boy or a girl. They said it didn't matter, and they must have taken him from me."

"I am so sorry that happened to you," he said. "She's open to talking to you about it, she said, if you want to."

"I don't," Jodi lied. A day had not passed in the thirty years since she was forced to give her baby up for adoption by the school her parents had sent her to that she had not thought about that baby, wondered where the child, now an adult, was.

"She told me that they aren't supposed to tell anyone where their child's been placed but that this rule has bothered her all her life, and now that she is—well, she's not healthy. She said she was very sick. She doesn't have long to live, and she wants to make things right. She said she would be open to helping us find him. If you want."

"Well, fuck."

"Do Mom and Dad know?"

Jodi scoffed. "Do they know? Oscar. They're the ones who sent me there."

"Right. Of course. I mean, I figured. But I thought I'd ask, just in case. They never talked about it."

"Why would they? They lied to everyone in the family just to save face."

"I get it. Even I thought you'd gotten a poetry scholarship to Menaul School in Albuquerque. I had no idea. Just—how come you never told me? You know you can trust me."

"Um, have you met your religion?" Jodi asked.

"If you think I'm going to judge you—" he started, but she interrupted him.

"You are a Catholic priest. Judging other people is pretty much your job, Oscar. So."

"A baby boy," he said, his eyes filling with tears. "I have a nephew somewhere. And you never told me."

"Yeah, well, I don't know where, or if he's even alive, and they won't tell me anything, so. I really don't want to talk about this. At all."

"Does Mila know?"

"No. And I'd like to keep it that way. I can't believe I'm even having to talk about this. I feel completely violated."

"I'm sorry. Anyone else around here know about this?"

Jodi nodded. "Diana," she said, referring to her childhood best friend, who now worked as a research physicist at the Los Alamos National Lab down south.

"Good. I'm glad you at least have her."

"She's a good egg," said Jodi. "You don't have to worry about me, Oscar."

Oscar had a pained look on his face. He reached out to hold her hands. "Jodi, if you want to talk about it, and I am speaking as your brother here and not as a priest . . ."

"There is nothing to talk about," she said, pulling her hands back from his. "I got pregnant at fourteen, because I knew nothing about anything because our parents don't talk about real-life shit. When I went to them for help, they acted like I was the worst person in the world, and they made me go to that school, where—I can't even talk about what happened there."

"I know. I've heard stories over the years. I'm so sorry. My own sister."

"They made me have the baby under general anesthesia. They said it was for my own good. I didn't even get to hold him. They just took him and gave him away. You know what's crazy? I had even changed my mind, halfway through. I wanted to keep him. But they said it was too late, that my parents and I had already signed the forms, and they had a nice home for him all picked out. Not a day has gone by that I don't think about him, Oscar. And now they won't tell me anything about him."

"It's different now," he said. "Let me see what I can find out."

"You'd do that for me?"

"I mean, for us. I would like to know where he is too. Jodi, you should have come to me first with this. I could have helped you. I still can. If you want."

Jodi sat with this for a long moment. "Okay, but promise me you won't tell anyone else. Please don't talk to Mom and Dad about it. I can't deal with them on this. I just can't. I am still so angry at them. I don't even know how to talk to them."

"Of course. I do have one question, though."

"Yeah, go ahead."

"Do I know the father?"

Jodi took a deep breath and blew it out while looking up at the night sky. She did not like to feel things like this, whatever this was. Melancholy. Pain. She'd spent so many years pushing all of it down, masking it in other outrage, in poetry. Not in real life.

"Yes," she said with a heavy sigh. "You know him."

"Who is he?"

"Kurt Chinana," she said, and his jaw dropped.

"The same Kurt Chinana who's the president of the Muelles Apache Nation?"

"Yeah. We went to school together. Mom and Dad hated him because, well. You know how they are."

"Does Kurt know about his baby?"

"The 'baby' is thirty years old now," she corrected him. "And no. He doesn't. Mom and Dad made me break up with him in a letter, and they never let me see him again."

"If you'll excuse my French, but holy shit, Jodi. He's one of the most powerful men in the state."

"I know. Can we drop this for now?"

Jodi turned on her heel and headed for the kitchen door. Oscar followed, catching her by the elbow just before she opened the screen door.

"I like how you handled the vegan thing with her tonight," he said, smiling gently. "I meant to tell you that."

"Thanks."

"And I thought she responded with grace too."

"She's a good one," said Jodi.

"What you told her, about moms sometimes exceeding your expectations of them. I want you to know that brothers can do that, too, if you give them a chance."

She smiled, softening just a little, and squeezed his hand.

"You're a great brother," she said. "And you have never done anything but impress me. Honestly, it's a relief to have someone to talk to about this. Now, let's get you back to the abbey before I get too tired to drive."

10

The next morning the clean-shaven, dark-haired man chose Celia.

Standing at the edge of a deep, wide hole in the ground, he pointed at her where she huddled with the other two women and said, "Her. The chubby one. Get her out."

The other man, the tall bald one with the beard, squinting against the smoke rising off the tip of his own cigarette, lowered the rope ladder and told her to climb up. They took the youngest one, Natalia, last week, in this same way. She had not come back. And now it was Celia's turn, for whatever it was they were doing.

"Climb up," said the bald one.

"No," said Celia, eighteen.

Her full name was Celia Maria Soto, and she was fully bilingual. She was originally from Guatemala, where the murder rate for women was three times the global average and jobs were nearly impossible to find if you happened to be female. She had come to the United States with her mother and younger sisters six years ago, but they had all been separated at the border, and she never saw any of them again. Celia had been sent to live in a dirty, cluttered apartment with a fat white foster family in Minneapolis, but they had treated her like little more than a slave, so she left at sixteen and started cleaning hotels, sharing an apartment with two other Central American women while going to the community college in hopes of one day opening her own insurance agency. She had been afraid to ask the government about her mother's whereabouts because of her undocumented status and had lived in the shadows of society until the day the skinny man with the knife and the bad teeth had kidnapped her from the hotel where she worked in Saint Paul. After she'd spent several days locked in the trunk of his car, he'd brought her here.

Paola and Altagracia, the new one who had been brought in to replace Natalia, had held on to her, and she had held them. They were filthy, cold, tired, and hungry.

The dark-haired man pointed his gun into the hole and fired off one shot. It did not hit anyone, intended to scare them. It worked.

"Next one will not miss," he said. "Climb up."

"What do you want from us?" Celia cried as the other two women began to weep.

The men grumbled together a bit, and then the bald one jumped down into the hole. The women huddled together as far from him as they could get, which wasn't far at all.

"What the hell is wrong with you?" screamed Celia.

"Shut the fuck up," said the bald man.

"Any of you talks back, or fights back, you will get a bullet to the head," said the dark-haired man. "Cooperate, and no one gets hurt."

In no time at all, the bald one had grabbed Celia by the throat and told her to do as she was told. He tied the rope around her, under the armpits, and the other men pulled her out, like some sort of trussed cow. After that, the bald man used the rope ladder to climb out himself, cursing the whole time.

The men used the rope to tie Celia's ankles and wrists together; then, as she screamed, they dragged her over to the firepit, where the dark-haired one withdrew a long metal poker. Celia saw that this was a brand. The kind you might use on cattle.

"Which part should be our calling card this time, gentlemen?"

"We already did a hand. How about a foot?" the one with the yellow hair suggested.

"Foot it is. Left or right. Ron? You decide."

The skinniest one, with bulging eyes, smiled. "Right, of course."

"Travis, you hold her still."

The bald one sat on Celia now as the dark-haired one removed her sneakers and then held the burning end of the brand against the skin on the top of her foot. She shrieked in agony, which made the men laugh.

After that, they dragged her across the rocks and dirt to lift and heave her into the back of an old white pickup. Her face landed in a pool of dried blood and hair. Short hair, like a dog's, maybe. Animal hair. It stuck to her cheek. The truck began to move, bumping noisily over the rough dirt road. Each jolt sent her bones crunching against the metal of the truck's bed. Everything hurt. She prayed for a miracle. To be rescued, found, something. Anything. But these prayers went unanswered.

The truck finally stopped, and she heard the men get out. They came around and lowered the tailgate. They were still in the forest, just a different part of it. She had no idea where they were. They untied her, stripped off her clothes, and threw them into a trash bag. Then they shoved her off the back of the truck like a sack of flour.

"Run," said the dark-haired man.

Celia was confused by this.

"Go," he said. "We're setting you free. We'll give you an hour to get ahead of us; then it's hide-and-go-seek."

She looked around and saw nothing but miles and miles of trees. Her burned foot now bore the same symbol these men had on the patches on the arms of their matching camouflage jackets. A pyramid, with an eye in it.

"I said run." The dark-haired one smiled at her, clearly enjoying her fear.

"What are you, stupid?" asked the bald man. "He said go. Now, git."

"I can handle this, Travis," said the dark-haired one. "If I want your help, I'll ask for it." He chambered his gun.

Celia ran.

11

Deputy Ashley Romero was new to the Rio Truchas County Sheriff's Department, but she was not new to law enforcement. She had gone straight into the police force in Albuquerque after graduating from high school and had worked her way up to become a detective, level two, by the time she was twenty-nine years old. Now, just past her thirtieth birthday, she was an experienced, seasoned, big-city law enforcement agent, who, due to the circumstances of her father's rapidly declining health, had chosen to relocate back to the rural county where she had been raised to help out at home. None of this impressed her new boss, who had hired her mostly because she was the only person without a criminal background of their own to apply for the job. Sheriff Lorenzo Gurule, sixty-something, with a buzz cut and washboard abs that he still liked to invite the other men on his team to punch as a way to test him, still enjoyed hovering over her desk to see if she was making any "rookie" mistakes. He never tired of reminding her she was the first woman he'd ever trusted enough to hire to work under him, other than his wife. He thought this was hilarious. It was his lurking obnoxious presence that had inspired her to head out on a call that ordinarily she might have ignored altogether. Anything to get away from him, and now that he was battling the vending machine for a pack of cheese crackers that had decided not to fall, even though he'd paid, this seemed like as good a time to sneak away as any.

"I'm going to head out on that ten twenty-seven five," Ashley told the dispatcher, Karina Jaramillo-Gurule.

"The one at Madame Esmeralda's place?" Karina asked, raising her painted-on eyebrows in surprise.

"Yeah."

"Uh, why, though?"

"Protocol to follow up on a call of a burglary," said Ashley as she strapped on her duty belt, trying to hurry before her boss came back.

"Well, I mean, sure," scoffed Karina. "When the call doesn't come from the crazy lady who makes the same call every day for the past ten years."

"A person called to tell us someone broke into her house," said Ashley. "We are obligated to check into it. It doesn't matter how credible we think they are."

"Did you miss the part where the person she said broke in and stole all her canned goods has been dead for seventeen years?"

"Maybe she made a mistake."

"Hey, babe!" She called out this last bit to the sheriff, who happened also to be her husband. "Your new girl here wants to head over to the psychic's place, to investigate her dead boyfriend breaking in again."

Lorenzo stopped beating up the vending machine to shake his head at Ashley in disappointment. "I already told her to ignore that woman's calls," he said.

"I'd like to check it out anyway," said Ashley. "Even if she's wrong ninety-nine percent of the time, there could be one time when she's right, and I wouldn't want to be the officer who ignored the call."

The switchboard lit up again, and Karina, still seeming to be laughing at Ashley, turned her attention to the incoming call.

"If you want to go talk to a crazy lady, be my guest," said the sheriff. "You're just lucky it's slow right now. But I don't want to have to be the man who said I told you so. You'll have to see for yourself. She's nuttier than a squirrel turd."

Fifteen minutes later, Ashley steered her cruiser into the driveway leading to the decrepit pink adobe house registered to a Maryanne Tina

Garcia, a self-proclaimed seventy-something curandera and psychic who went by the professional name Madame Esmeralda. The house was located in the small town of Zarigüeya, just through the Coyote Pass, near the Colorado border, its front porch decorated with several pots of plastic flowers and three cats who roosted on the sagging armchairs, most likely meant only for the indoors, that had been placed outside as a sort of waiting area.

Madame Esmeralda opened the door just a crack, but it was enough for Ashley to see her burgundy kimono and silver turban and the neon-orange lipstick, applied thick as frosting, that leaked lines above her upper lip.

"I am only taking walk-ins if there is something you must urgently know," said the psychic.

"Hi, Madame Esmeralda. It's Deputy Ashley Romero with the Rio Truchas County Sheriff's Department."

"Oh," she said, pulling off the turban and dispensing with the fake smile. She seemed disappointed Ashley was not a paying customer. "What do you want?"

"You called us to report a burglary?"

"I did?" Madame Esmeralda looked confused. Ashley knew this look well. Her own father was battling dementia.

"Yeah. A little bit past noon today."

"What day is this?"

"Wednesday."

"What time is it?"

"A little past two in the afternoon, ma'am."

The psychic considered this for a moment; then her face lit up as something took root. She opened the door completely and stood aside to let the deputy enter. "Oh, yes! That's right. Come in, come in. I have to tell you about it."

The living room of the small house had been converted into the equivalent of a home office for a curandera and psychic, complete with a round table, upon which rested a large crystal ball. The blackout curtains were drawn, and the only light in the room came from a small lamp with a red lampshade. The ceiling's vigas had dozens of bundles of dried herbs hanging down from them. The rest of the cluttered decor seemed to be a mix of Catholic and Native iconography. There was a smell of incense and bacon in the air, and somewhere in one of the back rooms, a television was on, to what sounded like a lowbrow daytime talk show, something about paternity tests.

"Please, have a seat," said Madame Esmeralda, motioning to the table.

"I prefer to stand," said Ashley, removing her notepad. "But feel free to sit if you're more comfortable. Could you tell me what happened?"

The psychic waddled to the table, in a way that made Ashley think one of the woman's legs was shorter than the other, and plopped down in a chair with a humph. "He comes around all the time," she said. "It don't matter how many times I told him not to come here; he still comes here, trying to pick a fight. I don't fight. I'm a lover, not a fighter. He knows that. So he's started taking things from me instead, like he's trying to egg me on. You know how it is when a man wants to fight with you? It's like that."

"Who are you talking about?"

"Craig," said Madame Esmeralda, as though this should have been obvious.

"Last name?"

"That is his last name. First name is Billy."

"Billy Craig?"

"Billy Craig," spat the psychic, as if the very thought of this person made her sick.

"Do you know this man?"

"Know him? I was married to him."

"So your ex-husband is stalking you and breaking into your home?"

"That's right. That's right. Except we never got divorced."

"Are there items missing?"

"Yes! Yes! I can show you."

Ashley wondered how she planned to show the missing items, but she was fascinated by mental illness and tried to treat everyone with the respect and kindness she herself would like to be treated with if she were in a similar circumstance.

"Come with me, dear," Madame Esmeralda said, rising with some effort.

Ashley followed her through the hanging beads that separated the living room from the hallway, and then they took a quick left into a hoarder's kitchen and out a back door. The backyard was as cluttered as the rest of the house, and there was a small shed at the far side of it. The door to this stood open.

"There," said Madame Esmeralda, pointing to this shed. "In there. He came and took my canned vegetables. I had over a hundred cans in there. I get them discount on account of my granddaughter working at the Sam's Club. I had beans, and corn, and Hatch chiles. Everything. And now, look. Ten cans left."

Ashley's own father often forgot if he'd eaten, and unless someone was there to monitor his meals, he could eat all day long and make himself sick, thinking he was starving.

"Worst thing is, the last time he did this, you know, I asked him to at least pay for the food. You want to take some food, you're hungry, fine, I understand. I'm a nice lady. I will help you out. But I am not making as much money as I used to, and the social security, it doesn't go as far as you think. So I asked him, I wrote him a note, and I left it here, I said, 'Billy Craig, if you are going to take my cans, the least you can do is leave me some money. Pay me.' But do you know what he did?"

"No, ma'am, I don't."

"He left me a foot."

"A foot?"

"Yes, a foot."

"Like a lucky rabbit paw?" asked Ashley.

"No. Come on. I'll show you. Right over there, under the cotton-wood tree by my little pond. Used to have more water in that pond, but we don't get the runoff from the snow like we used to. I am worried about my little fish. I have some carp in there."

Ashley started toward the small pond and tree, just the other side of the backyard fence. "Can you show me this foot?" she asked.

"It's hard to miss. It's a foot and nothing else. You don't see that every day. I mean, I know Billy Craig lives at the cemetery now, and so I figured maybe that's all he could find. But if he thinks I want a thing like that, he has another thing coming."

Madame Esmeralda shuffled and waddled across the yard, in her house slippers, and led Ashley to the tree. There, she pointed, and pushed her lips together in great annoyance with her dead ex-husband.

"Oh my God," said Ashley.

"Well, I told you that," said Madame Esmeralda. "What, you didn't believe me? Nobody up at the sheriff's believes nothing I say no more."

Ashley Romero took the radio from her duty rig and pressed the button to call Karina. "Yeah, hi. I'm out here at Madame Esmeralda's place in Zarigüeya? Looks like I'm going to need some backup. Medical examiner too."

"You're shitting me," said Karina. "You got a body?"

"Part of one, anyway."

12

Travis, Ron, and Eric sat side by side in the middle of the dark forest, on a downed log beside the firepit they'd built with found stones, listening to General Zeb's evening lecture as the fresh-caught meat roasted and crackled. Javelina, the General said it was. Wild boar. Just tasted like pork, and they had it damn near every meal out here. The corn and beans they'd found on the psychic's land had come in handy and would round out the meal just fine.

The General had them leave their calling cards in places frequented by touchy-feely woo-woo liberal types but that weren't crowded. Hot springs. Local psychic. People would start to get the picture, pretty soon. The Zebulon Boys were here, and they meant business.

Travis hated sitting next to Ron, because he was scrawny and sniffly and smelled like a dead rat. All that stringy hair. Looked like a god-damned pedophile from one of them cop shows. Eric was all right, but Travis wasn't sure the guy could be trusted. Something shifty about him. All that yellow hair, bleached like a weirdo. Too quick to agree to everything. The kind who bottled it up and stabbed you in your sleep. The General, who was leagues better than these other losers, looked like a leader was supposed to look—strong and assertive, a total alpha male ready to defend his people. Travis loved this man and would do anything for him.

"We are down to two girls, but I have more recruits on the way," said General Zeb. "I expect you troops to welcome them in a friendly manner, but report to me if anything at all seems abnormal about them.

We have to be careful, and you are my eyes and ears on the ground when I'm not there. Understood?"

"Understood," Travis, Ron, and Eric replied. Travis hoped to God these new recruits, whoever they were, would be stronger and better than these two sacks of shit. You couldn't take down the reconquista with a gang of misfit goddamned toys.

Somewhere in the darkness, off to the side, came the muffled sounds of the two remaining women, Paola and Altagracia, crying in their hole in the ground. The General did not tell them to quiet down when they cried, because he said he liked that sound. Found it "nourishing." He only told them to pipe down if they tried talking to him. He was pacing back and forth, on the other side of the fire, singing Eric's praises for successfully finding a Mexican wolf den. It had long been a dream of the General's, to kill a Mexican wolf. To let its spirit inhabit him. He liked the symbolism of it but also the spirituality of it.

When Travis had come to camp two weeks ago, from Arizona, seeking to join the movement, thrilled to have finally been invited, he had known that there might be some hunting involved. That's what the General had liked most about his application, that Travis was an experienced hunter and not afraid to break the law to take what he needed from the land. He'd answered the poaching question honestly, which he guessed a lot of applicants probably didn't. They probably thought Zeb would want them to be law abiding, seeing that their job with Mexicans was just to enforce the laws against the illegals. But Travis knew what kind of men were needed for this job. The kind who took what was rightfully theirs, no matter what the hell the liberal laws had to say about it.

"Anything you'd like to share with the troops this evening, Private Lee?" the General asked him about halfway through dinner.

"I found out where the Mexican woman cop lives. The one that ticketed me. We can keep an eye on her now."

"Well, good," said General Zeb. "I don't like how she talked to you."

"I visited with her a little."

The General sized him up, chewing thoughtfully, looking like he wasn't entirely pleased with this information. "Now don't you go getting reckless, Lee. We need cool heads out here."

"No, sir," said Travis. "I kept it cordial. Just checking out what she knew. It was just as I thought. I think she's onto us."

"Why do you think that?"

"She mentioned us by name."

The General smiled and nodded like he'd done something special. "Hell, Lee. That's good. Why do you think we're leaving the calling cards? People need to know who's responsible when the New Gettysburg comes. What else you learn about her?"

"I mean, she seems smart. For a Mexican chick. We should keep an eye on her."

General Zeb went back to slice more meat, this time a plate for Travis. "You think she'll get in the way?"

Travis shrugged. "I wouldn't put it past her. She thinks she's tough. Got a mouth on her."

"If that's the case, then we need to take care of the problem."

"She has a daughter, looked like. Same age as them two, maybe a little younger." Travis pointed his fork toward the pit.

"Mexican?"

"I mean, the mom is, so. At least half."

"Interesting," said the General. "I want you to go back there. You and Ron. Friday night. Get the daughter for me. We'll use her as a bargaining chip if need be. Good find, actually." The General put a hand on Travis's shoulder, patted him with affection. "Proud of you, son."

"Thank you, General Zeb." Travis felt a frog in his throat. To have his idol appreciate his work like this was almost too good to be true.

"All right. That's enough talking. Finish your supper, boys." The General chinned toward the folding tables set up by their tents, with the bomb components all spread out on top of them. Hunting the girls was just the entry point, to prove you wanted to be in the army. The real battle was going to be much bigger than that. "We've got work to do."

13

Eric waited until Ron and Travis were sound asleep to leave. It was two in the morning when he finally felt safe enough to peel himself out of his sleeping bag, to slip silently into his boots. He held his breath as wolves howled in the near distance, hoping this wouldn't wake the others. They snored on. He took only his gun and his cell phone. He could replace everything else, in time. Zeb said he had sold his truck as soon as he arrived. He said it was a way to erase any tracks leading to them, but Eric now believed it was a way of keeping him captive too. He had to go on foot, and quietly.

Once he'd gotten a quarter mile down the mountain, Eric broke into a run. All-out, 100 percent sprinting for the first few minutes, putting as much distance as he could between him and that lunatic.

He didn't have an issue with killing Mexicans. He'd killed enemy combatants in Iraq and Afghanistan. He had no problem killing invaders, and he'd do it again in a heartbeat, for God and country. But no matter how he figured it, chasing down unarmed naked females in the woods wasn't war; it was crazy. If Zeb wanted to hunt down Mexicans in battle, he should have gone after some of the men down there on the border. That's what Eric had thought he'd be signing up for, that kidnapping the girl was maybe so they could use her as a decoy or something. But no. Zeb wanted to chase them like wild animals, brand them, cut their body parts off. Sick shit. Also, Eric sure as hell wasn't interested in killing endangered animals. He was an outdoorsman and a conservationist, and he'd left the poaching question blank on the application because he knew that some of these good families out in the rural places, they could have times when money was tight and the only meat they'd have would be something caught out of season. He could understand that. But this poaching for the hell of it, and the thing with these women. It was all too weird. Not to mention the new plans to plant bombs at the casinos and the city hall. Eric knew there were a lot of Mexicans living around here, but they weren't the only people who might be in those places. He wasn't a goddamned terrorist. He was a patriot. He'd come here to help keep America safe from alien invaders. That was it. Not to kidnap women—at least one of them, the one who smelled like marijuana when they brought her in, she wasn't even Mexican, she was Indian, she said, supposedly some daughter of some big chief somewhere—and chase them through the woods. He'd thought this paramilitary outfit was more serious than that. General Zeb was fixated on killing him a wolf, and while Eric wasn't opposed to hunting legally, he did not see what poaching a wolf had to do with protecting Americans from Mexicans. It was just plain stupid. This Zeb guy was more about himself and his rage than about honestly wanting to help out their people. Online, General Zeb was strong and well spoken. But out here, he was basically like your crazy-ass uncle, an absolute unhinged lunatic. He would have killed the man in his sleep, if he hadn't thought his little lackey Travis would have defended him. He'd have killed them both, if he thought he could.

Eric had no desire to tell the police about the General, however. It was none of his business anymore. Eric was as libertarian as they came and did not get up in other people's business. Plus, all the cops around here were Mexicans, anyway. They'd never treat Eric fairly. That was a given. He did not care what happened to those women up there; it was none of his business now. All he wanted was to get the hell out of New Mexico, to go back to Hemet, California, maybe change his name, go back to his job at the Jiffy Lube.

When the floodlights came on him, hot and white enough to blind him, Eric was so startled he almost crapped his pants. He hadn't even seen the house, but there it was, behind the lights, along with the silhouette of a man in a cowboy hat.

"Who are you and what are you doing here?" came a gruff man's voice, with a western twang Eric had not heard too much of around here. He sounded white. This was a relief to Eric.

"Who wants to know?" he asked, squinting to try to see the figure behind the light.

"That's none of your business," said the man's voice. "Now I'll give you ten seconds to figure out whether you're going to answer me before I shoot you dead for trespassing on my land."

Eric heard the gun cock. He did not need ten seconds. He only needed five seconds.

"Are—are you a white man, sir?" asked Eric.

"Ten, nine, eight," came the reply.

"My name is Eric," he said. "I come in peace, sir. I'm just lost."

14

Shortly after sunrise on Thursday, Jodi went horseback riding with Mila along the grassy banks of Ovejitas Creek for a little mother-daughter bonding time. Afterward, they both caught up on chores around the house, including Jodi finally getting around to butchering the roadkill deer from the casino that she'd brought in from work earlier in the week. Mila, naturally, wanted nothing to do with any of this now that she'd gone vegan. She went in the house to clean the bathrooms, which was a damn first for that, and as good a reason to support her dietary life choices as Jodi could think of. Because Jodi was meeting up with the handsome new wildlife veterinarian to do a check on the wolf den later in the day, she would be starting her workday closer to noon and wanted to get as much done around home as she could before then. She was not good at staying still and doing nothing, even during her downtime, and preferred to be outside keeping her little homestead running.

With the deer hung head down from the game hoist and gambrel behind the barn, Jodi worked to get it skinned and dismembered, setting bits and pieces down on the tarp draped over a plastic folding table she'd set up nearby. It was nice to do this good, honest labor without neighbors watching her in horror, as had been the case when she lived in Andover. All the other wives in that neighborhood had actually seemed to enjoy things like tennis, and seemed to regard Jodi as something of a murderer. Every fall, following a tradition she had developed growing up on a ranch with parents who hunted, Jodi went on solo hunts up north, to harvest most of the organic, grass-fed meat she, Graham, and

Mila would eat for the rest of the year. The neighbor ladies reacted as though she were a serial killer the first time Jodi came home with a dead buck tied up in the back of her Jeep. She'd butchered it in the backyard, much in this same way, and because the yards in Andover didn't usually have fences between them, some of the neighbors had watched this from behind discreetly gripped curtains. The tennis invites stopped coming after that, but that was just as well. Jodi had never seen the purpose of hitting a ball back and forth for nothing but imaginary points and the meaningless domination such points conveyed. People used to be skilled because skills were needed for survival. Now, people couldn't do anything real for themselves. They still had an instinctual drive to feel accomplished, but they aimed it at worthless pursuits, like taking selfies, complaining about injustices on Twitter, or subscribing to the *New Yorker*. The modern world had gone to pure bullshit.

A little past 4:00 p.m., Jodi pulled her work truck up to Henley's house, up the mountain past Uquiba Lake, near the bluffs where Oscar's abbey could be found. The house was a square log cabin, recently built from the looks of it, encircled by fir trees, not too far off one of the state highways leading south into Gato Montes. He owned a Subaru Outback, olive green, complete with a bike rack in the back and a ski or snowboard rack on top, and this was parked beside the house. Just beyond that, she spotted the veterinarian breaking down some large cardboard boxes, stomping them into flattened submission. Jodi did not envy him. Moving was stressful, even under the best of circumstances. When he heard her pulling up, he waved and trotted over to the truck.

"Is it four already?" he asked, rhetorically. "Been fighting with boxes all day. Give me ten, to get changed and gather some things? You can wait inside if you like."

More because she was curious about what the young veterinarian's decorating style might be than because she minded waiting in her truck, she agreed. Inside, the house smelled like miso soup and oranges and was decorated in a manner that surprised Jodi. She'd been expecting the decor to match the outside of the cabin, but it was contemporary and bright, all beiges and grays, expensive furniture in a Bauhaus midcentury modern style she associated with hipster bachelor lofts back east. She'd gotten used to the usual southwestern art people favored around here and was surprised and pleased to see his collection of framed prints, and maybe an original or two, by excellent artists she recognized but had not seen in a while, including Kehinde Wiley, among others. The place was spotless and, like her own house, held no shortage of books on a wide variety of subjects.

"Can I get you something to drink?" he asked. "Haven't really stocked up yet, but I've got bubbly water, unsweetened but flavored with, I forget what. I think it's lemon or lime. And coffee. I've got iced tea, and coffee."

"I'd love some coffee," Jodi said, taking a seat on one of the chairs.

"Cream and sugar?"

"No, thanks. Just black."

A minute later, he handed her a thick, handleless pottery mug of steaming coffee, with a promise to be right back. "Make yourself at home," he said. "Sorry about the mess." There was no mess. Jodi did make herself at home, using the time to peruse the collection of framed photos on top of the upright piano. Lots of pictures of Henley with wild animals, wolves most of all. And a couple of shots of him with what appeared to be his parents, a college graduation picture, maybe, and some family get-together photos. No girlfriend or wife that she could see. Not that she was looking.

They engaged in small talk as Jodi drove them to the trailhead. He asked about the area, what it was like to grow up there, and she told him the good parts. Close community, lots of family, solid values that did not seem to be too corrupted by the outside world. Lots of people who were land rich but money poor and grew what they needed, giving away the surplus. She told him she noticed his degrees from Berkeley and Stanford, and he told her that all the book learning in the world was less important than the year he'd spent living amid a pack of wolves in Canada, for field study. She listened, fascinated, as he described having given up everything in life to literally live with wolves in their den, how the alpha male and female brought him food, how he ate only what they ate, which was mostly raw deer and elk and sometimes fruit. He helped the pair raise their pups. She had so many questions, about how he had gotten them to trust him, and he said it was easy. Wolves weren't like people, he said. If you hung around long enough and were cool, they accepted and cared for you.

The conversation continued as Jodi led him up the trail, past the hot springs, up over the top of the mountain, and down the other side, to the meadow where Lyle Daggett sometimes grazed his herd.

"Wow," said Henley, taking in the sweeping views of this pristine wild place. "Don't tell me where the den is. Let me see if I can guess."

"Okay."

He took his time, looking over the entire stunning panorama. The sun was still fairly high in the sky. "We might want to hunker down a minute, till it feels like the right time."

"The right time?"

"I want to check on the pups without the parents there," he said. "At least until they get to know me. And this doesn't feel like hunting time, yet. I'd bet everything I own that they're all still in the den."

"Okay," said Jodi.

Henley folded his legs beneath him and took a seat on the trail. He closed his eyes and breathed in deeply. Jodi remained standing, aware that she was on the clock, and alert for anything unusual out here. After a minute or two of what appeared to be meditation, Henley removed a set of binoculars from his backpack and continued to search for the den.

"There," he said after a while, pointing to a large downed aspen in front of a rocky outcropping at the top of the escarpment that sloped up the mountain from the valley.

"That's amazing," said Jodi. "How did you know?"

"That year gave me a wolf sense, I think," he said. "It just looks like the best place to be a wolf. You're up high enough to see your enemies coming. The tree is a natural entry, protective. They can slip under that tree, but a bear can't. You're near a river, so lots of fresh water whenever you want it. The plateau is where prey animals graze. It's paradise, really."

"Nicely done," she said.

He continued to watch the entrance of the den until he saw what he was waiting for. "There they are!"

Jodi removed her own binoculars, and sure enough, she saw the alpha pair, along with three younger adult wolves, rangy and lean, leaving the den.

"Have y'all named them yet?" he asked.

"I mean, they have numbers. And a couple of them have been tagged."

"I'm going to name them, then," he said. "The papa, he's the biggest one, with the darker fur? That's going to be Amadeus. And the mama, she's actually the second-smallest one. She's going to be Virginia."

"Wolfgang and Wolfe?" asked Jodi.

"Of course."

"The other female? Naomi. And the two brothers? Blitzer and Tom."

"Are you always so literal?" she asked.

"No. From time to time I am downright figurative. Shall we?"

Jodi's radio crackled to life just as they began walking along the edge of the valley, and Becky's voice broke through. "Hey, hon. Jodi, you there?"

"Yep," Jodi answered as quietly as she could.

"Hate to bother you on the wolf date, but just got a call from Hafeez. Thought you'd want to hear this."

"Okay. You're on speakerphone, by the way." Jodi wanted to make sure Becky didn't blurt out anything she shouldn't.

"Hey, Dr. Bethel."

"Hi, Becky."

"He's family now, Jodes. He can eavesdrop. I know you kids have baby wolf-wolfs to see, so I'll be quick. Jodes. Hafeez got a call from Sheriff Gurule's office. A Deputy Romero—she's brand new, like you freaks—seems she went out on a call to that crazy psychic's place. Madame Emerald."

"Esmeralda," Jodi corrected her.

"Whatever. The one with those ridiculous billboards all along the highway? Her. Long story short, crazy lady said her dead ex-husband broke into her shed to steal some canned corn, and left a gift for her as payment. Are you ready?"

"Do I have a choice?" Jodi asked.

"No. Are you sitting down?"

"No."

"Okay. So, the gift? It's a severed foot."

"Fuck," said Jodi, and she turned away from Henley a little out of a sense of protectiveness.

"Here's the kicker, though. You see what I did there? Kicker?"

"I see."

"You're not the only one who's got puns, hon."

"I wish I were."

Becky laughed. "The kicker is, it has that same symbol on it. Burned into the skin. *Branded* is the word Hafeez used."

"Branded."

"Branded. He thinks the hand was probably branded too. And he said it's a different person than the hand. Totally different DNA."

"Jesus. Do we know whose it was?"

"Not yet. He's still running tests. When you get done there, I set a dinner date for you with Deputy Romero, so you two can compare notes."

"Okay."

"I don't know how much of that you got into during your training, but playing nice with the sheriff and the state police is part of what makes your job as a game warden suck so bad."

"Yeah, I know."

"This deputy's got a chip on her shoulder too. Loves to tell people how she was a big shot detective with the APD."

"Great."

"I'm like, 'If you were that hot shit, girl, what are you doing working for Lorenzo Gurule in Rio Truchas?'"

"I bet she loved that."

"She's all yours now. Meet her at Goldie's. Call me when you're on your way, and I'll let her know."

Jodi put the radio back into its holster and gave Henley a "welp" kind of a look, to counteract his measured astonishment.

"Dude. Paying for stolen creamed corn with a severed foot, though," he said. "That's more like some Oakland shit. I thought I was leaving that behind when I came out here to Rio Truchas County, New Mexico."

"You have much to learn about our ways, young man," she said. She hadn't meant for this to come out sounding flirty. Or maybe she had. Either way, it did. And Henley ran with it.

"I ain't that young."

"That's a matter of perspective."

He grinned with only one side of his mouth as he picked up a stick. "I bet you could teach me some things, though. As an elder."

"I'm sure I could. Like how you shouldn't hit on women old enough to be your mother."

"Ouch."

She grinned back. "Let's go see some baby wolves."

"I think that's a great idea," he said. "Because after that disturbing call, I think I need a spiritual palate cleanser."

15

Lyle Daggett had learned one thing in his years as a military interrogator: the less a man talked to his suspect, the better.

This is why, as the flinchy blond man who said his name was Eric flapped his lips about this and that, Lyle just leaned back in his chair at the kitchen table and listened. You learned more that way. He'd been listening to the guy talk a mountain of shit all day long as he put him to work fixing fence.

"Eric," he learned, was dumber than a bag of hammers and truly did not like Mexicans. Last night, when Lyle had dragged him in from the night at the business end of a rifle, this man had talked about how glad he was that a white man had found him instead of Mexicans. Lyle had kept quiet, because it would not have done him any good to mention that his beloved late wife, Renata, had been from Guadalajara. Nor would it have been useful for him to tell this stranger that Lyle's three grown children, Monica, Laura, and Tomas, were half-Mexican, and that two of them had married full Mexicans, and now he had four grandchildren who were more Mexican than anything else.

Truth was, Lyle had not found this man at all. Lyle had been out putting his dogs up in their kennel when this man came crashing out of the forest onto his land. This man had trespassed. He had invaded Lyle's land and did not see one ounce of irony in it when juxtaposed against his hatred of what he called "illegal invaders."

Lyle had let this man spend the night on some straw in the locked barn, mostly so he could sleep soundly knowing Eric was contained.

He'd put him to work mending fences during the day, to earn his stay, and also to see what kind of a person this was. Turned out Eric was the kind of person who didn't know how to mend a fence, or do much of anything. A city guy. Claimed to work at a Jiffy Lube in Hemet, California.

Lyle filed all this information away in his head.

Now, the man was talking about Mexicans again. He talked through mouthfuls of the steak and potatoes Lyle had been kind enough to serve him for an early dinner. Lyle had fed him because it was hospitable to do so, not because he liked him. He did not, and he was still trying to figure out what to do about that. Some of the things Eric had said sounded downright illegal, as in criminal, as in he might have killed some people. Lyle was taking his time before deciding what to do with all that.

Lyle had noticed a few other things about this fellow. He was jumpy as all get-out. And he didn't know how to interact with a person in a normal way. He had a robotic way of talking, like all he ever did was talk to a computer. The camo clothes were all brand new but had patches on them, with that same symbol he'd seen on those traps set up out by the wolf den. This man's hands were dirty but had no calluses.

Everything about the man seemed fake as a six-dollar bill.

And Lyle should know, because most things about Lyle were fake too. The only difference was Lyle was smart, and careful, because he had no desire to ever have his past found out. And this man was not any of those things.

"They're taking over through the birth canal," said the man. "Come here just to shoot babies out their hoo-has like bazookas. They think we won't fight back, if it's babies, you know? But a Mexican is a Mexican, no matter what size."

Lyle had so many things he would have liked to say in response. For instance, he'd have liked to point out that this last bit sounded like the worst Dr. Seuss book ever written. But instead he just laced his fingers together on the table and nodded to let the man know he'd heard him. Not that he agreed with him, just that he'd heard the words. If Eric thought Lyle agreed with him, well, that was on Eric.

"Do you let roaches grow in the walls until they're full grown?" asked the man in an attempt at rhetoric.

"I don't reckon I do," said Lyle. It was an honest answer. Lyle was a meticulous man. There were no roaches, rats, or mice to be found in this trailer, or in any other building on the two-hundred-thousand-acre ranch.

"Exactly. You exterminate them."

Lyle had been on the fence about whether this man was truly a dangerous racist until he heard that word. *Exterminate.* Now he knew for sure. This was not a person he wanted anywhere near his house: not because Lyle feared for his own safety but because he worried for the man's.

"We should get going, Eric," he said with a sigh. "I like to be home before dark, and it's a long drive out to the bus depot. If you want to keep drinking your coffee, you can put it in one of the thermoses in that cabinet there."

The man took his plate to the sink and even rinsed it. He thanked Lyle for the food, patted him on the back. Said, again, how surprised he was that in a county with this many Mexicans, there was at least one real true American still ranching the land. You do not ranch the land, Lyle thought. *Ranch* is not a verb.

Half an hour later, as Lyle steered his Chevy pickup onto an old logging road up the back hill, the man was still talking about Mexicans. Didn't even seem to notice they weren't leaving the ranch at all, just getting deeper back into it. The supposed Mexican invasion was a goddamned obsession with him. Lyle disagreed with every word, but he chose to chew on a toothpick instead of engaging with a moron. As often was the case, the fool took his white silence to be xenophobic camaraderie.

"There's a camp up there," he told Lyle, pointing north. "If you run across them boys, don't do it."

Lyle wasn't sure what this meant. The sentence was as poorly constructed as the man's brain. He did, however, suspect that this camp had something to do with the missing calves he'd been puzzling over. And the random shots he heard from time to time.

"And why's that?" he asked.

"I thought the guy in charge was one of us, but he's not."

Lyle nodded. "Terrible when you realize someone isn't actually on your side." He pulled up to an old rock shack that didn't get much use, next to a splintered and weathered old pen that used to hold sheep a hundred or so years ago. The shack used to be where cowboys settled down for the night, before there were trailers. Now and then, if a storm came in or if Lyle was particularly tired, he used it to take a siesta.

"He's just crazy, is all."

Lyle nodded again, wondering how crazy a man had to be to have this unstable person consider him crazy. "Good to know. Listen, Eric, I need to do a little chore here in the rock house. Give me a hand."

"Sure thing," said Eric, eager to help his comrade.

Lyle opened the cabin door with a key and stood to one side to let Eric go in first. "After you, sir," he said.

"Thanks, Captain," said Eric.

Lyle chewed his toothpick and waited until the man was inside the little windowless building before closing and locking the door behind him.

"Hey!" called Eric from inside the rock house. "What's going on?"

Lyle watched for a moment as the doorknob jiggled. Eric's voice grew more panicked. "What the fuck, man? C'mon."

"Boy, I'll tell you what, Eric," said Daggett, in a regular tone of voice, his mouth close to the door. "I never met a nicer bunch of people than my Mexican in-laws. Most upstanding, religious people you'd ever find. Loved the Lord. Prayed to him every day."

Lyle waited for a response but was met only with silence.

"I'd suggest, Eric, that you learn to do the same. On your knees, the way they do."

Lyle walked back to his truck, noticing a rainstorm starting to build. He'd call Becky over at Fish and Wildlife once he got back up the hill and had a signal. Until then, Eric would be all right. There was a cot in there, and a gallon of water. A saddle blanket or two. Nothing to eat, but a day or two without food never killed a man. The cabin didn't get much use, but it was in good condition, because, as a responsible man, Lyle Daggett took care of things.

He hadn't been to town in the evening for a drink in a long while, but after the stress of dealing with another person all day, and especially one this stupid, Lyle needed to get lost in a crowd and drown his sorrows. He went back to shower and put on a nicer hat before heading in to Goldie's.

16

Kurt Chinana was on the last mile of his five-mile run. He'd run six tomorrow, seven the next, and then eight, as part of training for the first inaugural Inter-Tribal New Mexico Relay Ultra Marathon, slated to launch next summer. He was forty-seven, and would be forty-eight by the time the race came around, but as the president of the Muelles Apache Nation, he felt it his duty to run at least the first leg of the race, through his own territory up here in the north. Though he preferred to run outside, it was threatening to rain this evening. He pounded out the miles instead on the high-end treadmill, in the new gym he'd had built as an addition to his expansive corner office at the government center, and watched the storm roll across this beautiful enormous land through his floor-to-ceiling windows. The podcast he was listening to on his smartphone, *It's Native Business*, was interrupted by an incoming audio call from his wife, Gina, who had finally decided to grace him with her almighty presence and actually call him back. He had been texting and calling her all day. She'd ignored him or sent him straight to voice mail. He could hear the commotion of the airport in the background on her end as he said hello.

"Make it quick," she said.

"That's what she said," he joked back, hoping to disarm her at least a little.

"Only when he's good at it," she snapped back, as if to imply that Kurt was not. She could get mean when she didn't get her way, and the tranquilizers she took to fly tended to loosen up her already loose tongue.

"You guys boarding yet?" he asked.

"Not yet. Probably soon. I don't have much time, so let's make this quick, okay?"

"I've been trying to reach you. We wouldn't be rushed if you'd picked up. Where have you been?"

"What is this? You some kind of overseer now? Don't have Paola to control anymore, so you have to control me now? God, Kurt. You're so predictable. I shouldn't have even called."

Kurt was glad there was no one around to overhear this call. His frequent verbal jousts with his tempestuous wife—who tended to accuse him of all the things she actually was doing—were one of the main reasons he was less and less comfortable using the company gym on the third floor. He'd had this private exercise room built mostly so that he could fight with his wife in isolation. Word got around fast on the reservation, and as the public face of his people, he was not in a position to be the subject of gossip right now. Not with three big mineral-exploration deals on the table. There was too much at stake.

"Well, that's what I'm calling you about," he said. "I wanted to know if you'd heard anything from our dearest daughter today."

Gina sighed, and he could almost see her rolling her eyes as though the world were ending. "God, Kurt. No. I haven't heard from her. She doesn't have to check in with us all the time anymore. In case you haven't noticed, our daughter is an adult now, living in her own place."

"She's eighteen, a legal adult, but that doesn't mean she's an emotional adult yet. Or a practical one," he said. "She can't even cook for herself."

"Oh, is that all women are good for? Cooking?"

"That's not what I'm saying, and you know it. She's living on ramen and apples."

"So? Do you remember what you lived on in college, Kurt?"

"No."

"Well, I do. Snickers and pizza."

"She keeps getting parking tickets. Speeding tickets. She can barely drive. She's spoiled."

"Whatever. Is that why you've been harassing my phone all day? So you could insult our daughter? I have to go."

"Listen. I think we need to report her as a missing person. It's been a week! This is getting to be too much."

"You know what? I'm not doing this right now. I have to calm my mind for this flight, and I need to review my notes for the finance committee meeting tomorrow."

"How can you be so nonchalant about this?" Kurt's face twisted with frustration, even though she wasn't there to see. "I can't believe you don't care about your own daughter!"

"I care, Kurt. I just don't think she needs to report back to us every minute of every day like you do. I happen to trust her. She is a grown woman now. Let her live her life, for fuck's sake!"

"I have a bad feeling," he said. "She always texts me back, at least that. She texts. But nothing, for a whole week. That's not like her."

"Jesus, Kurt! Leave her alone, already. She's on her own, enjoying her life, and I suggest you do the same."

"I can't relax knowing she might be hurt," he said. "I'm going to drive to her apartment in Albuquerque and see if she's okay."

"Don't you dare. She will never forgive us if you do that!"

"Then she should answer her phone and texts."

"Right. You do realize that's what you just said to me? You try to control the world, Kurt. You can do that with your government but not with your family. We are sick of your shit."

"I'm still going down there."

"Oh, Jesus. Because she's just dying to talk to her control freak of a father. I swear to God, you're so clueless. Do you not remember what it's like to be eighteen?"

"I remember exactly what it was like. And I would never have made my parents worry like this. Sorry. Parent. One of us is just fine."

"I have to go. They're boarding."

In the distance he heard the airport intercom announcing that the flight to Washington, DC, would begin boarding with first-class passengers. That would be Gina. She refused to fly anything else.

"Have a good flight," he said.

"I'm sure I will. And I have been meaning to tell you this, but I didn't know how to bring it up."

"What?"

"You don't have to pick me up on Saturday, like we'd planned."

"I don't?"

"No."

"Why not?"

"I—I'm sorry, Kurt, but I've decided I want to stay out there for a while."

Kurt stopped running and jumped off the treadmill as the news hit him. "I'm sorry, what?"

"I have to go. I'll send you an email explaining it. But—the short version of it is that I can't take this anymore."

"Take what?"

"You, Kurt. Us. All this fighting. Your constant micromanaging everyone and everything. Just . . . you. I can't take you anymore. I want a divorce."

"Where will you be staying?"

"Not that it's any of your business, but if you must know, I will be staying with Alan."

"Alan? As in, Alan Goldstein, your other college boyfriend? Alan with the douchey Porsche? Alan you were seeing at the same time you were seeing me? That Alan?"

"I'm done talking about any of this," she said.

As he stood there trying to think of something to say back, Kurt heard the line go dead.

17

General Zeb had Ron and Travis dress in their infantry greens in order to greet the new recruits at the appointed rendezvous point, by the old fire-lookout station twelve miles from base camp. This was where all the men in the army had parked their vehicles in a little culvert and covered them by pine boughs and other vegetation. They rode to the spot together, on abandoned logging roads and even over some rough raw terrain, in Travis's old white pickup. As they pulled up to the van with the couple from Arizona standing outside it, he warned his two soldiers.

"I don't want you boys saying anything about Eric, you heard me?"

"Yes, sir," they said.

"Keep your eyes peeled for that little fucker. See if his truck is still here. If it is, we need to be very alert for an ambush from him. If you spot him, you have orders to shoot to kill. We do not bargain with deserters. We do not have compassion for traitors. Understood?"

"Yes, sir."

General Zeb led his troops, in formation, to greet the new recruits, who did their best to salute him in the manner in which they had been instructed in the disappearing video he'd sent them over a social media app.

"Troops, introduce yourselves."

Travis spoke first, saluting with enthusiasm, and clicking his heels together. "Sir! Private First Class Travis Eugene Lee, sir!"

Ron went next, barking, "Sir! Private Ronald Bailey Martin, sir!"

General Zeb nodded to the newcomers to let them know to follow suit.

"Sir, Levi Novak Barr, sir!"

"Say it again with your rank, son."

The recruit looked at him with fear, because he did not know what
his rank was.

"Private," said General Zeb, helpfully.

"Sir! Private Levi Novak Barr, sir!"

"And you?" General Zeb regarded the female with a smirk, because
it was not his belief that women should serve in any army. He had
brought her here mostly out of a morbid curiosity, to see what would
happen if he admitted a couple to the ranks. Would they remain loyal
to one another, or to him? He needed to work these sorts of puzzles out
before he began to admit large numbers of soldiers to the army. There
were thousands waiting for an invitation. What the ones here with him
now did not know was that they were a test run.

"Sir!" shouted the woman, with more heart than he'd seen in her
boyfriend. "Private Marjorie Morgan Anderson, sir!"

General Zeb paraded back and forth in front of them, rubbing his
chin in thought. Everyone waited at attention. He enjoyed this power.

"Very well," he said. "At ease. As the other soldiers here today
already know, part of your initiation will be to listen to me tell you why
I chose to name our group the Zebulon Boys. I will quiz you on this
after supper this evening, back at camp, so I suggest you pay attention."

The woman raised her hand now, as though she were in a class. This
was so annoying it took away any fondness he might have felt for her
a moment before.

"This is not a school," he said. "It is an army. We do not raise our
hands."

Misunderstanding him, the woman took this as permission to speak
freely, and blurted, like a real Chatty Cathy, "I already know why you
called the army the Zebulon Boys. I have watched every speech you've

ever given, and read every essay you have ever written. You can quiz me right now if you want to. I am just one hundred percent thrilled to be here. This could not be more important, to be doing the Lord's work at your feet, General."

General Zeb had always found women to be much too talkative, and far too poor at managing their impulses, and she was proving him right on both counts.

"What I meant, Private Anderson," he growled, saying her name like it was a joke, "is that this is not a school, and if I want to hear from you, I will ask you to speak. Otherwise, you are to remain silent. Is that clear?"

"Yes, sir, General Zeb, sir. I am so sorry. I didn't know. I promise you, it won't happen again."

General Zeb grew furious now, from her incessant talking, after he had just given her orders to be silent. He put his face only inches from hers before shouting, as loud as he could, with as much red and twisted-up anger as was possible to see on another person's face, "Shut the fuck up!"

The woman's lower lip began to quiver, like she was a toddler you'd taken a cookie from, once the shock of the moment had faded a bit. She was about to cry. This was why women, and men who acted like women, did not belong in the military. General Zeb looked at her boyfriend very closely to see how he would handle seeing another man berate his beloved in this manner. To his credit, Private Barr stared straight ahead as though nothing had taken place. The man was clearly of better character than the woman. She was common as a weed. General Zeb stepped into this man's space now instead and, with narrowed eyes, examined every inch of his face.

"I suggest you get a handle on your woman, Private Barr," he said. "Or I am going to have to do it for you. And I promise you, I won't be near as nice as you will."

"Yes, sir, General Zeb, sir," said Private Barr. General Zeb lingered a moment longer, savoring this power. This man would be fine. But the woman had to go.

"Zebulon Baird Vance was born on May thirteenth, 1830, in Buncombe County, North Carolina. He was the third of eight children, and his grandfather was a wealthy man and a congressman. At the time of his birth, the family owned eighteen slaves. Young Zebulon was a genius and was sent to college at the age of twelve. When his father died two years later, he was sent home to help run the family's affairs. He later impressed the governor of the state so much that the governor himself paid for young Zebulon to go to law school. He was a prolific reader and writer, and when the time came to serve his country and people in the Civil War, he stepped up. Zebulon Baird Vance was an officer in the Confederate Army, and a two-time governor of the state of North Carolina, as well as a United States senator. He was a proud member and Grand Dragon of the Ku Klux Klan and, in my eyes, the last great leader the United States has ever seen. It is in his name that we come together now, because it is not too late to rescue this great country from the jaws of the Tyranny of Wokeness. We have made it our current mission and cause to protect the nation from being overrun by Mexican invaders, and we have chosen Rio Truchas County, New Mexico, because there are more Mexicans per capita here than anywhere else in the nation. This is where we will start the war, and we will do so on July third, as Operation New Gettysburg."

He could have gone on and on, but it was starting to sprinkle, and he was eager to see what they'd brought him.

"Did you bring me a Mexican female?" he asked the man, resolving then and there to stop addressing the woman directly at all unless he could not help it. She needed to learn her place.

"I did, sir," said Private Barr. General Zeb connected eyes with the new recruit and saw that the man was deliberate in using the first-person singular. He saw that the woman was upset about this. Women were always upset about something. This Private Barr, though. He had what was needed in a good soldier. He had read the General's curiosity about his loyalty and was already doing what he could, within the confines of his station, to prove himself a good soldier.

"Well, let me see her," said General Zeb.

The woman ran to oblige him, still hoping to fall into his good graces, even though there was not a chance in hell of that happening. She opened the back double doors of the cargo van without first checking with her boyfriend, which irked General Zeb. But all that ire disappeared the moment he saw that the woman they'd brought him—the small, brown, skinny, terrified woman who was scooted up against the wall of the van as far from him as she could get—was, in fact, pregnant.

"Well, I'll be goddamned," he said, a smile spreading across his handsome face as he patted Private Barr on the shoulder. "You done brought me a two-for-one special, son. Color me impressed. Well done."

18

Ana Luz Hidalgo felt like she was still learning English, but mostly she had become fluent. Her first language was Tzotzil. Her second was Spanish. Once she'd learned two languages, the third felt easier. But even if she hadn't spoken their language, she would have understood the intentions of the couple who'd come up to her behind the restaurant where she worked, pointed a gun at her, bound and gagged her, and dumped her in the back of a van for many hours without water or use of a bathroom. Ana Luz believed she was about to die, along with the unborn child in her womb. This did not bring her as much angst as it might have brought other girls of sixteen, because death had been following Ana Luz for four years, ever since the day it had first found her in Chiapas.

When she was twelve, Ana Luz had given birth to her first child, a girl, alone in an outhouse. She had been too young and ignorant to even understand what pregnancy was. The father was a friend of her mother's boyfriend, an old man, with ugly teeth, and mean. The closest thing to a father Ana Luz had, her own father having never been mentioned. He'd breathed his oniony molded rot into her when her mother was at the market. She did not tell anyone at first, but then they all saw the bump and the way she had stopped talking or smiling. They all pretended nothing had changed. She gave the baby to her mother, still covered with goo. She didn't know what else to do with it. Then she had a fever and a lot of bleeding because the sac the baby had been in was still inside her and was supposed to come out. The woman doctor at the hospital told the police about the birth, and the man who'd caused it. The police put the man in jail, but his family was mad about it, and so they killed Ana Luz's mother, and the baby, who was not quite one year old then. They would have killed Ana Luz, too, but she wasn't home the day they came over. Neighbors told Ana Luz she was next, and that the murderers would be back, and so she left in the night when everyone was asleep. She went north. She walked. She begged. She did whatever she could to survive. Slept in ditches. Drank water from rancid puddles of mud swimming with tadpoles. She made it to Phoenix and found work. She lived in a room with some other Mayan girls, some from Mexico and others from Guatemala, and they were all learning to read from the one who knew. She had met them through the coyote who'd brought them here. All of them had that same look in their eyes as she did, the way a wick looks after you blow out the flame, sort of dark and bent over and fragile. It wasn't just that they were physically tired. It was that their souls, too, were tired, from so much pain and hopelessness. At night, after they'd worked on their letters and words, they watched TV. A Spanish-language telenovela from Colombia, where all the actors were white, about the nobility of poverty and the evils of cartels, a story so obvious Ana Luz wondered why anyone found it worth telling.

The man who collected money from them for having gotten them to the United States did different things, all of them horrible, if they didn't pay him. This wasn't fair. They'd all paid him what they owed him, two or three times over. But he told them to keep paying if they wanted to stay, or he'd report them to the government, and they'd be sent back to certain death. One month, Ana Luz didn't have enough money, and so he did what he did, and now here she was, pregnant again. She did not love the baby that grew in her, and she tried not to think of it as anything more than a stomachache that would eventually be over. She had never been to a doctor in the United States, because she avoided anyone and anything that might end up with her being noticed and sent back to Mexico and certain death.

She did not cry, or scream, or fight anymore, because sometimes a woman was just too tired, in her spirit, to do any of those things. She did not rage against what was happening to her. Instead, like a woman who has been adrift in the ocean for many days and has learned that she needs to find ways to conserve her energy if she wants to have any hope of being rescued or surviving, Ana Luz just tried to float, and breathe, and sometimes, if she had a burst of energy, pray.

Then the van had finally stopped. In addition to the kidnappers, there were three other men now. The most deranged looking of them was in charge. She had known many men in her short life with this same kind of crazy eyes. She understood enough English to grasp that this was some kind of army, named after someone who owned slaves. Whatever this was, it was not going to end well.

Ana Luz was dragged out of the van, thrown into the back of a white truck with her kidnappers, and, after more rough driving through the forest, brought to a small clearing, where there were two tents, both of them camouflage. She saw a cook fire and some rope with meat drying on it. The man in charge spun her around. Looked at her. He touched her everywhere, as though she were a melon at a market and he was deciding whether to buy her. She felt the nausea boil up, and tried to stop herself from throwing up, but failed. When she was done, no one offered her water or a towel, or helped her at all.

Instead, they yanked her by one arm, dragging her off in the trees, to the lip of a deep hole in the ground, about ten feet across. There were tree branches over this, to hide the abyss, but once they were moved aside, Ana Luz saw that there were two other women down there, brown like her, scared like her, dirty and afraid as animals in a trap. Someone shoved Ana Luz once, without warning, and she fell into the hole. It was about three times as deep as she was tall, and the fall hurt. She twisted her ankle on the hard earth, and it popped. Her leg felt strange, electric, and she worried that something might have happened to the baby because she could not protect it. The worry wasn't for the baby itself so much as it was for what carrying a dead baby around inside you might do to her. There were many terrible ways to die, but that seemed like one of the worst.

The branches were put back over the top, and the hole became dark. It was damp and smelled rotten, like urine and feces, and something worse. It smelled like death. Ana Luz knew what death smelled like, and it was here.

The other women in the hole, filthy, their hair matted, came to help Ana Luz once the branches were back and the white people weren't looking in at them anymore.

"Are you okay?" one asked, in Ana Luz's own language, Spanish.

"I don't know," said Ana Luz.

"I'm Altagracia," said the woman, and Ana Luz just nodded. "And that's Paola. She doesn't speak Spanish."

"What is this place?" asked Ana Luz, in English. "Where are we?"

The one called Paola hugged herself. Her eyes darted, paranoid and afraid. "This place is hell," she said, shivering. "We are in hell."

"They hunt women here," said Altagracia.

Ana Luz was not sure she'd heard this correctly. "Sorry, what?" she asked.

"There were two others before you," said Paola. "Natalia. And Celia. They hunted them."

"They compete to kill us," said Altagracia. "They get points."

"Are you sure?" Ana Luz asked.

"They bring back pieces of them," said Altagracia. She removed some branches to reveal a human ear, shriveled and wrinkled like a dried apricot, and a foot, and several fingers.

"I hope they're still alive," said Paola.

"Yeah," said Altagracia. "I doubt that."

"Celia was mad cool," said Paola, rocking back and forth. "She has to be okay. She has to be. I told her to call my dad. He'll come for us. I know he will."

Ana Luz had felt despair for much of her life, but none of it compared to the yawning horror that now opened in her heart.

Altagracia slid down the wall of the hole and sat in a hopeless way upon the floor. "They were talking earlier today about taking one of us out of here soon," she said. "For a new hunt."

Paola added, "They haven't decided which one yet."

"My God," said Ana Luz.

"But they will."

19

Jodi piloted her truck along the slick and twisting two-lane highway, through a punishing rainstorm that, this high up, had decided to toss down some nuggets of hail. As she drove, she wriggled out of her filthy, soaking-wet shirts and into the spare undershirt and uniform shirt she kept in the back seat. It was a little past seven in the evening and would be dark in an hour or so. At six thirty, she had dropped Henley back at his cabin, still aglow after finding himself in a cozy hole in the ground with six sweet little wolf pups. That was two more pups than Jodi had realized were there, and she was glad she'd been there to see them. Because she'd had to shimmy into the den on her belly, like a snake, and run a good mile-plus through a deluge back to the truck, Jodi was soaked and mud steeped, and in no position to have a work meeting with the new deputy. Henley had kindly offered to let her borrow some women's clothes he had in his cabin and thought "might be about your size," but Jodi had declined the offer. She was surprised to find herself stabbed by a pang of jealousy at the mention of the clothes, even though she had zero evidence they might have belonged to a girlfriend. Jesus Christ, she thought. I might actually have a crush on someone. She had not been sure that would ever happen again, and here it was. Happening. And he was dating someone. Probably. Because of course he was.

She was now headed toward Goldie's Bar and Grill in Gato Montes, to meet up with the new deputy from the sheriff's department, Ashley Romero. The scanner was quiet, as often happened in a good soaking monsoon. Summer afternoons often brought these kinds of downpours to the mountains of New Mexico. No one in Massachusetts had ever really seemed to appreciate rain the way Jodi did, having grown up with these monsoon storms as sacred, rare, and powerful things. She never felt the power of the universe, or God, or whatever you wanted to call it, more than she did in the middle of a summer thunderstorm in the high-desert Rockies.

As she drove, she called home to check on Oscar and Mila. She'd wondered if it was reckless to leave them there alone, given that Travis could be lurking around. But Juana was there to alert them to any prowlers, and Mila could certainly handle herself with a gun.

"Everything's fine," Oscar told her. "And you'll be happy to know, my niece is helping me brush up on my own shooting skills, in case I need them."

"Is that even allowed?"

"By who?"

"Pues, the Vatican. Rome."

"I'm a priest, not an orphaned child," he said.

"Well, what's the pope's stand on firearms?"

"Jodi. The catechism of the Catholic church allows Catholics the right to use arms for self-defense. Jesus himself said, 'I did not come to bring peace, but with a sword.'"

"Ah, yes. Right. The Jesus sword. I forgot for a second that you were the guys behind the Inquisition. My bad."

"Stop. That was more than five hundred years ago."

"Which gun you using?"

"We've been out in the back field, doing target practice with a few weapons. The sniper rifle with the scope. That thing is cool. Pistols. The shotgun. De todo."

"And what about dinner? You guys eaten yet?"

"We were thinking maybe we could have us a snack while you finish up, and that if we were super nice to you that you'd maybe agree to bring us back some of Goldie's tacos and rellenos, some refritos and queso. But, tú sabes, no pressure."

"Text me exactly what you want, and I'll bring home some take-out," she said as she pulled into the restaurant's parking lot. She spotted the sheriff's cruiser already there and parked next to it.

Goldie's was a landmark, a legend, and the busiest New Mexican food restaurant in the entire county, despite its being a bit out of the way from the bigger towns and cities. People came all the way up here from Santa Fe just to taste Goldie's famous homemade salsa, and sometimes you'd even see visitors from as far away as Durango. The building itself was nothing to write home about. Kind of a weird-looking place, to be honest. It used to be a house, back when the current owner's grandfather had started selling his mother's homemade burritos and tacos on the street for a few cents, with his siblings. He had only been, like, seven years old back then. It was local lore that those little kids loved their mother's cooking so much they set up a little stand and hawked those delicious spicy packets of meat and vegetables and beans and corn like the best carnies on earth. The truth, of course, was that it was the Depression, and the kids were probably starving like the rest of the family. But the food was good, because old Oralia "Goldie" Dorada was a damn fine cook, and the business grew, and grew, generation to generation. The house it started in grew, too, by fits and starts. A rock building stuck onto the side over here. An adobe addition above the garage. A hollowed-out double-wide mobile home across the back patio added to accommodate parties and events. There were strange murals painted on the outside walls, some of them excellent, and others really quite bad. But one thing never changed—the recipes and the satisfaction of the people lucky enough to eat them.

The inside of the main building was dark but not exactly cozy. It had something of a dungeon feel to it, if dungeons had wagon wheels hung on the walls as decoration. There was a rock foundation in one corner that probably would have been a lot happier outside somewhere.

The nicest spot in the room was the group of tables near the large, almost medieval fireplace, and Jodi was pleased to see that this was where Deputy Romero had decided to set up shop and wait for her. Just the other side of the fireplace, which opened on both sides of the half wall into which it was sunk, was the bar portion of the bar and grill, and though it could sometimes get noisy and rowdy in there, for the time being it wasn't too bad, most likely on account of the storm keeping people home.

Jodi could not help but notice everyone in the place staring at them as she and Deputy Romero shook hands, the latter standing up to greet her. The old-timers, especially, seemed like they weren't sure what to make of the pair.

"Nice to meet you, Officer Luna," said the deputy.

"Same. You can call me Jodi."

"Ashley," she said with a smile. They both sat down, and Ashley leaned closer to Jodi. "You'd think they'd never seen a woman police officer before," she said.

"Many of them probably haven't," said Jodi.

"Well, they'll just have to get used to it."

A server named Barbarita came to the table, with two glasses of ice water and a shot of whiskey that she set down with a satisfying pop in front of Jodi.

"Good evening, Officers," said Barbarita. "Officer Luna, we saw you coming, and I hope you don't mind, but we'd like you to have this shot of your favorite, on the house." She nodded to the bar, where Goldie herself stood smiling and waving. She held up a bottle of Dead Guy Whiskey.

"I ordered it like you asked," she yelled across the room.

Jodi wanted to hide. "I shouldn't," she said. "I'm on the clock, but thanks."

Barbarita shrugged and left the shot glass where it was. "What else can I bring you?"

"Iced tea for me," said Ashley.

"I'm good with water, thanks," said Jodi.

After Barbarita walked away, Ashley picked up the shot glass and sniffed it. "Dead Guy Whiskey?" She wrinkled her nose.

"It's a brand I like, out of Portland," said Jodi. "But not while I'm working."

Ashley shrugged and downed the shot in one gulp, making the twisted face most people make after swallowing anything eighty proof. "Wow," she said. "That's . . ."

"Great whiskey?" Jodi asked.

"Terrible, just terrible," said Ashley.

Jodi grinned. "You say that like a woman who doesn't know a thing about whiskey."

The two women exchanged a few scraps of small talk before getting down to the business of sharing what they each knew about the severed women's body parts they'd found.

———

As Jodi told Ashley, as discreetly as she could, what she knew about the Zebulon Boys, Lyle Daggett nursed his second whiskey, neat, Jameson. He didn't mean to eavesdrop through the fireplace, but his years in the military had made him acutely aware of all the conversations around him at any given time, and what they said interested him—as did the older of the two women, herself. He indulged in a third glass, and once he heard that the to-go order Jodi placed was ready, and then the scooting of the women's chairs across the floor as they stood up to end their meeting, he pulled out a fifty and left it on the counter. Topping himself with his hat, and lowering it in such a way that no one would be tempted to try to stop and chat with him, he followed them to the door. As Jodi held it open for the deputy, she noticed him just behind her, shrugging into his jacket. He acted surprised to see her too.

"Wish I'd known I was going to see you," she said. "I saved some backstrap and tenderloin for you, deer I got on the job. A thank-you for the veggies, which were great. Have you met the new deputy?"

"I haven't had the pleasure," he said, removing his hat again, in the vestibule. Jodi introduced them, and they shook hands. Ashley was just getting called out on a car accident and apologized for rushing, but she had to leave. Lyle stepped forward and took Jodi's place holding the door as the rain came down outside.

"Before you head out," he said, "I wanted to see if you had some time to spare, to stop by my place real quick."

She eyed him suspiciously, like maybe he'd suggested something untoward. "How much have you had to drink, exactly, Lyle?"

"Not enough to do something as stupid as you think I'm doing," he said. He looked outside to make sure Ashley was gone, and when her cruiser drove past, he came closer. "I overheard you two talking about the Zebulon Boys. I think I have one of them trapped up at my place."

Jodi's eyes widened. "You *what*, now?" she asked.

"I can keep him as long as you like, but I think it might be nice if you came and had a chat with him."

Jodi looked at the white plastic bag of takeout and sighed. "I need to get this back to my kid and my brother before it gets cold," she said. "But if you're sure you can hang on to him, I could swing by in the morning."

"That's fine," he said. "He was wearing out his welcome, though. It's why I ended up here. But I'm glad I did."

Jodi gave him a strange look. "When you say you have him trapped, what do you mean, exactly?"

Lyle capped himself with his hat again, grinned in a charming sort of way, and turned the collar of his jacket up against the rain he was about to walk into, without an umbrella. "He's been doing some work for me out on the ranch, and we've had some conversations, that's all. We'll see you in the morning."

"You mind if I bring Deputy Romero along? We agreed her department should handle most of this, given the nature of the crimes we appear to be dealing with."

"Bring whoever you like, but I do think you might get more out of him if it was just one of you, for now."

"I'll think about it. I have so many questions, but it's been a long day as it is, and I really need to switch over to my mom hat for a little while."

"Have three kids of my own," he said, "so I do understand. They're grown and gone now, but I still have days where I wonder if they're eating right. Giving Mila Goldie's takeout, I'd say you're a damn good mother."

They smiled at each other, a beat longer than they might have if there weren't a little something between them, and Jodi wondered what the hell was happening to her that she was finding herself interested in men again. It still felt like cheating, but not as much as it used to.

20

Eric Parker's hair was greasy as warm cheese and the color of the inside of a banana peel. He sat defiantly in the center of the old ranch cabin, arms crossed over his chest, staring Jodi down from his seat on the small folding cot, as the morning sun cast a block of light upon the dirt floor of the small rock bunkhouse. The room smelled of human waste, and Jodi, who was glad she'd come without the young deputy for now, saw the plastic bucket he'd apparently been using as a toilet. So Lyle had actually been keeping the man captive. Trapped. She'd have to ask him more about this later.

Jodi stood just inside the room, near the open door, hand over her weapon just in case. Lyle stood behind her, to one side.

"How could you do this to me, brother?" Eric asked Lyle. "I thought you were on our side?"

Lyle said nothing. Jodi was starting to think this was his super-power. His lack of a response seemed to unnerve Eric, who grew more agitated, vibrating with anxiety until he couldn't contain it. Like a jack-in-the-box, he popped off the cot and began to pace, running his hands through his hair in despair.

"Really? It's like that, huh? I can't believe this, man! Can't fucking believe this. You fed me. Gave me a place to rest my head. You acted like my friend."

Jodi heard Lyle sigh, and it made her smile a little. If she'd had any inclination toward bringing the ranch manager in on kidnapping charges, the trapped man had just exonerated him.

"So I hear you were part of a group camping out in the forest," said Jodi. "Going to war against the reconquista. That right?"

"I don't have to answer to you," he said, spitting in Jodi's general direction.

"That's true," she said. "But I'll arrest you either way, based on that Zebulon Boys insignia you're wearing on your sleeve."

"On what grounds? I'm the one being held captive here! Can't believe you locked me in here, man! I thought we were friends."

"Trespassing," she said. "For starters. Mr. Daggett here tells me he did not invite you to his property. I will assume he was holding you here in anticipation of my arrival."

"He fed me!"

"That is not a crime. Dismembering women is, however."

"I want a lawyer," said Eric. "I plead the Fifth."

"Suit yourself," said Jodi, removing the handcuffs from her belt before snapping them open with a satisfying crack.

"No, hey, what do you think you're doing?" said Eric, backing away from her. His eyes scanned the room frantically, trying to find a way out or a way to protect himself.

"Officer Luna," said Daggett, stepping into the cabin now. "If you don't mind, I'd like to have a word with Eric, alone, before you take him in."

It was then Jodi noticed the large screwdriver in Daggett's hand. Eric saw it too.

"Hey, no," said Eric. "What the hell is this?"

Jodi figured Daggett was just bluffing, to help her out, so she played along. "Sure thing, Mr. Daggett," Jodi said. "I'll just be right outside if you need me."

As she moved toward the door, Daggett stepped closer to Eric, slapping the screwdriver against his palm like a billy club.

"Hold—hold on," said Eric. "You guys can't do this. You can't physically hurt me. It's illegal."

"As I recall," said Daggett to Eric, "you shared some details about your time in the camp that did not seem all that legal to me. And bombs, from what I understand of them, hurt people too. Why the sudden interest in the law now?"

"I told you all that because I trusted you," he cried like a child. "You weren't supposed to rat me out! What we were doing out there, it was for you. It was for all of us. I trusted you like my brother, man!"

"Can't imagine why you'd do that," said Daggett.

"Because you look like a solid guy!" cried Eric.

Daggett motioned for Jodi to close the door and leave. Eric cracked.

"Okay—hold on. No! Don't go. Fine. I'll talk to her."

She came back into the bunkhouse and stood next to Daggett.

"Just—just, can I get some kind of immunity or something?" Eric asked. "If I tell you what I know?"

"Depending on what you tell me," said Jodi, "I might take some sympathy on you."

"What do you want to know?" he asked.

"Daggett tells me you don't like Mexicans much," said Jodi. "And he thinks you were at a camp of people who share that view, and that they're still out there, planning something big."

Eric looked scared but nodded. Jodi tried not to react personally, though she was disgusted by him.

"What can you tell me about it?"

"Okay. Look. It's not Mexicans I dislike, necessarily. I'm sure some are good people. You're probably one of the good kind. It's that the other ones, the bad ones, they're taking over my country. I'd feel that way no matter who was doing it."

"So you guys planned to fight back, for your country?" asked Jodi.

Eric nodded vigorously. "Yes. That's exactly it. That's what I thought we were doing. I've done two tours in Iraq, and I was in Afghanistan. I'm a good guy. I did that because I love my country."

"Fair enough," said Jodi. "Thank you for your service."

"You're welcome," said Eric.

"So tell me about this camp."

He looked uncomfortable, so much so that she almost pitied him. "It's headed by a guy named General Zeb," he said.

"Oh, you mean Atticus Everett?" asked Jodi.

Eric looked stunned. "How did you know that?"

"Same internet where you learned stuff."

"I was like a lot of guys out there on the forums. I saw his videos and heard his podcast, and he got me all riled up, you know? I wanted to help. So I came out here."

"Out where?"

"Here, to New Mexico," he said.

"From where, Eric?"

He hesitated before saying, softly, "California."

"Okay, so where, exactly, here in New Mexico, might I find the rest of your group?"

"Whoa. Hang on. Ask Mr. Daggett there. I left the group. I ended up here because I left. It's not my group, okay? Let's just get that clear."

"Let me rephrase, then," said Jodi. "Where, exactly, here in New Mexico, might I find Everett's group that you used to belong to?"

Eric looked terrified. "I can't tell you that."

"Okay," said Jodi.

"I mean, he moves the base camp all the time, in case people like you are looking for him. But he's in the San Isidro National Forest. Somewhere out there."

"And what do they do there?" asked Jodi. "In the camps?"

"They're planning to bomb some buildings in Gato Montes and Hispaniola," he said, looking ashamed.

"What buildings?"

"I don't know, man."

Jodi stepped closer and unlatched her Glock from its holster.

"Okay, okay!" said Eric. "The Walmart Supercenter, that's one. City hall, that's the other. And the casino. Out by the Indian reservation."

"Got a date in mind?"

"Same day we lost the Battle of Gettysburg."

"We didn't lose that battle."

"Well. General Zeb feels our side did."

"Is there a guy named Travis Eugene Lee in your group?" asked Jodi.

Another wide-eyed, drop-jawed look.

"Let's just say Travis and I talked."

"You're that Mexican lady officer he talked about."

"He mentioned me?"

Eric looked uncomfortable. "He didn't say, but he told us about you."

Jodi decided to bluff. "Well, good. You know, he's an informant for us."

Eric took this bait without questioning it. "I knew it! I knew there was something off about him!"

"And when we told him we had you here, he told us everything you did. Everything with the dismemberment, he pinned that on you. And he is willing to testify. What do you make of that?"

"It's a goddamned lie! I didn't want to be part of that. It's why I left."

"That's not what Travis said."

It was then that Eric broke open like a sweaty white supremacist piñata. As he began to talk, Jodi discreetly began to record the statement with her cell phone. He named the people who were there, what kind of bombs they were making, the buildings they planned to destroy. He told her there was a place where the General had them all hide their cars, the meetup point for new recruits. He said he'd driven there but that part of the agreement he had was that the General would sell his truck. He did not know if it was still there or not.

"Where's this meetup point?"

"I don't remember exactly, but it's in the same forest, near an old watchtower for fires or something."

Jodi knew of three of those in that area. It wasn't much, but it was a start.

He said there were new recruits coming in. That if you waited long enough at the old fire tower, you'd eventually catch all of them. He also told Jodi, when she asked, that they had subsisted off "meat from poached game animals," and some canned goods, and that the General was obsessed with killing endangered wolves. This last part he said with disgust, and Jodi could tell that as misinformed and tragic as this man was, he actually did care about conservation and wildlife.

When he was finished, Jodi thanked him, arrested him for confessing to wildlife poaching and conspiracy to commit acts of domestic terrorism, and slapped the cuffs on his wrists.

"Hey, you can't do this," he said. "You promised you'd go easy on me."

"This *is* me going easy on you, Eric," she said.

21

Sheriff Lorenzo Gurule sat with his feet up on his desk as he ate the second of three McDonald's sausage-and-egg breakfast sandwiches he had picked up for himself in Hispaniola when he went down there on a rollover-vehicle call an hour ago. Deputy Romero was out on a call from some Instagram hippies whose van had accidentally run into an elk as they were trying to find the turnoff for the Zopilote Cliff Dwellings, and the sheriff was enjoying the quiet moment in the office with his wife. While she manned the switchboard and took care of some paperwork, he put the earbuds in and pulled up the Fox News app on his phone to see what was happening in the world.

His blissful breakfast break was interrupted by the arrival of game warden Jodi Luna, who burst through the door dragging some poor handcuffed fellow in.

"Deputy Romero here?" she asked Karina, as though the sheriff himself were not right there. He took this as an act of disrespect, and so did his wife. Rather than answer, Karina rolled her eyes over to her husband and asked him if he wanted to handle this.

"Guess I don't have much of a choice, do I?" He popped the remainder of the sandwich into his mouth and swallowed it without much chewing. He left the third sandwich on his desk and felt a kind of pain in having to do so. He pulled his pants up after standing, hooked his thumbs through his belt loops, and came to the counter. "What you got for me, Luna?" he asked.

As she explained that she and Romero had been collaborating on a case involving the Zebulon Boys and the severed women's body parts, Gurule listened as objectively and dispassionately as he could. Both these women were green, and he did not quite trust their conclusions and would come to some of his own. When she finished explaining the situation, he thanked her and said he'd handle it from here. She seemed grateful, because the Fish and Wildlife offices didn't have much by way of holding cells.

"I can share my interview notes with you," she said.

"Not necessary," said Gurule, taking the prisoner by the elbow. "I'll have a little heart-to-heart with Mr. Parker here myself in a bit."

"I'd like to compare notes after you do," she said.

"We'll be in touch," he said, and that seemed to satisfy her enough to get her good and gone.

The sheriff took the suspect to the interrogation room, removed his handcuffs, offered him a cup of coffee, and told him to have a seat, promising to be back in a few minutes. Then he went back to his desk to finish his breakfast.

"What do you make of all that?" asked Karina, jutting her chin toward the window to the parking lot, even though Jodi had already left.

"Well, from what I've heard of the Zebulon Boys, they're not that bad," he said, gesturing to his phone, where a Fox News host was talking animatedly. "And sometimes these liberals can overreact."

"That's what I was thinking too," she said. "You should talk to him, get his side of it."

"Agreed. These city slicker cops have all been corrupted by the Black Lives Matter radicals," he said. "Then they come up here and start seeing enemies everywhere. But I tell you what. If the Zebulon Boys are trying to keep illegals out, I say more power to them."

"Exactly," said Karina.

"You want to come here, great, but do it legally."

"What part of *illegal* do people not understand?"

"I don't know what this world is coming to," said Gurule, who finished the last bite of his final sandwich, belched into his fist, then headed off to see whether one of America's patriots had been mistreated by the county's newest touchy-feely game warden.

22

Later that day, Jodi stood in her closet, freshly showered, wearing the fuzzy white robe Graham had gotten her for Mother's Day four years ago. She ran her fingers over the Andover clothes she'd shoved far in the back. She hadn't worn any of these things in years. She didn't know what you were supposed to wear to a retirement party for a game warden who was also your favorite uncle, but she figured she should make an effort to look nice.

She chose a black boatneck cocktail dress, the one from Barneys that she'd worn to her most recent book launch party in New York, four years ago. Another lifetime ago. She added turquoise jewelry and a concho belt, to make it seem a little less pretentious for Rio Truchas County, and a yellow shawl, with a pair of black Justin cowgirl boots that looked a little strange but would draw less attention than a pair of pointy Blahniks with the crowd she'd be seeing.

When Jodi came to the edge of the living room, Oscar and Mila were already dressed and waiting for her. She hovered in the hallway, unnoticed, to eavesdrop for a moment. Part of her was worried he might tell her about the baby Jodi'd had thirty years ago, her mother's darkest secret. Another part of her, though, was just curious about how they interacted when she wasn't around.

Mila had chosen to wear a very pretty pink-and-white sundress and a pair of espadrilles, both sent to her by Grandma Amy, Graham's mother, in one of her many Boston Brahmin care packages. Mila had a matching pink sweater tied around her shoulders, and would have looked just right at Amy's private yacht club in Cohasset. Her long, dark-brown hair was up in a high, shiny ponytail, decorated with a white ribbon. Jodi had to admit that she and Graham had created a lovely creature, a girl as at ease in bungee jumping clothes as she was in a party dress meant for a fancy sailboat. She felt that old familiar gut punch of sorrow as she realized, yet again, that Graham was missing his daughter's transition from girl to woman. He'd have had a lot to say about it, some of it right.

"Okay, so, like, Zero, he's a vampire," Mila was saying as Oscar leaned forward in his chair. He'd ditched his usual robe and sandals for Wranglers, cowboy boots, and a plaid button-down, because Jodi had finally convinced him that seeing a priest at a party could ruin it for lots of people. Mila was on the sofa just across the coffee table. "Only he doesn't know it, at first. Then he's awakened, and his vampire nature is revealed. And he is, like, so overwhelmed. He wants blood, you know? But he knows that's the worst."

Jodi smiled to see how hard Oscar was trying to be supportive of Mila as she described the plot and characters of one of her favorite anime shows to him. Mila, meanwhile, did not seem to be concerned at all that talking about bloodlust and vampires might not be all that much fun for a Catholic priest who actually believed in demons. She just saw Tío Oscar as her best friend, and that was a beautiful thing.

"And Yuki, who is, like, just this totally cute girl, you know? She is all, 'Screw taboos, man, I'm gonna let super-hot Zero feast on my blood to his cold vampire's heart's content, because he's just that hot and I'm just that self-sacrificing.'"

Oscar's eyes grew wide, and Jodi decided it was time to intervene. She stepped into the room and clapped her hands. "All right! You guys look great. We ready to go?"

At that moment, Juana began to bark madly outside.

"Uh-oh," said Mila, of the barking. "Wonder what's got her all tied in a knot?"

They all waited for a few seconds, and the barking stopped.

"I think we're all on edge because of the Travis stuff," said Jodi. "But it was probably just a skunk or something." She stopped off at the gun locker and selected the smallest weapon there, a Ruger LCR 9mm. She tucked this into her fancy sequined party purse. "Let's go have some fun for a change."

They arrived in the covered outdoor parking area to the side of the house, where Jodi's work truck and Oscar's TIPSY MONK van rested next to Jodi's family car, a cherry-red Jeep Rubicon perfect for both rock climbing expeditions and hunting and camping trips. Jodi pressed the key fob to unlock this vehicle, which, she noticed, someone had washed recently in her absence. She was looking forward to driving it again.

"Jodi," said Oscar, touching her arm. He looked worried as he pointed toward Jodi's detached garage/workshop, just beyond the barn. It was big enough to house several cars, and high enough for one of them to be an RV. And at the moment, the bright-green side door stood wide open. None of them ever left it open, and in fact, Jodi had locked it up right before she showered, after having gone in to take two packages of venison, wrapped in white butcher paper and neatly labeled in black Sharpie, to bring to Lyle at the party, in a cooler.

"Was it like that earlier?" asked Oscar.

Jodi shook her head, frowned, and sprang into action.

"Here," she said, handing Oscar the keys to the Jeep as she took the pistol out of her purse. "Both of you, get in the Jeep. We keep a Rock River AR-15 under the back seat—Mila knows how to use it. Hopefully you won't need it. But if you do, it's there. Go out past the gate, lock it, and wait for me there. If things get weird, call Deputy Romero and go to safety. I can handle myself."

"Let me come with you, Mom," said Mila.

"Not this time, sweetheart. I need you to look after your tío. It's probably nothing. Just taking precautions."

Mila nodded, and as they got into the Jeep, Jodi took cover along the side of the house and made her way toward the garage. Once she was sure her daughter and brother were out of harm's way, she approached the open door to the metal garage building with caution, gun drawn. Before entering, Jodi listened for sounds inside, but she heard nothing. She looked at the ground to see if there were any new or suspicious footprints. There did seem to be a few that were too big to be hers or Mila's, and too treaded to be Oscar's sandals or boots. Someone has been here, she thought. Or maybe Oscar has just begun wearing better outdoor shoes in my absence.

Slowly, she eased the door open a little wider, to squeeze herself through. She held her breath as her heart hammered against her sternum. She looked everywhere, listened—all her senses on high alert. She smelled something odd. Just a hint of what might have been cheap men's cologne or deodorant. It was so faint, and disappeared so quickly, that she wondered if her mind was playing tricks on her.

Jodi tiptoed through the spacious building, staying close to the walls. She'd set it up as a workshop: woodshop in one corner, metal shop in the other. She had a lift in the center, to work on her vehicles, and was proud to be disciplined about keeping them in top shape, and clean. This was also where she kept her butchering equipment when she wasn't using it. She noticed the pulley line for the game gambrel swinging, ever so slightly. There was no breeze in the building, and no reason it should have been moving. Jodi inched closer, turning in circles as she went, to alleviate the sense that someone was following her. This was when she saw that one of the small side windows had been left open. She didn't remember doing this, but she did recall Oscar telling her that Mila had been trying to figure out a way to build a rock climbing gym inside the large building, for rainy days. And she had left windows open before. Maybe even doors. The breeze from the window would certainly explain the moving cable. And it might even explain the door, if she had not closed it as tightly as possible, which might have happened, given that her hands had been weighed down with packages of meat. Just to be safe, Jodi did a complete check of the building, the barn, and even the house again. She checked the chicken coop and Juana's pen. Everything seemed fine. Glad she'd chosen the boots over the pumps, she walked across the front yard, down the long driveway, to the gate to the property, and ducked underneath it, joining her daughter and brother at the Rubicon.

"False alarm," she said. "I think someone might have left a window open."

She didn't want to point fingers, so she looked at Mila and smiled.

"Oh God," said Mila. "Did I? I might have. It was hot in there earlier."

"The breeze probably kicked the door open, because I might not have pulled it tight enough. Not a big deal. Everything's fine."

Oscar sighed. "Should I still drive?" he asked.

"Sure."

"You know," he said as he eased the Jeep down the road, "I love having you back home and all, Jodes, but I kind of miss when you were just a boring college professor and I didn't have to worry about you so much."

"You don't have to worry," she said. "You choose to worry."

"Exactly," said Mila. "It's all in your state of mind."

As they neared Goldie's, the traffic—if that's what you could call twelve cars in a row—got heavier than normal, because everyone who loved Eloy Atencio (and that was everyone in Rio Truchas County, just about) was showing up to thank him for his many years of service. It also meant that the Rubicon slowed down to a near stop as it passed the post office, which, as so often happens in small towns, also doubled as a Greyhound bus station twice a day. At the moment, the bus for El Paso, Texas, was just pulling in, to pick up the exactly three people waiting for it, one of whom, to Jodi's complete dismay, was none other than the yellow-haired Eric Parker, whom she had delivered to the county sheriff just that morning.

"Hold on," she told Oscar. "I need you to turn around."

"What? Why?"

They were passing the post office, and Eric was stepping onto the bus.

"I just need you to turn around! Now. I need to talk to someone boarding that bus."

Oscar was a nervous driver under the best of circumstances, and with his sister shouting orders at him, after the stressful and frightening past few days, he sort of froze.

"What are you doing? Pull a U-turn!"

"But it's a double yellow line," he said with a shrug.

"I realize that, but this is police business. I'm sure if anyone catches us, they'll understand." Jodi watched helplessly as the bus door swung closed and the brake lights flashed once, then went off, as the thing went into gear and began to pull out of the post office parking lot.

"Hurry!"

Oscar tried to pull out but got stuck, right in the path of Deputy Romero's sheriff's department cruiser. This made him more flustered, and he just let the Rubicon sit in the middle of the road for a few seconds, which upset everyone.

"Mom, you're upsetting Tío," said Mila.

Jodi whipped out her phone and called Ashley, who had just flipped on her blue lights.

"Hey," she said, looking right at Jodi through the windows of their vehicles.

"Sorry. I was trying to get my brother to chase the bus. I just saw Eric Parker get on."

"Yeah, I know." Ashley sighed. "I was going to tell you about it at the party."

"What happened?"

"Get your car out of the middle of the road, and I will meet you at Goldie's."

"Can you go get him off that bus? You have your work vehicle."

"No. Gurule let him go. He didn't press charges."

"What the hell?"

"You need to move your car."

"I know." Jodi hung up.

"I don't know where to go," said Oscar.

"Just keep going like you were before. You were fine. False alarm."

The bus was on its way down the highway now and would not be stopping until it reached Taos, or Santa Fe.

"You sure?"

"Forget it," said Jodi. She didn't have her truck. She couldn't just pull up next to a bus in the Jeep and demand that it stop. "Just—just get to Goldie's."

Oscar was so nervous she could see him trembling. She realized, and not for the first time, that being her little brother was draining him.

"I'm sorry I yelled. I'm not mad at you. I'm mad. But not at you. First round's on me."

23

Travis wished to God the General had let him do this assignment alone. But no. He had to bring skinny, smelly Ron with him. Ron, who chain-smoked in his truck all the way to Hispaniola, even though the little perv didn't have any cigarettes of his own. Just kept taking Travis's smokes, one after the other, lighting up by scraping matches against his pants zipper like some kind of a degenerate. When Travis asked him what the hell he thought he was doing, Ron reminded him that the General said everything they owned became the property of the Zebulon Boys army the second they signed the contract.

"What's yours is mine now, brother," he said. Travis didn't trust this guy further than he could throw him, and he kept an eye on him.

It was a little past seven in the evening when they got to the Walgreens. Travis hated being in this little city, the county seat, because everywhere you looked was another carful of Mexicans joyriding up and down the main street. If he could have gotten away with it, he would have shot every single one on sight. But that wasn't allowed. At least not yet. A day would come when the war was in full effect, and then it would be us against them, but it would be a while yet. For now, things had to be done in secret.

"I'll wait here," he told Ron. "Keep a lookout. You go get the stuff."

Ron seemed surprised by this. "Me? Why me?"

"Because I said so."

Ron scoffed and looked out the window. "I did not realize you were in the position to make these kinds of decisions, Travis."

"I am a private first class, and you are just a private. In the absence of the General, I call the shots."

Ron appeared to think about this and flicked the cigarette butt out the window into the parking lot. "Yeah, I guess you're right. How am I supposed to pay for it, though?"

"Don't you have any money?" asked Travis.

"I do, but I don't see how I am supposed to spend it on this."

"Not five minutes ago, you told me you were entitled to my cigarettes because what's mine is yours, but now you want to stake a claim to your money?"

"Fine. What am I supposed to get again?"

Travis couldn't believe this guy. He wondered if there would be some kind of way for Ron to have an accident before they got back to camp in the morning. "Don't you listen?"

"I listen, but I have that thing, whatever you call it. Attention deficit. I don't retain things."

"Where I'm from that's not attention deficit—that's just plain stupid," muttered Travis.

"Look." Ron sighed and turned to face Travis a little more head-on. "I know you don't like me much, and I can't say as I have much use for you either. But we should try to be united in the mission. We can't let personal feelings get in the way of doing the important work of the Zebulon army."

Travis mulled this over. "I guess you're right. But time's wasting while you're sitting here talking. We need to get the shit and get to the bitch's place before they get back."

"No, I know, brother. You're right. Tell me what I need to get again?"

Travis sighed. "Melatonin. Couple bottles of it. Some kind of soft dog food or treat that we can put it in. We need some rope, but you should probably get a couple of dog leashes and collars so you don't make people suspicious."

"Melatonin? What's that?"

"It doesn't matter what it is. Jesus! It's a vitamin thingy. It helps people sleep, but it works on dogs too."

"I don't understand why we don't just kill the dog, though."

"Because, genius." Travis scrunched as much of his own face toward his nose as possible as he glared at his comrade with utter contempt. "We don't want them to know we were there or are there. She's going to come home, maybe check on the dog. It needs to be asleep when she does that, not dead. Your mother feed you lead paint chips for breakfast when you were growing up or something?"

"Melanin," said Ron.

"Not melanin, you dumb shit. Melatonin."

"Fuck you. Soft dog food. What is that? In a can? How will we open a can out there?"

"Just use your brain. Buy whatever a dog will be excited to eat. Get some cheese then, or lunch meat."

"How about bread?"

"Bread? This is a dog. A carnivore."

"Pepperoni?"

"I don't care. Something we can put the pills in."

"And leashes? Why? Are we taking the dog somewhere? Can't we just kill it if we're taking it away?"

"Jesus Christ," said Travis. "No. We're using them to tie up the girl. The tape might be good enough, but just in case, the General said get some rope, but I think rope might look too suspicious."

"Why is rope suspicious? People use rope all the time, or they wouldn't sell it at the damn Walgreens!"

"They might not sell it at the Walgreens," said Travis. He was losing his temper.

"Melatonin, cheese, and dog leashes."

"Yeah."

"Do you have any cash?"

Travis glared at his passenger. "What's wrong with yours?"

"You seem like you have more. I need mine more."

Travis got his wallet out of the glove box, angry, and took a few twenty-dollar bills out. "That should do it," he said.

"Cool," said Ron. "Okay if I get me a pop while I'm in there?"

"No," said Travis.

Ron left then, went into the store, and returned fifteen minutes later, drinking a plastic bottle of Mountain Dew. When Travis asked him about it, Ron said he thought Travis had told him to get it.

"My bad, brother," he said. "Want me to go back in and get you one?"

Travis ignored the question and pulled out of the parking space in his usual road rage kind of way before Ron had a chance to put on his seat belt.

24

The modest lot for Goldie's was full, so Oscar had to park Jodi's Rubicon a block away and across the street. Goldie's lot only held about ten cars, but still, the size of the crowd descending upon the place—maybe fifty cars or so—was unusual for a town as small as Gato Montes, and an indication of just how much Officer Atencio was beloved by this community. People were driving up in whatever they had, including someone, now inside, who had parked their frog-green John Deere 4650 on the shoulder of the highway not too far off. Oscar was as hopeless at parallel parking as he had been at pulling a U-turn midstream, and after some discussion, he agreed to let Jodi take the wheel to show off the parking skills she'd had to develop in Boston, a city whose streets made zero sense and were clogged with cars.

As Jodi, Oscar, and Mila hurried toward the front door of Goldie's, Jodi saw that they weren't the only ones who were arriving a little bit late. Her childhood best friend, Diana Sandoval, was hustling across the street, too, from a few cars up, where she'd parked her BMW SUV. She was a highly regarded research scientist at Los Alamos National Lab these days, but she'd apparently decided to cut loose for the night and was wearing hot pants and a sparkly leopard-print shirt with red cowboy boots that matched her lipstick. Her bleached platinum-blonde hair had been newly cut into an A-line bob with black lowlights.

Jodi waited for Diana to catch up before going in.

"Well, damn, girl, don't *you* look all stuck up," Diana called out to her, approvingly, adding a wink just so Jodi wouldn't take it seriously.

This was a typical teasing Northern New Mexico compliment, designed to keep you humble.

"Not as stuck up as you, all blondie now," said Jodi, code-switching easily back to the local vernacular and intonation of her childhood.

"Yeah?" Diana countered. "At least neither of us are all, like, trying to be a sexy priest y todo eso, míralo. Qué chulo."

Oscar blushed. "I suppose I should say thank you," he said, uncomfortably.

"Oh my God," said Mila, of Diana, to Jodi. "I love her."

Jodi smiled, because Oscar's ears were flaming red as Hot Tamales candy. That almost never happened.

"Diana's my girl," said Jodi, looping her arm through her friend's, the way they had as children.

"Aww," said Mila, and Jodi surmised from her daughter's mixed expression of surprise and joy that she was not used to seeing her mother have female friends. In Andover, she hadn't had any, not really. The neighbor women disliked her, and her own colleagues were always sort of backbiting and competitive, even if they smiled to her face. She always remembered, whenever she saw Diana, why the two had hit it off back in the second grade, when they were identified as "gifted and talented" by a social worker at the school and pulled out of class once a week to go to a special room to read books the rest of their classmates still couldn't understand. They had made each other laugh like crazy back then, and this had not changed. Jodi and Diana could still make each other laugh like no one else.

The group went through the front doors, greeting friends and family along the way to the open french doors that led to the outdoor patio and the event trailer behind it. Hundreds of people were here. Everyone who was anyone had decided to attend, from the mayor of Hispaniola to the president of the community college, from state senators to the local farrier—and, of course, at least two dozen members of the Luna-Atencio clan, who'd come in from all the neighboring counties, wearing their Sunday best on a Friday night, and ranging in age from zero to their late nineties.

Jodi was happy for her uncle that so many people appreciated his years of service. She thought of the sterile retirement parties she had attended for others at the university where she'd taught, the polite, measured speeches, little more than an obligatory reading of someone's curriculum vitae. The rubber-chicken dinner no one liked. The uninspired slideshows. The polite laughter and gossipy whispers. The United States, once you left the rural places like Northern New Mexico, was a cold and competitive place, where people mattered only insofar as they could raise money for somebody else. She felt enveloped in a warmth and acceptance and love in that moment, which was exactly what she had hoped to regain by returning home. This was why she'd come. To stand in this room, with these people, arm in arm with her best friend, watching her brother and daughter accept hugs and kisses from person after person who was connected to them through blood and by this land. She vowed again, and not for the first time, to do the best job she could as the county's new game warden, to forge relationships as meaningful and honest as the ones her uncle had cultivated. She hoped that one day the community would come out to pay her the same respects when she finally retired.

As they stepped outside, Jodi saw Becky and Catalina frantically putting up the last of the silver streamers and Mylar balloons along the rock-and-adobe wall under the wide wooden veranda. Jodi loved the way this community just accepted them, too, without asking any questions. She remembered her grandmother talking about a couple of great-aunts she'd had, "spinsters" back in the 1800s, who had homesteaded out in this wilderness with just each other. Everyone knew. No one cared. As long as they shared in the community and were useful and kind, like everyone else. Along the wall beneath the little roof were several long tables set up with the evening's buffet, and the air was redolent with the smell of grilled meats, tortillas, green and red chile, pinto beans, and spanish rice.

"Oh, there's Marcus!" said Mila. "Mom, can I go say hi?"

Jodi followed her daughter's gaze to the young man she had been dating for about six months. He had grown since Jodi last saw him and was finally taller than Mila, probably five foot seven now, dressed in the same black Wrangler jeans, yellow cowboy boots, black button-down, and red cowboy hat as the rest of the men in his family's band. They were lugging gear in from a truck, through a side gate, onto the little stage on the patio of the restaurant. Marcus spotted Mila and smiled in a way that made Jodi not hate him *that* much. They waved at each other and seemed equally shy and adorable.

"That is quite an outfit," said Jodi.

"He doesn't love it. His mom picks their costumes. I think he looks amazing."

"Tell him I said hi," she said to Mila.

Diana grinned at Mila as she skipped over to her little boyfriend with youthful exuberance and said, with an elbow dig into Jodi's ribs, "Kind of reminds me of you and a certain track-and-field star, Kurt Chinana, back in the day."

Oscar shot Jodi a knowing look at the mention of this name—Kurt Chinana—and she shut him down by changing the subject, as though she had not heard this at all, and suggesting they go say hello to the man of the hour.

Atencio, wearing a fancy cowboy shirt and a bolo tie, was holding court at the head of the largest table on the patio and was dwarfed by the stack of gifts on either side of him. One of his younger grandsons, about two years old—Jodi had not met this one yet, meaning he must have belonged to the daughter who had moved up to Wyoming—sat in his lap. His wife and three of their five children, plus a bunch more grandkids, rounded out the happy, well-dressed crowd at the table. Jodi and her group greeted and hugged him.

"Do we have a good-looking family or what?" she asked, waving hello to everyone.

"I always thought it was unfair that one family got all the pretty genes," he joked back. "How's your first week been?"

She was about to answer, but he held his hand up and said, "On second thought, I don't want to know. I am enjoying my freedom. You can tell me all about it another time. Go get yourself some food."

Jodi was relieved. She had not wanted to ruin the party by telling her uncle anything about severed body parts and terrorists hiding in the forest, and she knew he knew her well enough to have already seen in her eyes that there was bad news. He had earned a break from the madness, and this evening was all about him.

"I expect you to dance with me later," she said, squeezing his arm.

"If you can keep up!" He smiled and returned his attention to the people at his table.

Jodi, Oscar, and Diana piled food onto plates at the buffet, ordered three margaritas at the open bar, then found an empty table near the bandstand. After a few bites of food, Diana, being relentless as a dog after a bone, went back to the former subject.

"Speaking of Kurt," she said. "My sister is friends with his wife's sister, you know? And word is, there might be trouble in paradise."

Jodi tried not to show any emotion and said, "I am sorry to hear that."

"Why? You know you and Kurt were destined to be together."

This is when Jodi spotted Henley, looking awkward and lost in the doorway. Her eyes lit up, and Diana was the first one to notice him noticing them.

"Well, hello, handsome," Diana muttered into her margarita. "Who is *that*?"

"Henley!" Jodi called, waving. "Over here!"

Diana looked at Jodi the way only a best friend who can read your mind does. "You did not tell me about this one," she said.

"Because there's nothing to tell," said Jodi. When Henley arrived at the table, she introduced him to Diana and Oscar and told him to get a plate and a drink and join them.

"You cradle robber," said Diana once Henley was out of earshot.

"Stop," said Jodi. "He's a colleague."

"Did you guys see your mom and dad?" asked Diana as she shoved a tortilla chip dripping with melted queso into her mouth. She tipped her head toward a table for two behind a tree, in a back corner. Jodi and Oscar had not seen them, and they briefly got up to say hello.

Gloria Luna wore a pale-blue dress with a matching suit jacket, stabbed through the lapel with her little American flag pin. Walter Luna, who was always most comfortable in ranch wear, tolerated a dark-gray suit with a blue tie he kept fiddling with. They were rumored to have been the best-looking couple in high school back in the 1950s, and they still looked perfectly put together, like a boxed set. Gloria's short hair was freshly cut, and Walter's was slicked back, the way he'd always worn it.

When Jodi, caught up in the moment, hugged her mother to greet her, Gloria seemed surprised and, still one of the best grudge holders Jodi had ever known, offered a tepid air hug back, with her butter knife still in one hand. Walter—who, despite his having been the rough-and-tumble cowboy, was the more considerate and cuddlier parent—noticed this and stepped in to ease Jodi's pain, as he had often done.

"Jodilynn," he said with a stoic pat on her back. "Nice to see you. You look healthy." It was as close to a compliment on her physical appearance as she would ever get from him. She had realized long ago, when she first needed a training bra, in fact, that it made her father very uncomfortable to have a daughter, much less a pretty daughter, because prettiness, like femininity, was a form of power that he could not master nor control. He had tried, from the time she was a toddler, to raise her as a son instead. Not consciously, probably, but nonetheless.

Gloria appeared much more pleased to see her son and set the knife down to hold Oscar's hands while smiling up at him. Having a priest in the family was a source of great pride for her. It was Oscar who saved them both from the hell of standing there trying to seem like a normal family.

"We'll catch up in a bit," he said. "Our tacos are getting cold!"

"Okay, son," said Gloria with a pat to his hands.

As they returned to their table, Jodi saw Ashley, still in her uniform, get into the buffet line behind Henley. Probably still on the clock but just popping by to be seen. Jodi also noticed the two of them noticing each other. This made her feel weird. Jealous. She didn't like this about herself at all. But, she had to admit, they were more age appropriate. She saw them chatting, and he pointed to Jodi's direction, as if to tell Ashley where he was sitting. Ashley smiled, waved, and came to the table, then asked, "Got room for one more?"

"Of course," said Jodi. "I need to talk to you anyway."

"Yeah, I know. I'm pissed too. You have to understand, my boss, he's, like, one of these guys who wants to build a wall. You know?"

"I have Parker on a recording, admitting to being involved in . . . you know. All that."

"Gurule doesn't want to hear it," she said. "Said it's inadmissible."

"That's not true."

"He makes his own truth. This is his little kingdom. He literally told me that he doesn't see anything wrong with the Zebulon Boys, that he heard on the news they were some good guys, they endorsed his favorite presidential candidate, and he thinks me and you are liberal city bitches trying to frame some all-American boys for an unrelated crime."

"The hand and foot literally have the group's symbol branded on them."

"He doesn't believe it. Says that could have been done after the fact."

"This is insane."

"The entire posttruth world is insane," said Ashley.

"Yeah."

"Would you mind coming to the restroom with me?" Ashley asked, and from her facial expression Jodi knew this was a fake request, an excuse to go talk somewhere more private. They excused themselves, and Jodi followed Ashley to the parking lot out front.

"So here's the thing," she said. "I moved back here to take care of my dad. He's all alone, and he's older—he was in his fifties when I was born. I'm an only child. So I took this job because it was available. I can't stand the sheriff any more than you can. And I plan to run against him in the next election."

"Does he know that?"

"No. And I think I'd like to keep it that way. But I'm keeping really good records of him on this Zebulon case. I think me and you need to bust it open, and then, when the time comes, let people know that he let one of them go."

"So you don't want me to confront him?"

"No. I want me and you to handle this without him in the loop."

"I see."

"I wish you'd let me know you were going to bring Parker in. I would have told you not to. To keep him in your own lockup."

"I was just trying to follow protocol."

"No, I know. I get it. You're new; you need to follow the rule book. But sometimes you have to bend the rules a little."

"So what do you think comes next? I mean, he's just getting away."

"I'm on it. I have contacts in Albuquerque, and they'll let me know where he goes."

"Okay," said Jodi.

At that moment, feedback screeched through the speakers as the band took the small stage on the patio. This also happened to herald the arrival of Lyle, in his black Ford F-150.

"Handsome guy," said Ashley, of the old cowboy. "Amazing that men can just keep looking better with wrinkles and gray hair."

Jodi tried not to feel offended by this comment, because she didn't think the young deputy meant to indicate Jodi herself was getting worse looking because she was older. "Yeah. Well. I think my daughter's going to try to sing a duet with her boyfriend tonight, in honor of her great-uncle," said Jodi. "I need to get back in there."

"Just try to let it go, for now," said Ashley. "These kinds of cases can take time. We'll get these guys."

As they walked back toward the front door, Lyle trotted to intercept them and hold it open for them.

"Hope I'm not too late," he said.

"Party's just getting started," said Ashley.

They got to the patio as the sixty-something patriarch of the band took the stage. "Testing, one two," he said, tapping the microphone. Satisfied it was all in working order, he announced, "Hello, damas y caballeros! We are Grupo Barela, the best New Mexico music band in the state!"

The crowd roared their agreement as Marcus stepped up onto the stage and stood behind the man. Jodi and Ashley went back to their table, with Jodi motioning for Lyle to join them. He removed his hat and smoothed down his hair as he took a seat. Jodi noticed Henley looking from Lyle to Jodi as though trying to figure out whether they had something going on.

The patriarch continued, "We are very honored to be here this evening, celebrating the career of Officer Eloy Atencio, who I am proud to call a friend—even if he did catch me taking a turkey out of season once and gave me a ticket. Thanks a lot, cabrón!"

The crowd laughed, and Atencio shrugged and smiled, like, *Just doing my job, boss.*

"Tonight we have a special guest to introduce to you. Come on up, sweetheart, don't be shy." He wheeled his hand at Mila, who, blushing, took Marcus's outstretched hand and joined them onstage. "This is Mila Livingston, and even though her name don't sound like it, she's pura Rio Truchas County, the daughter of Officer Jodi Luna, and the great-niece of old Eloy. Where is Jodi?"

He searched the crowd for Jodi. She waved, not thrilled to be getting the attention but fully knowing that it would help her in her new post to be regarded as an authentic local. Being Atencio's niece, and Mila's mom, certainly helped. She knew that many who'd known her as a kid wondered why she'd thought so much of herself that she had to leave, and it would take things like this to win them back over.

As the kids began to sing, Jodi felt her heart lurch. She was so proud of Mila, of how she was healing, and growing into this new community, as though she had always lived here. She fought back tears as she wished Graham could have been here to see this moment. As couples started making their way to the dance floor in the middle of the patio, she felt even more emotional, more alone, strangely—and this made her want to run and hide.

"Shall we?" came the man's voice, near her ear. She turned to find Lyle standing behind her chair. She had been so wrapped up in the performance that she hadn't noticed him get up. But he had been watching her, closely, and seemed to be stepping in to rescue her from her own pain.

She smiled, and accepted his hand, and said, "Sure."

25

As the party wound down, and Jodi, Mila, Oscar, Lyle, and Diana made their way to the vestibule with goodbye hugs to friends and family all the way along, Jodi realized just how exhausted she was. Her bones felt like they'd been replaced by steel rods. It had been a hell of a long week. Ashley had left on a car-crash call about an hour ago, with a promise that they'd regroup in the morning to discuss next steps on the Zebulon Boys case with clearer, more rested heads.

"Hey, sleepyhead," said Diana in response to Jodi's constant yawning. "How about I take Oscar back to the abbey on my way home, so you and Mila can get on home and rest? You look like you are dragging."

Oscar perked up when Jodi asked him if that would be okay.

"Of course," he said.

"Isn't that kind of out of your way?" Jodi asked.

"I'm just in it for a free six-pack of priest piss," said Diana. It was how she referred to the beer the brothers brewed.

"Just go easy on him," said Jodi of her brother. "He's fragile."

Lyle moved close to Jodi now and said, "If you don't mind, I think I'd like to follow you home."

Jodi was shocked by this and at a loss for words.

"Not like that," he said, clearly embarrassed by her assumption. "With Eric Parker on the loose, and knowing these boys know where you live, I just—as a friend, I want to make sure you get home safe."

Jodi took a long moment to consider this before agreeing to it. She had never felt like Graham had her back, not in this old-fashioned big-brother kind of physically protective way. Graham had been supportive of her work and loved to listen to her poetry, which was everything, for a time. Graham had been hard core about feminism and felt that it was important to give Jodi agency, not infantilize her by opening her doors, or asking her whether she had changed the oil in her car, or whatever it was other husbands did. She had loved him for it, at first, because she had been raised in such a rigidly structured world with regards to gender roles. But, she realized now, maybe it was okay to let people help you. Maybe it was okay for a man to offer to look after a woman he cared about. Maybe Lyle's offer to see her home safely wasn't any more sexist or controlling than Diana offering to help her out by driving Oscar back to his monastery. Friends help you out, she reminded herself, and this is what community feels like.

And seeing Lyle's pickup headlights in the rearview mirror as Jodi piloted the Rubicon through the twisty mountain passes that led her home as her dear, sweet, beautiful daughter fell asleep against the door, trusting her mother with every ounce of her soul, felt good. She found her mind wandering to imagined kisses with him. She wondered what it might feel like to have a man hold her again. It had been a long two years of complete celibacy and only fleeting moments of physical closeness with friends and family, limited, of course, to quick hugs or walking arm in arm with Diana. She missed intimacy.

When they got to the gate, Jodi got out to open the padlock. She hated to see Lyle go and needed to admit it to herself. She came up to his window, and he rolled it down to talk to her.

"I don't have any whiskey," she said. "But I've got a few Tipsy Monk beers, if you'd like to come in for a minute or two."

"You up for that?" he asked, and she nodded.

"The drive gave me a second wind. I don't feel ready to sleep just yet. Be nice to get to know you a little better."

Lyle grinned, mostly with his eyes, and said, "Lead the way."

Mila was awakened by the truck stopping at the gate, and as Jodi drove them up the rise toward the house, she told her daughter that Lyle would be coming in for a drink. Sleepy and warm and probably still feeling the glow of the evening's socializing, Mila mumbled, "Good for you, Mom," in a sincere way. "You need to get you some."

"Mila!" Jodi barked. This made Mila laugh.

"Oh my God, Mom, relax. I'm just teasing you. You don't need my permission to have a grown-up life. But if you want it, you have it. You don't have to become a nun because Dad died."

Jodi parked the truck, and in the commotion of guiding her guest to a parking space next to her Rubicon, she did not notice that Juana was not barking up her usual storm. She was too nervous about having a gentleman over, hoping she didn't do anything stupid.

Mila didn't linger in the main part of the house and seemed eager to give her mom space with her new friend. Jodi remembered the comforting feeling of being a child and hearing the adults talking in some other room in the house, not being able to quite make out what they were saying but feeling protected and taken care of. She told herself that was how Mila felt about this visitor. Silently, Jodi apologized to Graham's ghost. He would understand, wouldn't he? Now that it finally had sunk in that he wasn't going to come bursting through the door at any moment, with a bag of Thai takeout and a bottle of wine. Now that he was truly and really starting to seem gone.

"Nice place," said Lyle, who removed his hat and set it on the entry table, upside down.

"Still needs a lot of work," said Jodi. "Need to update so many things. I'm getting to it, slowly but surely."

Lyle joined her in the kitchen and leaned against the counter as she rummaged in the refrigerator for a couple of cold bottles of Catholic beer. "You always so bad at taking a compliment?" he asked.

Jodi stopped midtwist with one of the bottle's caps and stared at him. Graham had often accused her of this same flaw. Not taking compliments well, answering any nice thing anyone said about her with deflection and countercriticism.

"Yeah," she said. "I am." She finished opening the bottle and handed it to him. He waited till hers was likewise opened and then held his out for a toast.

"Here's to new friends," he said.

"Cheers to that." Jodi clinked her bottle against his, and they both took a drink. Then she said, "It's a little chilly in here. Why don't we take this to the living room, and I'll get the fire going?"

"Sounds good to me," he said. She led him to the sofas and set her beer down on a pottery coaster on the table before opening the wood-stove and throwing some logs in from the bucket at its side. She took some newspaper kindling from the stash beside the bucket and lit it up beneath the logs. After blowing on it a couple of times, satisfied that it was not going to go out, she closed the door, dusted off her hands, and joined Lyle on the sofa.

"I mean it," he said, admiring the vigas and the walls. "I really like what you've done to the place. It looks a lot better."

"Have you been here before?" she asked.

"Few times, with your uncle, before you moved back. Y'all have some good fishing in that creek in your back pasture."

"Yeah, we do."

"Makes you see why they named this place Trout River County," he said.

"Indeed. Nothing better than fresh trout in the summer. You have just inspired me. I am for sure going to get out there with my flies tomorrow."

"These floors are really something. Were they like this, or did you put new ones in and make them look old?"

"That's what was under the carpet. Four layers of carpet."

"No offense, but it used to look like the seventies threw up in here."

"Yeah. I just sanded it and bleached it before staining it white."

"Looks great."

"Thank you."

"You're good at doing things yourself," he said, approvingly. "Not many people can say that anymore."

"I don't understand why people pay for gym memberships instead of just learning to fix things around their own homes," she said. "They pay contractors and gardeners, then go work out for two hours, staring in a mirror."

The conversation continued and ranged from books to movies to music and finally—as the yawning attacks returned—came around, though only briefly, to their shared history of loss.

"Last time I was up this late, talking to a woman, was the night Renata died," he said. He was three beers deep now. Jodi considered what he said and felt like crying. The beer had loosened up the place in her brain that gave her permission to feel things for other people.

"I'm so sorry," she said. "That must have been so hard."

"It wasn't fun. But we expected it. I had time to prepare. She was at peace with it, and she held my hand and she forgave me."

Jodi wondered what she'd had to forgive him about but was not tipsy enough to ask.

"I always wonder if it would have been better to have had advanced warning of Graham's death," she said. "Or if it's easier just having it happen all at once, like ripping off a Band-Aid."

Jodi was, however, tipsy enough to reach out and grab Lyle's hand. He squeezed hers back, without turning his eyes away from the wall in front of them.

"I'm not a perfect man," he said.

"Show me one who is," she answered. He turned his face toward hers now, and they looked into each other's eyes for a long enough moment to make it awkward.

"You seem to think that young wildlife veterinarian was something special," he said, with just a hint of jealousy.

"Who, Henley?"

"Nice-looking fellow. Seems like you two might have a thing?"

"No. No thing. We work together. We get along. That's all."

"So you're not seeing anyone?"

"Nope."

"Think you might maybe want to?"

"I think so. Maybe."

"You're really something," he told her.

"Something good, I hope?"

He scooted just a little closer and grinned. "Yeah. Something good."

Butterflies rippled through her chest and twinkled up and down her spine as she allowed him to kiss her. Just a peck at first. And then with more passion. She had forgotten what this felt like. She had not kissed many other men. Just Kurt, then Graham, and now Lyle. She let herself melt into the moment and felt for all the world like a teenager again.

When they came up for air, she was horrified to find herself yawning again. She was not bored with him by any stretch of the imagination, and she wished she weren't completely exhausted.

"That good, huh?" he asked.

"It's not you," she said. "I've been up—it's been a hard week. So much going on."

"And it's two in the morning," he said. "Should I get going?"

Jodi took a deep breath. She had enjoyed the kiss, but she was still afraid to go further than that. "Have you dated at all, since Renata passed?"

"No."

"So is this weird for you too?"

"A bit."

"I mean—I'd like you to stay. You can stay. It's late, and you've had a bit to drink. I feel safe with you here."

"Thank you. I could stay in your guest room, if you prefer."

"I wouldn't," she said, being fully honest with him. "What I'd really like is if you just slept with me. Like actually sleep. If it's not too weird, I'd like to fall asleep in your arms."

"Not weird at all," he said.

"It's not the sex I miss, so much as the intimacy," she said.

"You have sex awake," he said. "And if something's off, you can leave. But to sleep in the presence of another person? That's much more intimate, because you are never more vulnerable than when you're sleeping."

"That's it. That's exactly it."

"Do you feel safe enough with me to sleep with me?" he asked.

"Yes. Do you feel safe enough with me?"

He glanced around the room again and nodded his approval. "I have never known a woman more capable of being in the world," he said. "And I can't imagine a place I'd feel safer than sleeping next to you."

Jodi led him by the hand to her room, turning off lights and checking locks as she went.

"I don't have any more of Graham's clothes," she said. "And you're a bit too tall to fit into my pajamas. I have a robe or two that might cover you up."

Lyle was already stripping down to his boxer briefs and undershirt. "I'm a cowboy, Jodi. I can sleep naked on a bed of cactus."

And so they climbed, each in their underwear, underneath the warm white goose-down comforter, and Lyle took the position of big spoon. They did not talk anymore, instead just allowing their fingers to interlace at Jodi's sternum. Lyle's breath on the back of her neck was immensely soothing. As she began to drift off, wolves began to howl up the mountain, and she smiled to herself, thinking that the parents and older siblings in the pack were out finding food for those six sweet little pups.

"Good night, Mr. Daggett," she said, snuggling in harder.

"Buenas noches, Miss Luna," he replied.

———

Five hours later, at seven in the morning, later than she usually slept, Jodi woke to find Lyle curled up next to her, still sound asleep. She had a tiny bit of a hangover but could still remember the night perfectly. She loved seeing him there, and in sleep she could see the boy he'd once been. She eased herself out of bed and tiptoed to the bathroom to grab her robe, with plans to make pancakes and coffee before he woke up and, hopefully, to warn Mila that he was still here so that she would not be too shocked. Mila's door was still closed, and the house was quiet, so Jodi put the coffee on, then slipped into her boots. She headed outside through the side door and fed and watered the chickens, collecting a dozen eggs first. Next, she fed the horses. When she got to Juana's pen, she realized something was very wrong. The dog was usually up at the sound of Jodi coming out of the house, but she was not standing in her usual spot at the front of the dog run. She was still in the little house, asleep.

"Juana? Here, girl!" Jodi called, but the dog did not move.

Jodi set the basket of eggs down, opened the pen, rushed to the doghouse, and peered in. Juana was not asleep. She was having a seizure, foaming at the mouth and unresponsive. Next to the doghouse was a hunk of bright-orange American cheese, wadded up around several small white pills.

Regretting not having taken a firearm with her, Jodi quickly scanned the surroundings. She ducked and ran toward the house. This was when she noticed that Mila's bedroom window, which looked out over the garden on the dog-pen side of the house, was wide open, the curtains flapping in the air.

"No," she said, sprinting for the window. "Mila!" she screamed. "Mila! Mila!"

When she got to the window, she saw a trail of blood along the outside wall, leading across the garden pavers a few feet before it disappeared. Her heart sank with the kind of cold and nauseating dread only a parent can feel upon discovering something has gone wrong with their child. When she looked through the window and saw signs of a struggle in Mila's room, then ran into the house and burst into the room, trying to understand what could have happened, the fear intensified into absolute, bloodcurdling terror. Mila was gone, but left behind, on her pillow, was one severed human ear, with an earring pushed through it, bearing the Zebulon Boys insignia.

26

The bald man who smelled of cigarettes and his skinny sidekick, who smelled like a literal toilet, held Mila still and put a knife to her throat. Meanwhile, the short-haired man who gave everyone orders took photos of her. A fourth man, the one they called Levi, stood off to one side watching, because they told him he was supposed to "observe" only. The man taking photos, who had a gun, was laughing, as though this was great fun for him. The bald one, who did not have a gun, didn't say much, but Mila sensed he despised the skinny one and worshipped the short-haired one.

She stored this information away for future use.

"Say, 'Hi, Mom,'" said the one taking the pictures.

"Go to hell," said Mila. Yes, she was scared, but also strangely calm. She was already numb, and being grabbed from her bed in the middle of the night, gagged with someone's old filthy socks, tied up with dog leashes, dragged through her own window, and tossed into the back of a truck with a burlap sack tied over her head only served to make her even more numb. Like, it would have been funny if it weren't so terrible. Dirty socks and dog leashes? Who were these clowns?

She had roughly timed the drive, in her mind, though it was an imperfect science, not knowing how fast the truck was going. She knew enough of the twists and turns in the road to be able to discern that they'd gotten to the turnoff toward the more remote part of the San Isidro National Forest, near the falls. She loved this area and knew it well, because there were cliffs here that, now and then, her mom let her climb. The bed of the pickup was very hard and ridged, and there was no way to get comfortable, no position she could find, that didn't result in bruising. This was also okay, because Mila, having thrown herself off things all her life, was no stranger to bruises. She'd heal.

That said, there were limits to her bravery and confidence. And this place, whatever it was, was scary as hell. There were tents and a blazing firepit and slabs of meat hanging from the trees. There was a smell of rust, which she knew instinctively was blood, in the soil. And rot. It smelled like death here. Death and an outhouse. They'd had to walk for what seemed like an hour to get here from wherever they'd parked the truck, and she'd had to do this barefoot. So that sucked. Everything hurt. In addition to the men doing her photo shoot, Mila saw a woman, standing nearby and watching, with an ugly, superior smirk. She seemed to enjoy watching these men hurt Mila. Mila didn't want to think about what this group all together might find to do to a teen girl in a place like this. But if they were going to do it, she was going to make it as unpleasant for them as possible all the way through.

"Dig it in deeper," said the short-haired one. He looked normal, almost, except for the completely crazy look in his eyes. He reminded Mila of a television news anchor. All of these people wore hunting-type outfits and were white. Mila assumed the bald one was the guy who'd followed her mom home and that this short-haired one was the guy who was leading this stupid militia.

"The knife, or . . . ," said the bald-headed one.

"Shut your filthy mouth," said the short-haired one. In a sudden rage, he pulled his pistol out and aimed it at them. "We respect and obey miscegenation laws in this organization. To even hint at having intercourse with Mexicans is grounds for release from the army, and when I release you, you do not leave alive."

"Sorry, General. It was just a joke." This was the skinny one speaking.

"Last I checked, jokes have to be funny," said the bald one.

"Shut your face, Travis," said the skinny one.

"Enough, both of you!" cried the one she now knew went by General.

Okay, Mila thought. These guys are not that bright, but they are crazy, violent, hateful, and members of an armed white supremacist group. They are mean by nature. They are not even nice to each other.

She filed all of this away too.

"Now do what I said," said the short-haired one. "Cut her a little, just enough to draw blood for the photo. We want Mama to shit her pants when she sees this."

"My mother is not afraid of you, and neither am I," said Mila. "You cut me, that's just going to make her want to kill you more."

"Shut up," said the skinny one as the knife bit into the soft flesh of her neck. She counted backward from one hundred by threes, a stress-reduction technique she'd learned in counseling after her father died. She wanted to scream, or at least whimper, but she didn't. She would not give them that pleasure.

"We'll wait on the rest of it till tomorrow. She still looks too well. Give her a chance to get to know her roommates, adjust to the new circumstances, simmer down a little," said the General.

"Yes, General," said Travis.

"Throw her in the stalag for now," the General said. "Let's take Paola out later: cat-and-mouse time."

"I love cat-and-mouse time!" said the skinny one, like a child.

"Shut up," Travis told him as he dragged Mila, still bound at the ankles and wrists with dog leashes, across the encampment, toward what looked like a bunch of branches all in a pile under a tall pine tree. The others followed.

"You," the General said, to the lone woman among them. "Open it up."

"Yes, sir, General Zebulon, sir!"

The woman is way too into this, Mila thought.

Out of all the collected crazy people there, this one was by far the one she feared the most.

The woman knelt next to the pile of forest debris and began, with much grunting and effort, to remove several large branches from it. It was then that Mila saw what the debris had been covering: a deep, wide hole in the ground.

Mila heard something moving at the bottom of the hole and nervously peered in, but she was still too far to see the bottom of the pit. What was down there? Snakes? A bobcat?

"Move," said the General, pushing her forward as the others pulled in tight to contain her.

That was when Mila saw a woman's face, hungry, dirt streaked, terrorized, and blinking against the brightness of the morning light, squinting up at them.

"Holy shit," said Mila as her body began to tremble in fear. Her knees grew weak, and the sounds of the world around her were muffled by the booming of her own heartbeat in her ears. Any bravery she might have felt was instantly gone. This was much, much worse than she'd thought. She tried to wriggle free, to run, but she was surrounded.

"Adiós," said the General.

He grabbed Mila by the arm and shoved.

27

Lyle was watching over Jodi, just outside the dog pen next to the barn on her property, when that new wildlife veterinarian, Henley Bethel, pulled up in his Subaru. The guy looked worried, his forehead all creases and scowls as he walked over to them. He moved bent forward a little at the waist, like someone had pushed him. It was a too-fast, stressed-out walking style that Lyle associated with city slickers who were always on their way to somewhere important and running a few minutes behind. Like the world was ending. Out here, you didn't worry in quite the same way. You worried slower. You planned. You didn't stress out like a drowning person grabbing at the sky; you focused, and floated, and, when you could, swam.

"Good morning," said Henley. He was carrying several bags and boxes of things that Lyle figured a veterinarian might need on a house call.

"Morning, Doctor," said Lyle, tapping the brim of his hat. "You need help with any of that?"

"Nah, I'm good," said the doctor, but he looked nervous.

"Glad you're here. She's in there." Lyle tried to affect a relaxed posture in hopes some of it would wear off on the doctor before he got into the pen with Jodi and her dog. Dogs and women were both pretty good at sensing when a man was losing his shit; at least that had been Lyle's impression of things over the years. Jodi and the dog both needed this man to be a calming and reassuring presence.

Lyle watched as Henley entered the dog enclosure and walked toward the back, where Jodi was cross-legged on the ground next to the doghouse. Spilling from the opening of the doghouse was Juana's quivering, seemingly unconscious head. Jodi was on her phone and could not have looked more tired and upset if she tried. Her eyes were bloodshot, and her hair was a mess, and she was wearing a bathrobe that had been white before she'd sat in the dirt in it, with cowboy boots. When she spotted the doctor, her body language grew even more distraught. Lyle sighed and shook his head just a little, wishing the other man didn't wear his feelings so much on his sleeve.

"Hi," the doctor said, with an awkward wave. Jodi waved back distractedly and got to her feet to give him access to the dog.

"Are you serious?" she said into her phone. Her voice was louder now as she fed off his fear. "El Paso? You think he's heading to Mexico? Oh my God. The irony. Okay, Ashley. Thank you. Talk to you in a bit."

Jodi ended her call and filled Henley in on what they knew. The doctor was kneeling down now, inspecting the hunk of cheese and the dog both.

"I have to go," Jodi told him. "You got this?"

"Yeah, of course," he said, but she must have seen his bewilderment just like Lyle did.

"You sure?" she asked, in almost a motherly tone.

"Yeah. Go. I got this."

"All right. Thank you. Call me if you need anything."

Jodi came to Lyle now, moving in the focused, steady manner of rural people in a crisis.

"It's going to be fine," he reassured her. Her shoulders dropped down from where she'd scrunched them up by her ears, and she exhaled in relief.

"Yeah," she said, taking in his calm, slight smile.

"Sounds like they found Eric," he said, gesturing to the phone that was still in her hand.

"Yeah. Deputy Romero's contact in Albuquerque said he transferred there, to a bus to El Paso. She's on her way to intercept the bus now. She's about to board a flight."

"I like that Deputy Romero—she's good."

"Yeah," said Jodi. "She seems to be."

"So what's next on your to-do list, and how can I help?"

"Stay here and watch the house. In case they come back, or in case Mila shows up. She's a smart, strong girl, and I would not put it past her to find a way to escape. Someone from Hafeez's office is coming by for the ear. I'm going out to where he said the Zebulon Boys parked their cars. See if someone shows up."

Lyle noticed the young doctor's head snap around toward them at the mention of the ear. Looked like he wanted to ask questions but was too busy tending to the poisoned dog to interrupt himself. Lyle noticed the way the doctor kept sneaking glances in this direction. Looked like he wondered why Lyle and Jodi were standing so close. Why she was touching his arm. Why she burrowed into him for a comforting hug.

"I'm sure you can handle it, whatever it is," Lyle told Jodi as he answered the unspoken question for the doctor and bent toward her beautiful face, to kiss her goodbye, on the lips.

28

Eric had commandeered a whole row of seats at the front of the bus, and as the driver crawled the Greyhound along Santa Fe Street in El Paso, Texas, like a big slow slug looking for a place to have a nap, he had a full view out the front window of all the decrepit adobe buildings in the neighborhood. **PANADERÍA. CARNICERÍA.** All of them had signs in Spanish.

Oh well, he thought. Better get used to it.

Running away to Mexico was what all the best good guys did in the movies, when they were really just misunderstood, and it felt like the brave and right thing to do. The sun would be setting in a couple of hours, and there was something heroic about thinking of watching the sunset from the safety of Mexico. Even though that Mexican sheriff up in Rio Truchas had let him go, it would only be a matter of time before what he'd done with the Zebulon Boys caught up to him. Those fuckers were planning to blow up a whole town. He needed to get good and gone. He didn't know anymore whether he would be hunted down by those lady cops, or that ranch manager who'd betrayed his trust, or by the General himself. What he did know, however, was that he was not safe at all, going back to Hemet, or anywhere in the United States anymore. He'd be killed if he stayed. He'd let his family know where he was once he got across the border. He didn't know what he'd do for a living there, but car mechanics were needed everywhere. He'd figure something out.

"Is it far to the border crossing?" Eric asked the driver, who was another Mexican. They were literally everywhere you looked. "Do I need to take an Uber or something?"

The driver laughed. "You're joking, right?"

"No. I've never been here."

"You see that bridge?" He pointed to a low, terra-cotta-colored bridge that was about a block away. "On the other side, that's Juárez."

"Can you walk over it?"

"Yeah, bro. Thousands of people do, every day, back and forth."

"Is it expensive to cross? Do you need papers?"

"Fifty cents per person, pedestrian. That's ten Mexican pesos."

"Are you serious?"

"Yeah." The driver pulled into the dock for his bus and picked up the microphone. "Ladies and gentlemen, welcome to El Paso. Please don't forget your belongings. Have a great day."

Eric didn't have any belongings. Just himself. And he was the first one to disembark, going quickly toward what appeared to be the start of the rust-colored bridge, a block or two away. When he turned the first corner, he had the sensation that he was being followed, confirmed when he looked over his shoulder and saw a young Mexican-looking woman trailing him. She did not look away when he caught her eye. In fact, she sped up. Eric noticed the lump under her jean jacket and recognized it as likely to be a gun.

"Shit," he said to himself, and he began to run. The woman ran, too, but he was faster. The closer he got to the bridge, the more crowded the street became. He saw now that the bridge had a wide section along the side for people on foot. This was crowded, too, with people moving in both directions. He sped up, weaving in and out of the bodies as though they were nothing but obstacles, slamming women and children aside as he went. The woman who was chasing him was not as inclined to do whatever it took, and the crowd slowed her down.

"Excuse me, sorry, this is urgent. Emergency. I have family on the other side, dying, heart attack, I need to get through, please," he lied, and the people, being sheep like they always were, parted to let him through. As he paid the fee to get through the turnstile to the other side, he saw the woman stop nearby, to watch. She had a defeated look on her face, like she knew it was too late. He wondered if she would follow him to Mexico. He gave his ticket to the attendant and went through the port.

"Bienvenidos a México," said a deep male voice over the speakers in the ceiling of the open-air roof.

Eric took one last look backward, but the woman was gone.

29

Mila's fall into the hole had been broken by the arms of the three other women at the bottom, who had intentionally tried to catch her as an act of kindness. Mila might have landed on her feet anyhow, because she was born with a sort of kinesthetic genius for turning and twisting in midair, like a cat. It took a minute or two for her eyes to adjust to the dim light, after their captors had replaced the branches across the top of the hole. By the time she was able to make out their faces, the other women had removed the bindings from her wrists and ankles and settled her down on the ground, as far as possible from the area they had apparently been using as a latrine. They knelt or sat near her, asking her if she was all right, in English and Spanish.

"I'm fine," she said, trying not to vomit because the hole was basically the underside of an outhouse. "The real question is, How are you guys? And who are you? And why are we here?"

The young women, who all seemed to be less than twenty years of age, spoke in hushed tones, close to Mila's ear, and filled her in on everything they knew. The one who spoke perfect English was Paola Chinana, eighteen, the daughter of Kurt Chinana. Mila told her that her own mother had dated Kurt back in middle and high school, and Paola seemed surprised by this and also pleased to have some connection to the outside world who knew about her family, some semblance of normalcy in the midst of the madness in this hole. The pregnant one said her name was Ana Luz, and she was from Chiapas. Her English was good but heavily accented, as was her Spanish; she said that Mayan was her native language. The third one, Altagracia, spoke English very well and Spanish not that well, and she said she was a Mormon Puerto Rican college student from Utah and that she'd been kidnapped as she went for a jog. They told her about two other women who had recently lived in this same hell with them, adding that the captors had taken them out and hunted them like animals. They showed her the human ear, and she told them that her kidnappers had left the missing ear to the set in her room, on her pillow.

"They're taking me today," said Paola. She seemed numb. "I really hope all they do is take part of you, not all of you."

"Okay," said Mila. "Listen to me. It's going to be okay. First of all, my mom knows about one of these guys, Travis. And she has to know I'm missing by now, and I'm sure she will know who took me, because they aren't even trying to hide it."

"That's because they're building bombs and plan to start some stupid war against 'Mexicans' in Hispaniola in a couple of weeks," said Paola. "Even though only one of us here is actually Mexican."

"Which brings me to my second of all," said Mila. "These people?" She pointed up. "They're not the brightest bulbs on the string. I've met bear turds smarter than them. It won't be hard to defeat them if we're intelligent about it."

The others looked defeated and seemed to appreciate her optimism while also finding her foolish.

Mila stood up and started looking over the dungeon very carefully. "Okay. So we're about fifteen, twenty feet down. That's not too much. And we're in a forest, under some trees, and"—she picked up a couple of sticks that had fallen into the hole from the branches above—"we have tools."

The others watched her with interest but did not seem convinced.

Mila broke some smaller twigs off the largest branch, which was about two feet long, and began to use the thicker, stronger, sharper end of the branch to dig into the walls of the hole. She did this several times, each time a little bit higher, and was soon able to climb about five feet up the side of the wall, like a spider.

"Any of you girls ever rock climbed before?" she asked.

None of them had.

"Well, today you're going to learn how."

At that moment, just as the women had begun to feel a glimmer of hope they'd not yet felt down here, the branches were pulled aside again up above. Mila jumped down, dropped the stick, and hoped they would not notice the climbing holes she'd begun to build. She watched in horror as an orange plastic Sked rescue stretcher, attached to black ropes, was dropped into the hole.

"Paola, you're up," said the General. Mila squeezed her eyes against the light and saw that he was pointing a pistol at them, while Travis and the skinny, stinky one held the rope. "Get in, or die now."

"Fuck, you guys," said Paola, trembling.

"It's okay," said Mila. "Just get away from them as soon as you can, if you can, and find a place to hide. Stay there. My mom will be here soon, and she has an amazing rescue dog, Juana. She'll find you. You're going to be okay. I promise. Okay?"

Paola nodded and gave Mila a look of thanks before sliding herself onto the stretcher, strapping in, crossing her arms over her chest, and allowing herself to be hauled up to whatever came next.

30

Dressed in her work uniform once again and armed and prepared for war, Jodi drove her work truck from one old fire-lookout station to the next over the course of the entire afternoon and into the evening. This was made slower and more difficult by the fact that she had the horse trailer hitched to the back, with two horses in it, because she knew that vast portions of this terrain were inaccessible by motor vehicle.

Finally, toward sundown, she found the lookout with the hidden cars, far up a rocky mountain at a high-altitude, beautiful, and virtually untouched part of the forest she had actually never even seen before. Frantic to find Mila, she had talked to Becky and Ashley as she drove, trying to come up with the best plan of action. Because of Gurule's sympathetic stance toward the Zebulon Boys and his own apparent hatred for the Mexicans he believed himself to be different from—because he'd had the blind good fortune to have been born in the United States, even though a couple of generations back his own ancestors had been born in Mexico in this very same place—they decided to keep it to themselves for now, and to only alert other police forces such as state troopers if they did not make any headway in the next forty-eight hours. Ashley told Jodi what had happened with Eric Parker: that he'd run across the border and she'd decided not to chase him because she had no jurisdiction there, and he wouldn't have talked anyway.

"I'm flying back later tonight. I'll come find you. We'll find these assholes. I promise."

Jodi gave Ashley the exact coordinates of the lookout tower and said that her own plan was to camp out there all night and to head out on horseback early in the morning to look for clues about where the terrorist base camp might be when the sun came up again.

"If they're coming and going from here," she said, "there have to be tracks, or something. It can't be that far from here."

Jodi had done a quick once-over of the assembled vehicles. A van from Arizona, a sedan from California, an SUV from Nevada. She jimmied the locks open and looked inside, collecting the registrations and other documents she found in the glove boxes. At least she had the names of the others involved. She radioed these in to Becky, who shared with her the great news that the ear found in Mila's room did not, in fact, belong to Mila. It was not a genetic match.

Night was coming down quickly, and the temperature dropped fast up here. Jodi needed to get a fire going, get these horses out to graze a bit, and set up her tent before all the light was gone.

As she went back to her truck for the tent, she heard the distinctive crack of a gunshot echo through the forest. It stopped her cold. She stood, hair raised on her arms and neck, and listened for another shot, trying to place the one she'd heard. A second shot, then a third. Then nothing. She tried not to obsess over the terrifying thought of Mila being shot, told herself that she would find her daughter. People fired guns for all kinds of reasons out here.

"Keep a cool head, Jodi," she told herself.

She had taken the tent to a clearing behind the cars and trees, and was about to bring the horses out to eat some grass, when she heard the sound of a motor, distant at first but growing closer. This has to be them, she thought. Something is happening.

She abandoned the fire and left the tent only halfway assembled, drew her pistol, and went back toward the abandoned logging road to hide and wait. For ten agonizing minutes, she listened to that distant engine until, finally, headlights came into view, from up higher on the mountain. She was expecting it, somehow, to have come from below. She watched carefully as the truck came into view. It was a Chevy Colorado ZR2, kind of a truck-SUV hybrid, beige, and fully loaded. Not a cheap vehicle, and not remotely practical, really. She had never seen one in this area before. She took out her binoculars as it got closer, trying to see who was driving it, but the forest was dark now, and the headlights made it impossible to see anything. She fought with herself mentally, trying to figure out what to do. When she realized it was not slowing down and had no intention of stopping at this lookout tower, she decided she had to stop it herself. She had no idea who or what was waiting for her inside the truck, but thinking of Mila, and only Mila, she walked out into its oncoming path and took a shooting stance, aimed her Glock at the windshield, and shouted, "Police! I order you to halt!"

Jodi braced for being run over, or shot at, or whatever might happen next. She had a bulletproof vest on, and she hoped that her reflexes would be enough to get her to safety if whoever this was did not comply. The ZR2 slowed down, then stopped, but kept its brights trained on her. Jodi instantly pegged this as the type of behavior you'd find in poachers who spotlighted animals—spotlighting being the practice of poaching at night and shining your brights in the eyes of your target animal to disorient it and make it easier to kill. It was illegal pretty much everywhere to do this.

"Turn off your lights!" she screamed, hating the feeling that she was a prey animal being spotlighted by some anonymous asshole in the middle of nowhere. "And step out of the vehicle, hands up where I can see them. Do it now!"

"Jodi?" came a familiar voice as the headlights and engine both turned off, leaving them all in pitch blackness and silence. So familiar, and so out of context, that she was caught off guard and shook her head like a dog with water in its ear. "Jodi, what the hell are you doing out here?"

"Tío?"

The passenger door of the ZR2 opened, and in the chunk of bluish light ignited by the opening of the door she saw that it was, indeed, her uncle, newly retired officer Eloy Atencio, in civilian hunting clothes. She was at once relieved and confused, because she knew him to be a law-abiding man and did not think he would be out here hunting off season. She was also confused by the truck, and its driver, a white man of about forty, whom she had never seen before. There were two people in the back seats of the vehicle as well, but she could not see much more than shadows of them.

"Put your gun down, sobrina," he said.

"Who's with you?" she asked. "Are you all right?"

"I'm fine. I'm with friends. Put your gun away, and I'll introduce you and try to convince them my favorite niece isn't a crazy person."

Jodi sheathed her weapon and took out a flashlight, using it to make her way to the truck.

"Can we turn the lights on again now?" her uncle asked. He sounded awkward to Jodi, and she felt intuitively that something was weird here.

"Sure," she said. She went directly to the driver's side window, which was already rolled down, and shone the flashlight into the face of the driver. He put his hands over his eyes and laughed.

"Hey, now," he said. "No need for all that."

"To whom do I have the pleasure of speaking?" Jodi asked.

Atencio was at her side now, and he moved the flashlight by tugging on Jodi's arm. "What the hell are you doing?" he demanded. "I told you, these are friends."

"I'm Jonas Sauer," said the driver.

"Owner of the Sauer Brothers Ranch," said Atencio, almost as a warning to Jodi. "Which, last I checked, employs your new dance partner."

Jodi felt embarrassed but not entirely comfortable yet.

"Oh, you know old Lyle Daggett?" Jonas asked her, all fake friendly.

"Yeah," she said.

"Great guy. Hell of a guy."

She noticed her uncle's gaze kept twitching toward the bed of the vehicle, which was covered in a blue tarp.

"I'm Officer Jodi Luna," she said to Jonas. "I apologize if I gave you a fright, Mr. Sauer. I'm on a bit of a stakeout right now, and I couldn't tell who was driving."

"No worries. I have nothing but respect for our officers of the law; isn't that right, Eloy?"

Jodi made eye contact with her uncle and saw that, yes, he was deeply nervous.

"That's right, Mr. Sauer," he said.

"Who you got with you?" Jodi asked. "Mind turning on the cabin lights for a second, Mr. Sauer?"

"What's this all about?" said Jonas, growing angrier.

"Just being friendly is all," said Jodi.

He scowled but turned the cabin lights on, even as Atencio sighed as though this were going to end in some sort of doom for him.

"Just my wife, Marlena Sauer, and a friend of the family's."

In the light, Jodi saw two women. One who was tall and willowy, a blonde beauty, clearly the new trophy wife Lyle had told her about. She, too, was dressed in camo hunting gear, though hers was pink. Next to her, Jodi saw that the "family friend" was none other than the governor of the state of New Mexico, Cheryl Baca-Crichton, all five foot one of her, something like a shrunken, apple-headed version of Hillary Clinton, dressed head to toe in hunting gear.

"Governor?" Jodi blinked in astonishment as her uncle cursed under his breath in Spanish.

"Howdy, Officer," said the governor, who opened her door and stepped out to come around with that politician's smile to shake Jodi's hand. "Nice to meet you. I'm sorry we interrupted your stakeout. I hope you get the bad guys. We'll get out of your hair here, right away. As you know, I am all about safety and protecting New Mexicans from dangerous criminals. I just wanted to thank you, personally, for your service."

Jodi shook the governor's hand, noting the grip to be aggressive and stronger than you might expect from a woman her size and age—the latter being at least ten years older than Jodi.

"What brings you all up here this late on a Saturday evening?"

"Well, Mr. and Mrs. Sauer here are visiting our fine state, where they happen to be one of the largest private landowners, but I'm sure you knew that already, and they asked to have a guided tour of some of the lesser-known places up here. They really enjoy the outdoors."

"And you asked my uncle to come with you, why?"

"Eloy and I go way back, don't we?" she said, slapping Atencio on the back.

"That we do." Jodi's uncle looked at her as if to beg her to leave well enough alone, but once again, his eyes darted to the bed of the truck, revealing that he didn't want her to know what was back there.

"What you got here?" she asked.

The governor shot Atencio a stern look, and he said, "I'll talk to her. Jodi? Come with me for a second."

But Jodi was determined. She walked around the back of the truck and pulled back the tarp. There, dead from several inexpertly placed shots, shots that would have meant great suffering and a long, bloody death, was one of the wolves from the pack out by Lower Fresita Hot Springs. It was the alpha male, Amadeus, his ear clip and collar still in place.

"Tío? What the fuck?"

Atencio quickly pulled the tarp back over the wolf. Jodi saw the governor standing with her feet shoulder distance apart and her hands on her hips, directly facing them as though to challenge Jodi to give anyone there a citation. Atencio pulled Jodi farther away, into the darkness, and said, "Jodi, there are times when you, as a game warden, might have to look the other way."

"They poached a fucking wolf."

"Mr. Sauer is very powerful. He's in energy exploration."

"You mean oil and gas."

"Yes. And the governor, who I will remind you is your boss, is eager to make him happy about opening some new economic growth opportunities here in New Mexico."

"You mean she wants to convince him to drill for more oil here."

"Yes. It would mean a lot of revenue for the state. So she asked him what it might take, and, pues." Atencio gestured to the tarp. "That's what it would take. A Mexican gray wolf stuffed in his living room. She wasn't happy about it, either, but the pack is doing good, Jodi. They have four pups. They'll be all right."

"Six, actually, but that still doesn't make it legal or good. This is horrible. They are endangered! This is beyond illegal."

"Six? That's even better, then."

"How the hell did you end up with these people?" Jodi felt unbelievably betrayed, and he knew it.

"It's a very long story. But let's just say I owe the governor some favors, and she cashed them in today."

"You led them to Amadeus," said Jodi, her eyes filling with tears. "After all these years of him trusting you. Of you looking out for him."

Jodi saw tears in her uncle's eyes and realized there was much more to this story than he was letting on. "Come by tomorrow, and I'll tell you more. I know this is disappointing. I feel awful about it. But if you want to survive in this job, you have to learn to cut some corners sometimes, for the greater good."

"How is more oil drilling the greater good?"

"New Mexico is a poor state. We need the jobs."

"And what if I give them a ticket?"

Atencio shook his head. "You don't want to do that. The governor likes to get her way. Things happen to people who don't let that happen."

"What kinds of things?"

"You don't want to find out. I should tell you, too, that the governor is talking about putting Jonas's new wife on the state's game board."

"What? Our governor wants to put the wife of a man who poaches *wolves* on the wildlife game commission board? I thought she was a Democrat!"

"One wolf, who was getting old anyway."

"Amadeus was eight! He had another four years, easy."

Atencio sighed. "What I learned over the years is that political parties don't mean a whole lot when money and power are involved. These elected leaders, they aren't like us. They need power. When someone has the money and power to get someone like that elected again, they do what they're asked."

"And you help, apparently."

"There would have been consequences if I didn't."

"Like?"

"We'll talk about it another time."

"This isn't happening," said Jodi, heartbroken.

"But on the other hand, if you just go back to your stakeout and pretend we were never here, you'll get on her good side, and that's worth a lot. It could mean more money for the department down the road, so you can do more to protect the rest of the wolves from the real poachers."

"I can't believe this."

"It's just the way it is," he said. "It's how it is in nature, and politics, and life. I'm sorry."

"Just go," she said, realizing that she was outnumbered. First, it was the Hispano sheriff who hated Mexicans and did not think he had anything in common with them. Now, the Democratic governor helping an oil magnate poach endangered animals. She'd thought she'd left the complications of the worst of America behind by coming back home. Apparently not. She'd have to deal with all of this later. "I don't even want to look at you right now."

"Good call, hija. You want to tell me what this stakeout is about?"

"No," she said. "Not right now. Maybe someday."

She watched, in horror, as her uncle hobbled back to the truck, older than she'd ever seen him, and worse for the wear. He climbed in and allowed himself to be driven away by a man rich enough to kill an entire species and get away with it.

31

Lyle didn't love texting. He thought it was one of the worst things that had ever happened to human interactions, after headphones. Just one more way people pretended to connect but actually grew more distant from reality. But Jodi had asked him to text instead of call, because she was in the middle of the forest, in the middle of the night, listening for sounds of the terrorists who had her daughter. She was something else, for sure. Determined. But also hotheaded, at least at the moment. He understood this. He could not imagine what he might have done if some greasy pip-squeak like that Eric Parker had kidnapped one of his own half-Mexican daughters.

It was past midnight, and he had agreed to stay the night in Jodi's house, alone, in case one of the Zebulon Boys tried to come back for whatever reason. This was a risk for him personally, though he did not tell Jodi so, because the ranch owner, Jonas Sauer, had arrived the day before, with his newest former model wife. He'd be up at the ass crack of dawn, looking for Lyle to take him out to do whatever it was he thought cowboys did. Lyle had sent his boss an email letting him know he was needed on an urgent matter with a friend. He did not go into too much detail, and wouldn't. If there was one thing life had taught him, and especially a life as a military interrogator, it was to reveal as little about everything as you possibly could, to the vast majority of people, and especially to the people who thought they knew you but didn't. Old Jonas would have to figure out how to saddle a horse and thread a fly on his own.

Lyle was tired, but he sure as hell wasn't about to sleep. Not after last night. He didn't want to take the blame for it, but he had to wonder—if he hadn't been cuddling and drinking with Jodi, would she have been more alert to sounds in the house? Was she going to hold him responsible somehow? If Mila never came back again, would Jodi forever blame Lyle, at least viscerally, and despise him?

"Christ almighty," he mumbled, tired of the curveballs life kept tossing at him.

He sipped his coffee and tried to figure out what to text her back. He'd helped himself to some of the fancy ground piñon coffee in Jodi's cabinets and was about halfway through the ten-cup pot, all by himself. The Henley fellow had figured out what was wrong with the dog (she'd been given a whopping dose of melatonin and would continue to have heart arrhythmia and lack of consciousness until it worked its way out of her system), and after administering an IV of fluids, he'd taken Juana with him and gone back to wherever he lived and worked. Lyle liked the guy, but Henley had not seemed to warm to him at all. In time, he was sure they'd work it out.

You should come home and sleep in a real bed, Lyle typed, with thumbs that were too big and too calloused to strike the proper letter half the time.

Hell no, was her reply.

You won't be much good searching for her if you're half asleep, he texted, then thought better of it and deleted it. She wasn't the kind of woman who needed to be told what to do, or what was best. And he wasn't the kind of man to get in her way. Can I bring you anything? he typed out instead before hitting send.

No. Ashley's on her way here with burgers and energy drinks
Let me know what you need on this end, if anything, he typed.

Thanks, Lyle

He wanted to say all the things in his heart. To thank her for the best night he'd had in years. To tell her how sad and angry he was for her that these pathetic sons of bitches were out there. That he was afraid. Yeah. He wanted to tell her he was afraid she'd never forgive him, that he didn't know if his old worn-out heart could take another break in it. But he said none of it.

Yep, he texted instead.

32

By the time dawn broke Sunday morning, staining the eastern sky above the forest a pale-yellowish gray, Ashley and Jodi were running on whatever crazy energy it was that kicked in after pure exhaustion. They sat in Jodi's parked truck, Jodi in the driver's seat and Ashley riding shotgun, with the windows down, watching the clouds of their breath form in the cold air, trying not to think about how cold they were. Throughout the night, after Ashley's arrival at about two in the morning, they'd taken turns sitting vigil in the truck and warming up and resting a little in the living quarters at the front of Jodi's Cimarron horse trailer, which was like a small recreational vehicle, complete with a tiny kitchen and bathroom, living area, fold-out dining table, and platform bed that fit over the bed of the towing pickup.

Ashley had brought two blankets into the truck's cab from the trunk of her sheriff's cruiser, and Jodi had burned through all four emergency thermal blankets in her rescue kit. The car thermometer told them it was thirty-seven degrees out now, not an unusual temperature for a night in June up this high. Ashley had brought a large thermos of hot coffee with her, which they'd been rationing for the morning. She reached down by her feet now and pulled it onto her lap. Jodi watched as Ashley used her frozen hands to unscrew the cap, excited for the feeling of the warm brew in her throat and the kick of adrenaline from its caffeine. The younger officer poured the first cup into the lid of the thermos and handed it to Jodi.

"Thanks," Jodi whispered, surprised by the frogginess of her own voice.

"Be light enough to chase some tracks in a few minutes here," said Ashley, swigging directly from the thermos herself. "Weird as this sounds, being out here this early, in the cold like this, reminds me of when I was a little kid and used to go fly-fishing. We liked to get out on the river early, right at dawn. We'd be out there all day sometimes, till the sun went down."

"You still fish?" Jodi asked, trying to make conversation to keep her amygdala under control so it wouldn't spin off into worst-case scenarios. Nobody was of any use in a situation like this if they were all riled up on imagined horrors.

"I do," said Ashley.

"Well, once this is all over, we should head out to the river some morning," said Jodi.

Ashley smiled at her. "I'd like that. Haven't been in a while, not since my mom died, and my dad—well, he's not able to anymore."

"Brothers and sisters?"

Ashley shook her head. "Only child."

"Well, we're going to get through this, and then we'll hit the river, get some trout."

"Sounds perfect," said the deputy.

"Gotta check on the horses," said Jodi. They'd slept in their manger portion of the trailer, standing up as horses often did. The trailer was high end, one of the few big expenses Jodi had allowed herself to make with Graham's life insurance money, and comfortable, with rubber floors and walls and some padding between the stalls. Jodi had run the heater for a few minutes at the start of the night in there, then turned it off. Horses were most comfortable at between fifty and sixty degrees Fahrenheit, and with two of them in there, the body heat they generated would have kept them in that zone without too much help.

Jodi got out, stretched her legs, and went around the back of the trailer to lower the ladder. She climbed to the roof of the trailer, where several bales of hay were stored. She tossed one of them down and broke it up to put into their feed buckets. While they ate, she did her morning needs in the living compartment, splashed some water on her face, and focused on putting her fear for Mila out of her mind enough to stay calm and find her.

"You know," she said as she came around to Ashley's side of the truck, "I didn't even ask you if you knew how to ride a horse. We're going to need them out here, I'm thinking."

Ashley smiled. "I'm a 4-H kid," she said. "We had horses growing up."

"Well, good."

Together, they saddled up the horses with the equipment hanging in the tack room portion of the trailer.

"This is Frida," Jodi told Ashley, "and this is Diego."

Frida was a sorrel-brown quarter horse who, like the painter Jodi'd named her after, could be a little self-absorbed. Her boyfriend, Diego, was a chunky dun quarter horse who, like his namesake, was never satisfied with just one mare.

"Like the painters?" Ashley asked, with a grin.

"Yep. Frida's probably going to be a little easier for you," said Jodi. "Diego's finicky, but he knows me."

This was when a rustling sound broke the near silence of the forest. Jodi heard it first and instinctively froze. Ashley was about to say something, but Jodi silenced her by putting a finger to her own lips. Ashley immediately went on alert too. The rustling became a rhythmic crunching, a crashing sound of something, or someone, running through the woods. The noise was growing louder, indicating that whatever it was, was headed toward them.

Jodi and Ashley moved as one to the side of the trailers away from the sound. Jodi pointed to either end of the truck and trailer rig, indicating that they should each take cover at opposite ends. Ashley went to the front, while Jodi stayed in the back with the horses, which trusted her. Both women drew their duty weapons, and crouched, and waited.

Crunch, crunch. Crunch, crunch. From the sounds of the gait, this was a human being. Two feet.

"No, no, no," came the sound of a woman's voice. "God help me. God help me."

Jodi and Ashley both heard it and exchanged a look of surprise.

"God help me!" came the voice, even closer now.

And then, the sound of the footfalls stopped.

"Shit, shit, shit," said the woman's voice, very close now, almost in a whisper. Jodi peered around the corner of the trailer and almost immediately made eye contact with a naked young woman, standing on the other side of the logging road, just at the edge of the woods, bleeding from her head and, it seemed, her legs and feet, covered in dirt. Her long, dark hair was matted and streaked across her face, and her eyes were wild with fear. Upon spotting Jodi, she became frightened even more and began to back into the woods again.

"Hey," said Jodi, coming out into the open now. "It's okay. We're not going to hurt you."

"Are you with them?" the young woman asked. "Are you one of them?"

"I'm Officer Jodi Luna, and this is Deputy Ashley Romero. We aren't with them. We are here to help you."

The woman seemed to weigh her options and did not want to trust them.

"It's okay," said Ashley. "You're safe now. Come on. Let's get you somewhere safe."

This statement lost some of its weight, however, when the sound of a gun being fired rang out somewhere behind the young woman. The noise seemed to frighten her more than Jodi and Ashley did, and she ran toward Ashley, screaming.

"You see?" screamed the young woman. "That's them! They're fucking crazy! They're hunting me. Like I'm a fucking animal. I have to hide."

"Take her inside the trailer," said Jodi to Ashley. "I have some extra clothes in there, in the drawer by the bathroom. I'll stand guard."

Jodi took cover once again and tried to calm the horses, who were stamping and whinnying, fully saddled, in their stalls. The forest grew quiet, and then Jodi heard a man's voice off in the distance call out, "Retreat!"

33

From the sounds of things, the males had left the camp, to hunt Paola, whatever that meant, and they'd left only the woman, who Mila now knew was called Marjorie, to watch over the camp. Even her disgusting boyfriend, Levi, was gone. The General had barked orders at this woman to "make yourself useful and get this place spick and span, and have dinner ready for us by the time we get back later." This meant now was the time for Mila to get herself and the other women out of the hole.

Using the stick as she had before, Mila dug handholds into the cold, wet earthen walls of their dungeon. Though she was able to grip them and scale the side all the way to the top, it was only due to her many years of rock climbing and her finger strength. The other two were unable. Altagracia had been in this prison for too long and was starving, weak with hunger, and sick from being kept in this filth. The other, Ana Luz, was not as weak as Altagracia, but she was very, very pregnant and had a sprained ankle.

"Listen," Mila whispered to them. "I'm going to go out there and deal with Marjorie. And then, if I can, I'll come back for you. We have just a few hours. We're going to have to find a way out of here."

"God bless you," said Altagracia.

"Thank you," said Ana Luz.

"Just sit tight. This nightmare is almost over. Okay?" Mila smiled to reassure them, just as she'd had to encourage her mother to keep going after her dad died. Tío Oscar had told Mila she had a special gift for healing people, and she had never known what he meant, exactly, until right now. She had an ability to stay calm and to help other people to feel like things were going to be fine. This was because, deep down, Mila truly believed it. She believed in herself, and in her ability to overcome anything life could throw at her. Including Marjorie.

As quietly as she could, with the earth crumbling and falling under her weight, Mila dug her fingers and toes into the earth and climbed her way out. When she got to the top, she had to figure out a way to hang on while also pushing enough of the branches and other debris out of the way so that she could pull herself completely out of the hole. This was harder than she'd expected, and twice she fell back into the hole while trying. Each time she waited, in silence, to see if Marjorie had heard anything. If she had, she wasn't doing anything about it.

Finally, on the third try, Mila was able to squeeze herself through a small opening in the mess of branches atop the pit. She stayed low, on her belly, and had deliberately chosen to emerge from the side of the hole farthest from the part of camp where Marjorie was the most likely to be. The light was blinding for a moment, but her eyes quickly adjusted. Her pink pajamas were so encrusted with dirt at this point that they seemed completely brown, and they served as good camouflage. She did not see Marjorie anywhere and slowly, cautiously stood up before taking cover behind the nearest tree. There, she found a large stone and a small but solid and hefty fallen branch. She took these up as weapons. There she stood, listening. She heard nothing.

Mila tiptoed toward the camp, hoping to find something she could put on her feet. Even men's shoes ten sizes too big would be better than running barefoot through this forest, which, like the rest of New Mexico, was no stranger to cacti and stickers, sharp rocks and sticks. The campfire was still warm from that morning's breakfast, and judging from the sun's position in the sky, Mila figured it to be somewhere around eight or nine in the morning. There were three tents set up. Mila went to the closest one, slightly larger than the others, and, stick and rock ready, quietly peeked her head in. There was no one inside it, just a cot, with a sleeping bag neatly rolled up at one end, a folding chair, a camping lantern, some boxes lined up in a straight row, and a green army-type duffel bag, with clothes folded and stacked with precision inside. From this stash Mila took two pairs of socks, a long john shirt, and, to her excitement, a sharp hunting knife, found at the bottom of the bag in a holder. She found a belt, which barely stayed on her when set to the slimmest hole, and slid the knife into it. She found a baseball cap and tucked her hair up into it, then tightened the strap in the back. To her delight, she also found a long coil of rope, which she looped over one shoulder. She could try to lower this to the other women. They would not be strong enough to climb out, though, and she wouldn't be strong enough to pull them. There had to be another way. She was done with this tent and padded toward the opening. No shoes, and no gun, but this was better than nothing.

Treading as lightly as possible, Mila left the tent and checked out the next one. Two cots, no people, messier than the previous tent. She found a box of granola bars and a couple of bottles of Mountain Dew hidden under a pile of dirty clothes. Ravenous, she tore into the bars and downed one bottle of the soda as quietly and quickly as she could. No guns. A pair of combat boots, but they were much, much too big and would not be helpful. She left them on the ground but did shimmy into a too-big Carhartt jacket.

There was one tent left. Mila went to this one and, knife drawn, carefully peeked inside, thinking that if Marjorie was anywhere, it would be here. Sure enough, there was an ugly woman inside, sound asleep in a sleeping bag on the ground, faceup. Mila wasted no time at all. She dropped the coil of rope by the door, lunged across the tent, and straddled this hideous person, pinning her down tight, and held the knife to her throat as her eyes popped open in surprise.

"Don't fucking move," said Mila.

"What is this?"

"Don't talk either. There's no one here to help you."

Marjorie didn't listen. She resisted, calling Mila's bluff, and tried to push the girl off her. Mila was surprised by how strong the woman was, but she was undeterred.

"I told you," she said, driving her knee hard into Marjorie's sternum through the sleeping bag, knocking all the wind out of her. "Don't. Fucking. Move."

Marjorie went limp, gasping for air, and Mila used this moment to slam her elbow across the woman's face a couple of times, for good measure. Something in the back of her mind told her she should just kill this person. That this person had killed others, and would kill her in a heartbeat if given the chance. But Mila did not want to take anyone's life. Not unless she had absolutely no choice.

"Take your hands out of the bag, slowly, and don't try anything," said Mila.

This was when she saw Marjorie look toward a plastic bag pushed up against the wall of the tent, about arm's length away. No sooner had she seen Marjorie look at it than the woman slid one hand from the sleeping bag and made a desperate grab for the bag. Mila sprang into action by kneeing Marjorie in the head to stop her. She stabbed the hunting knife straight through the woman's hand, pinning it to the ground, then grabbed the bag herself.

Inside, as Marjorie screamed and writhed in pain, Mila found a pistol and ammunition.

"Well, well, well," said Mila. "What did you plan to do with this, Marjorie?"

"Screw you," said the woman.

Mila pulled the knife out of Marjorie's hand and backed away from her, loading the gun. She was quick at this and almost immediately had it pointed at her foe, who was now sitting up, wailing, gripping her damaged and bleeding hand with the other.

"Shouldn't have moved," said Mila. "I am asking that you listen to me this time. Don't move. Do we have a deal, Marjorie?"

Marjorie watched her hand bleeding, like she couldn't believe what was happening, then started talking to Mila like she was a human being. Begging. "Please, just help me," she said. "I'm going to bleed out."

"You're not going to bleed out." Mila went to the coil of rope and, keeping a wary eye on the agonized Marjorie, sawed a piece of it off, about two feet in length. She used this to bind the woman's wrists together. Then she unzipped the sleeping bag and did the same with her ankles. She found a suitcase with some clothes in it and used a pair of Marjorie's underwear and a bra to wrap the wounded hand, then to tourniquet it at the wrist.

"Do you want to get to a hospital?" she asked, and Marjorie nodded, desperate. "Then I am going to need two things from you. Three, actually."

"What's that."

"One, I need you to tell me how to get out of here. Two, I need your shoes. And three, I need your phone."

"I don't have a phone."

"Bullshit," said Mila.

"I don't! The General doesn't let us."

"If I find out you're lying to me, Marjorie, I will not be happy. And I am going to ransack this tent before I leave. I will find your phone."

"Fine!" screamed Marjorie. "There. In that purse."

"Thank you." Mila found the phone in the purse and stuffed it into the pocket of the jacket she was wearing.

"God, this hurts," said Marjorie.

"Not as much as having your ear completely cut off, I bet," said Mila. "Now, tell me how to get out of here."

"That I honestly do not know," said the woman, and Mila could tell she was probably being truthful. "They met us at the watchtower and brought us here blindfolded, for safety."

"Where's the orange stretcher board you freaks use to get people out of that hole?"

"I don't know. The General keeps it in the truck, I think."

"Where's the truck and the General?"

"Hunting."

"Hunting Paola. A person."

"A Mexican," she spat. "Who came to take what wasn't hers."

Mila laughed and, in anger, came closer and stuck the gun right in Marjorie's face. "How did you get this stupid?" she asked. "Paola is Apache. Her family has been on this same land for twenty thousand years, probably. Your people came and took it, by force. And you think she's trying to take something from you? Where do you get off, alien?"

"Well, she looks Mexican."

"You can't look a nationality, you moron," said Mila. "Everyone on telenovelas looks like you. Well, except pretty. Is there anything else I can use to help get those women out?"

Marjorie nodded. "There's a rope ladder, under the stump."

"Where's the stump?"

"By the hole."

"All right. Get up. You'll show me where it is."

"I can't walk with my ankles tied, dumbass."

"Try again."

"Sorry. I can't walk with my ankles tied, miss."

"Then I guess you'll have to hop like a bunny," said Mila as she found a pair of sparkly bedazzled sneakers, all American flags and Jesus fish, and slipped them over her feet. A perfect match in size, if not in style. Mila was ready to run.

Twenty minutes later, Altagracia and Ana Luz were out of the hole, standing with Mila, who still had the gun trained on Marjorie.

"Okay, ladies," she said. "There's just one last thing to do before we go."

Mila grabbed Marjorie by the rope at her wrists and dragged her, hopping, to the edge of the hole.

"No, please, take me with you," Marjorie begged.

"No can do," said Mila. "But we'll send someone to get you, later."

"Please!"

Mila smiled as she pushed Marjorie over the edge and into the dungeon.

"Bye, Marjorie," she said. "See you around."

34

"She's the daughter of the president of the Muelles Apache Nation," said Ashley, finding Jodi a little ways down the road from the truck and trailer, looking for tire tracks in the dirt road.

"Really? What's her name?"

"Paola Chinana."

"Wow." The shock of realizing Kurt's kid—or Kurt's other kid—was here hit Jodi hard.

"She was one of what she said were four women or girls being held at a camp in the woods, by some bad people who for sure sound like the Zebulon Boys."

"Did she . . . ," Jodi began.

"She confirmed that Mila is there, at the camp."

"Oh God. How is she?"

"She said she was fine. Has both her ears. And, you'll like this, was working on a way to climb out of the hole in the ground where they're being kept."

"Attagirl," said Jodi, feeling a sense of relief, however small it might have been, for the first time in many hours.

"I've called Paola's dad to come get her," said Ashley. "She gave me some very general directions about how to get to the base camp. South and west of here. She drew a map. It's not great, but it's better than nothing."

"This is good. We need to get up there, now."

"I agree. But I think we need to go up together. Right now, we need to wait with her until she's safe."

"I hate this," said Jodi.

"I know. It's agony. But from the sounds of it, they're busy right now trying to hunt this one down and won't do anything to Mila, for the time being. President Chinana is already headed this way, in a tribal police vehicle. It won't be much longer."

Jodi sighed, and Ashley put a comforting hand on her shoulder. "You'll get your daughter back, safe and sound, I promise."

"Thank you," said Jodi.

"Why don't you make sure the horses have everything we might need. You have panniers?"

"Yeah," said Jodi.

"Load 'em up. Make sure we have all the things. Flares, GPS, water. You know the drill."

"I'll do that," said Jodi, amazed by the confidence and composure of this younger officer. "Thanks, again. I'm glad you're helping with this."

"Well, I have my reasons too. Not entirely selfless."

"I hope you beat him," said Jodi.

"I will," said Ashley. "I'm going to head back into the trailer, to see how Paola's doing."

"Okay."

An hour later, Jodi was grazing the horses under the trees when the black Ford Expedition with the Muelles Apache Police logo in gold letters on its sides came crunching up the road. It had not reached a complete stop when the passenger front door flew open, and none other than Kurt Chinana burst from it, with much the same look on his face as Jodi had been wearing on hers for the past twenty-four hours.

"Where is she?" he demanded, evidently not yet recognizing Jodi and seeing only her uniform.

"In the trailer."

Kurt ran toward the trailer door before Jodi had time to assist him and had already opened it by the time Muelles Police Chief Vince

Coteen had gotten out of his vehicle. Jodi came to greet him. She started to fill him in, but he stopped her.

"Deputy Romero already told us on the way in," he said. "You should go now. I understand your own child might be out there."

"Thank you, Officer Coteen," she said.

"Hey, I'm a dad too. This is almost unbelievable."

Jodi found Paola in her father's arms on the little sofa inside the living quarters of the trailer. Ashley stood by, watching the happy reunion.

"I hate to rush you," said Jodi, "but Deputy Romero and I need to get this trailer locked up so we can try to find the rest of the women being held at the camp."

Kurt seemed to recognize something about Jodi's voice, and as he said, "Yes, of course, come on, sweetheart," to his daughter, he searched Jodi's face. She smiled, in a sad way, to let him know it was her and that these circumstances sucked.

"Jodi?"

"Hi, Kurt."

"Oh my God!" He stood up, with Paola, dressed in Jodi's sweats, leaning on him. He held one hand out, and Jodi took it to shake. "Did you—I mean. Wow. Oh, wow. Thank you. I had no idea. Last I heard you were in Boston?"

"Long story—I'll tell you another time. I'm just glad she's back safe."

"Thank you," said Kurt, again.

Jodi shut down, emotionally, as she did when there was just too much going on. She stepped out of the trailer and waited for everyone to get out. She avoided eye contact or interacting again with Kurt, because she was carrying more pain than she could handle. She locked the trailer and, more than ready, mounted Diego. Ashley followed suit with Frida, and, map in hand, panniers packed and ready for whatever they'd find out there, the women rode off into the trees in search of terrorists, and the women they intended to hurt.

35

The woman was so small, and so pregnant, so caked in filth and grime, that Jodi's heart lurched, horrified by the sight of her. They'd been riding for an hour when they found her, sitting alone at the base of a tree, staring up at the sky. If not for the swollen belly and breasts, Jodi would have sworn she was just a child, ten, maybe eleven years old. Maybe she was. Jesus. She remembered that Paola had described one of the other captive women as being "super pregnant" and knew this could be no other. The rage this produced in Jodi—that anyone would hurt someone this small, this fragile, this obviously in need of protection—made her furious.

She and Ashley were, about to bring their horses to a halt nearby when the pregnant girl looked at them and shook her head. She pointed toward her right, and when Jodi followed the line of her finger, she saw a man in full tactical gear and wearing a ski mask, trying to hide behind a different tree. Jodi jutted her chin toward the man at Ashley, who instantly grabbed her own rifle from where it was strapped over her shoulder, chambered it, and took aim at him. She took one shot, and he crumpled to the ground, grabbing his left knee. When he reached for the weapon he'd dropped as he fell, Ashley shot him again, in the hand.

"I'll get him," she said to Jodi. "You see about the girl."

Jodi appreciated that her younger but more experienced colleague was taking the lead on this. As she trotted her horse toward the girl at the tree, Jodi heard a third and then a fourth shot crack the air. When she turned to look, she saw that Ashley had killed the man after he'd tried to shoot her and, to her surprise, had also felled a second man who had come to his aid. Two less Nazis in the world, thought Jodi.

"Hello!" she called to the girl who now had both her hands and arms over her head, protectively. She tried to remember their names. "Altagracia? Ana Luz?"

"I'm Ana Luz," the girl said, clearly terrified.

"Hi. I'm Officer Jodi Luna. We are not going to hurt you. We are here to help."

The woman nodded with a bewildered look on her face.

"Are there any other men out there?" Jodi asked.

"Not here. But Altagracia's hurt. I am okay. Help her first," she said, pointing again to the woods. Jodi then noticed the second woman, lying on the ground with a wound and bleeding from the nose, mouth, and chest.

"Ashley!" Jodi called out, pointing. "There's a woman there, hurt!"

Ashley rode to the downed woman and jumped off her horse to help as Jodi got off hers to help Ana Luz.

"Please," said Ana Luz. "There's another girl back there. They have her. You have to help her."

"Do you know her name?" Jodi asked, feeling sick.

"Mila. Her name is Mila. Mila Luna. This is your daughter, yes?"

"Yes."

"She knew you'd come for her. She told us you would."

"Where is she?"

"She's the one who helped us escape. But they found us."

Jodi felt the world spin. "Who has her?"

"The one they call the General," the girl said. "And his stupid little Nazi army."

Jodi's pulse accelerated, and she felt herself grow extremely focused, the way only tremendous fear or rage can make you. "Where are they?"

"I don't know. They took her from us, at the river, down that way. I think she shot one of them, but I don't know."

"Ashley! I need you to help these two," Jodi called out to Deputy Romero. "Zeb has Mila. I'm going after them."

Jodi rode to where Ashley was just starting to help the badly injured woman up onto her horse.

"Catch," Jodi called out as she threw the truck's keys to her. "I have a feeling you'll be done before I am. Meet you back at the trailer in a bit."

"You shouldn't go after them alone," said Ashley.

"The only other choice is not going at all."

"Just help me get these two back, and then we'll go together."

"Sorry," said Jodi. "But I'm done waiting. I'm sure your mother would do the same for you. If you have a daughter of your own someday, you'll understand."

"This isn't how we do things," Ashley yelled as Jodi rode away.

"Sheriff's deputies might not work alone, but game wardens do!" Jodi called back. She spurred Diego toward the Rio Truchas, using a satellite GPS device. Her entire world had been reduced to a pinpoint of focus, and that focus was finding her daughter.

36

The creeps didn't know about the knife. When Mila had realized the gun she'd borrowed from Marjorie was out of bullets and that the phone she'd taken from her was actually dead as a snail shell, and when she'd seen the General and Travis descending upon her at the river, where she was waiting right out in the open for them as a decoy to give the other two women time to run—as much as they could, given that Ana Luz was limping and about to pop—she had thrown the holster in the river and stuffed the knife into the right sleeve of the men's long john shirt she was wearing.

"Okay, gentlemen," she said. She lifted her hands over her head in surrender and threw the gun down with her left hand, with great flourish so they could see. "I got no more bullets. I'm screwed. I give up!"

"Let me shoot her," growled Travis as they came nearer.

"No," said the General. "We need her to get to her mother."

"C'mon!" whined Travis.

"Put your gun away," said the General. "I'll let you shoot one of the other ones. Not the pregnant one. She's mine. The other one."

"Fine." Travis sounded whiny, like a little kid who hasn't gotten his way. Mila couldn't believe someone would be that disgusting, to be disappointed he wasn't going to be the guy who killed a pregnant woman. Fuck this guy, she thought, and for the first time since she'd been kidnapped, she felt herself really and truly afraid. For the first time, it hit her that she actually might not make it out of this situation alive. She realized she would have to do whatever was necessary to save herself. This was terrifying.

As they came up to her, Travis was on her right. Mila pretended to be injured and out of breath, too tired, almost, to stand. And then, when they least expected it, she took the knife and plunged it into Travis's throat, sawing it across his neck with a force she had not realized she had. It had a disgusting feeling up the hilt of the knife as it hit the cartilage of his windpipe. But it was his life or hers. After slicing through everything she could, she pulled the knife out. As the General took a few seconds to come to grips with the jarring change in events, Mila ran. Within moments, gunshots rang out as one of the freaks tried to stop her. She did not turn around to look and did not need to see him to know that Travis was a dead man. Instead, she began to bob and weave through the woods to make herself a moving target and harder to hit. She heard the sound of feet running through the leaves as the General took off after her, and strangely, she heard him laughing. He liked this. If the laughing man was the least bit upset about the loss of his buddy, whooping it up was a very strange way to show it. Total psychopaths.

And then, the unthinkable happened. Mila heard the shot ring out and then felt it pierce the flesh of her right calf. It was more of a thing she heard inside her body before she actually felt it. A hot, screaming noise in her muscle. She was unable to put weight on the leg at all now, and when she tried, she simply crumpled down to the forest floor. She tried to think of a way out. Crawl. She could crawl. She began to do this, hands and knees on leaves and pine needles. But the sound of the General's feet stomping through the detritus only got stronger. She would never be able to crawl fast enough. Climb? Could she climb a tree? No. This was an absurd thought. Rocks? Sticks? What did she have to throw at him? And the knife. If he got close enough and had not shot her by then, she could use that. Mila's mind flowed a million miles a minute as the General quickly closed in.

To her surprise, the General did not shoot her again. Instead, he came to stand before her with an insane grin on his face.

"This is better than I thought it'd be," said the General, like a hungry man at a buffet.

"Is that so," she asked, deadpan.

"You're good," he said. "A feisty opponent is always better hunting than one that just runs and cries."

"Whatever you say."

He laughed, clearly enjoying her refusal to show him any sign of fear.

"I was actually hoping to just graze the leg," he said. "Because now you can't run, and it's not as fun anymore."

"You must be very disappointed in yourself," said Mila. She ripped a strip off the thin pajama shirt and used it to wrap a tourniquet around her leg, just below the knee. "I know I, for one, am super disappointed in you."

He laughed again and took his phone out to take some photos of her. "Your mom is going to love this," he said.

Mila noticed something moving behind the General now and, to her intense surprise and joy, saw that it was her mother, Jodi, in the near distance. She got off Diego and tied the horse to a tree, with a finger to her lips to keep Mila quiet. Mila averted her eyes and tried to adjust her face into an absence of expression.

"What should we do with you now?" asked the General.

"Well," said Mila, stalling for time. "I mean, it's pretty clear that you can kill me whenever you want now. I'm trapped."

"True."

"So here's what I'd like."

He glared down at her in amusement.

"I'd like you to tell me why you do this. What's the philosophy behind your army? I mean, my dad was white, you know, so there's a part of me that might actually agree with you—don't know if you'd considered that. I could be an ally."

"Your dad, if he was white, was a filthy, disgusting race traitor," said the General.

"Oh, totally," said Mila, just to screw with this lunatic. "It's like you knew him."

The General scowled as if trying to figure out what she meant.

"I mean, I told him that, every day. Like, 'Dad, you are a stupid, filthy race traitor. Why couldn't you have just made me all white, like you? Now look at me. Just a pathetic mutt, with a much lessened tendency for skin cancer. Not fair.'"

From the corner of her eye, Mila saw her mom creeping up behind the General, who still seemed clueless she was there at all.

"Are you mocking me?" the General asked Mila.

"I would never do that."

"Is that sarcasm?"

"No. Absolutely not. My dad was the worst race traitor in the history of race traitors. Or maybe the best. I mean, he was really good at being a race traitor. I'm proof of that."

Mila turned her eyes to her mother now, in a way that caught the General's attention. He spun around, instantly suspicious, just in time for her mom to take a shooting stance and aim her sniper's rifle at him. He ducked and rolled out of the way just as she squeezed off a shot.

Like a coward, the General ran. Her mom sprinted to Mila's side and saw the leg. "Nice job on the tourniquet."

"I've had some practice today. Wait till you see the other guy."

Her mother scanned the forest, and Mila followed her gaze as she spotted the General, darting between two large pines, and took aim again. Again, she missed.

"Hold on to me, around my neck." Mila did, and her mother lifted her up, then ran as fast as she could back to the horse. "You're going to get on Diego," she told Mila. "And you're going to use the GPS in the right pannier, and you're going to ride back to the dot that I marked *Trailer.* You understand me?"

"I mean, yeah. You're speaking English, so." Humor was how Mila and her dad had always coped with pain, and her mom seemed to know and appreciate this, because she smiled at her.

"Deputy Romero is there. You tell her to get you and the other girls to a hospital. And then she needs to come back and meet me there."

"We can't leave you out here with that guy," said Mila.

"You can, and you will," said her mother as she lifted Mila onto the back of the horse. "I need to know I can trust you to trust me. That you're going to do what I just said."

"I promise."

"Good." Her mom untied the horse and, as Mila held on to the reins, slapped his rump and yelled, "Ya!"

Mila nearly fell from the horse in a daze of pain and frustration. But being Mila, she steadied herself right away and—knowing that her mother was right, that she did need to get some help for this leg, that she wouldn't be much use to her mom if she bled to death in the woods—fished around in the right pannier for the GPS. She found the pin her mother had mentioned and, terrified she might never see her mother again, rode like hell to get there.

37

In a dense grove of underbrush two hours later, Jodi finally caught up to the General. She spotted him on an overgrown deer path through some scrub juniper. He moved with speed and strength, like a large cat. She took aim with her rifle and fired.

And missed.

Alert to her presence now, he fired back, the shot from his pistol echoing through the forest. The bullet was close enough that Jodi heard it unzip the air near her head. She also heard the thump as it buried itself in the trunk of a large pine tree just behind her. Without her GPS, Jodi was no longer sure where she was. The sun was directly overhead now.

She caught a quick glimpse of the General as he scurried off the path, slippery as a snake but stupid, down a hill and into a ravine toward a little creek. If he'd known anything about the mountains, he'd have gone up. Jodi had the advantage now because she could see down into the ravine, but he'd have a harder time seeing up and behind the tree. Jodi crouched and ran for new cover behind a different tree. From there, she zeroed in on him again, aimed, and fired.

And missed. She was more exhausted than she'd realized.

"God damn it," she said as she watched him run for it now, away from her, along the edge of the creek. Fueled by pure adrenaline, she chased him down the hill and began to pursue him along the waterway. He fired off two more shots, over his shoulder, sloppy. They came nowhere near her this time. She liked how messy he was getting, how clueless he was revealing himself to be about the wilderness. Most of all, she liked the way he stopped firing because, if she'd been counting right, he had probably run out of ammunition. Jodi, meanwhile, had stuffed all her pockets with rounds before she got off the horse. She closed in until he was about fifty yards ahead of her, still bobbing and weaving, throwing a look over his shoulder every so often to see if she was still behind him. He looked tired. And afraid. It was a beautiful thing.

As Jodi closed in even closer, there were a couple of moments when she could have taken a clear shot at his head and been done with it. But that was not legal. Or desirable. She needed to find a way to get him secured, cuffed or tied down, and then she'd radio their coordinates to Ashley, and then someone could come help her bring him out of the woods to face justice. She could have shot him in the legs, brought him down, ended it now. But there was something that had been unleashed in her at seeing him standing over her daughter, toying with her before he would have killed her, that made Jodi want to drag this out a little longer. Knowing what she knew of this madman, she enjoyed seeing him run, seeing him afraid.

She wasn't quite ready to let up on that yet.

Jodi drove General Zeb deeper and deeper into the wilderness for several more hours. Now that he was out of ammunition and as lost as she was, now that it was just him against her, she could control the direction of where he went. Jodi finally recognized where she was when the small creek they'd been traveling down opened onto the flat, grassy valley near the wolf den. This meant they'd come a good fifteen miles.

The General did not seem to know what to do now that he was faced with a massive valley. If he kept to the cover of the trees alongside the creek, it would bring him right up to Jodi. If he went out into the open, he'd give her an even better shot at him. So he just stopped and stood there. Jodi stopped, too, and watched him.

After a few minutes he looked back at her as she walked toward him with her rifle on her shoulder, watching him in its scope. She had it all planned out how she'd arrest him now. How she knew where to tell Ashley to find them. But as he smiled at her, and flipped her off, and yelled out, as soon as she got close enough to hear him, that he had done certain things to her daughter that he knew would have broken any mother's heart, Jodi decided not to let that darkness stay hidden in her heart.

She didn't have to shoot him, probably. He might have just stopped his bullshit all on his own, if she read him his rights and slapped on the cuffs.

But there was no one here to know any of this. No witness but the forest. "No witness," the poachers loved to say, "no crime."

Jodi shot him anyway.

Once, in the left knee.

And it felt good.

38

Jodi traipsed in triumph toward the General. She saw a blossom of red seeping through his left camo-pant leg and stood over him as he rocked on the ground in agony, clutching his leg and whining like a child. His true name came to her, like a little information bubble popping open in her brain. Atticus Everett. No wonder he'd changed his name. And yes, this man was no general of any army, and Jodi would not validate his obsession with a Confederate colonel by using the pointless words he'd decided to drape over his insane hatred.

"Atticus, Atticus, Atticus," she said. She felt herself smiling like a crazy woman, high on her own rage and power. "I hate to say this, but I do believe you've brought this upon yourself, son."

His chest heaved as he sucked in breath after quick breath. He bared his teeth like some sort of cornered animal and squinted his dark eyes at her. Dark eyes that lacked the fire of intellect, dark hair cut in a military buzz, an otherwise pleasant, handsome face.

"I need water," he said. "I need a doctor."

"You'll be all right," she said, coming closer.

"You," he panted, scooting sideways, "are a dead woman." Jodi realized he was leaning to one side to get more stability as he raised his pistol and pointed it at her. As soon as the crack of his firearm discharging broke the air, the bullet entered Jodi's left side like a searing-hot arrow, right at the waist.

Stunned, she just stared down at the place she knew the bullet had entered her body. She saw the blood before she felt it. She watched it come and tried to rewind time in her mind, tried to figure out what to do. How had she been so stupid? Why had she assumed he'd run out of ammunition rather than considered he might have been hanging on to his last bullet—or was it his last? Nothing had prepared her for the possibility that he could still shoot at her. She was relieved, though, to realize that while the shot had not grazed her, exactly, it had only pierced skin, and maybe the thin layer of fat beneath it. This would not be a mortal wound, but it was going to prove debilitating enough to be goddamned inconvenient.

Jodi's brain went into some kind of a fugue state, and as the survival self—which was efficient and knew what to do—leaped into action, another self watched as though from a great distance. Jodi saw herself take aim with her own pistol at Atticus Everett's left hand, which still held his gun, and with a steadiness that surprised her, she watched as she shot him straight through the palm and wrist. The bullet hit his gun on the way in, and the small golden spark it created seemed to rise into the air in slow motion, like a Fourth of July sparkler's ember. She heard him howl in pain and watched as he curled in on himself, like a pill bug poked by a stick. Good. He would not be shooting anyone again.

To her horror, however, Atticus hoisted himself up onto his one good leg and began hopping down the hill, toward the valley. He was in good shape and able to cover a fair amount of ground this way, whereas Jodi was immobilized for the moment, trying to figure out how badly she was injured. He was getting away. Jodi knew she had to hurry up and figure out how to make herself whole enough to chase him.

She set her pistol down and unwrapped herself from the rifle strap. She removed her jacket and then her work shirt. Grimacing against the pain, which now cut straight through her, she wrapped the shirt tight around her waist, like a belt, to apply pressure to the wound. She put the jacket back on, thinking that she'd probably need it if she was still out here after night fell, and she reminded herself that the ammunition for her weapons was still in those pockets, as was her satellite phone.

She rehung the rifle over her shoulder, wincing and cursing, and then picked up the pistol.

"You should not have done that," she told him, though he could hear nothing. She saw him, fifty yards from her now, hopping like mad along the scrub brush at the edge of the meadow. Jodi's mouth was dry. It felt stuffed with denim. She'd not thought to bring her canteen—only the whiskey flask that she'd stuffed into the side cargo pocket when she left the house. She had not brought a first aid kit. She had left everything with Mila and Diego. She had not planned any of this at all. And yet, here she was. She could call for help. But she was not quite ready yet, because she had not decided what she wanted to do with this man. She could have picked him off from here, shot him. But that was what he would have done.

As Jodi stood there, cringing in pain and trying to decide what to do with this terrorist, the universe decided for her. He let out a sharp, loud cry and fell to the ground. He folded in over himself and curled into a fetal position, wailing. Jodi began to hobble toward him, focused against her pain, to see what had happened.

Several minutes later, she was close enough to see that he had stepped into a leghold trap, one of the larger variety, designed to capture bears or wolves. It looked very similar to the others she had confiscated at Lyle's place.

"Please," said Atticus Everett now, scooting pathetically away from her, an inch at a time. He couldn't get far, due to the chain to which the trap was attached. "Get this off me."

Jodi came and stood next to him now. Close enough to smell his blood, and urine. She kicked his gun out of his reach. He watched it go, looking panicked.

"Please, take this off. It's breaking the bone."

He wasn't such a big shot now, was he?

"Give me one good reason to let you live," she said as she grabbed him by his hair and yanked his head so hard that he had no choice but to look her in the face as she stared down at him.

He steadied himself, and she saw the panic in his eyes shift to a frantic manipulativeness. "Because," he said, trying to sound like a nice and reasonable gentleman, "you're better than me. Look at you. You are a game warden, an officer of the law. A good mother. You respect the law. That's why."

"Oh, I see," she said. She released his hair and went to pick up his gun. She opened it up and saw that there was one bullet left. He'd been saving it to kill her at close range. "Now you're all about law and order?" She returned to him and searched his pockets. She removed a knife, and his phone, and kept them.

"I'm saying, you wouldn't be able to live with yourself if you killed me," he said. She detected a hint of panic in his words now. "I'm fine with killing people—done it many times. If this situation were reversed, I would definitely kill you. But you're better than me. You're a police officer. Killing me won't correct me. I need rehabilitation, not death, and you know it."

"And what does the law say about self-defense?" she asked him. "Seeing as you're so well versed in the law, *Atticus.*"

The pain in Jodi's side had faded into the background again. She knew it was there, but it wasn't life threatening, and her survival mechanism allowed it to slip from her consciousness, at least for the moment.

"Yes, yes," he said. "I understand. And I need you to understand that from my perspective, from our perspective as an army, that's all we're doing too. We are defending ourselves. Our land. Our heritage."

"From pregnant girls who weigh less than my dog?" she asked. "My dog whom you poisoned? Tell me again why I shouldn't kill you right here and now, for what you did to my dog alone."

"A man's life is not worth a dog's."

Jodi reached into her pocket and took out the satellite phone. But as she was about to call Becky, to radio for backup in arresting this man, she saw the lone alpha female from the wolf pack leaving the den, across the meadow, without her mate. She saw two of the younger pups standing at the entrance to the den, watching her. She remembered her uncle, and the governor, and the rich landowning oilman whose wife was now going to be on the commission deciding the fate of the very animals her husband had poached. Is there any justice to be found in a world like that for a man like this? she wondered.

The clock on the phone said it was five in the afternoon. Jodi would be able to walk, even with this injury, to the Lower Fresita Hot Springs trailhead in two, maybe three hours, if she left now. She could also trace her way back to the trailer by sundown, though she was less sure of the route and might not have the energy or stamina to make it that far. She could drink creek water, but that might bring its own set of problems without a sterilizer. In any of those scenarios, there was a good chance that, if she didn't call for help, this man could bleed to death or, perhaps, be eaten by wolves. What he would not be doing, without a tremendous amount of help, was getting out of that meadow alive. He would never leave this mountain unless she wanted him to.

Jodi moved a few feet away and sat down, cross-legged, to watch this man writhe in pain. She wondered why she didn't feel worse for him. She felt nothing at all. Maybe even a little thrill of pleasure at seeing him twist in agony. Maybe she would feel worse about this, eventually. Maybe she was just numb, and tired. Maybe she, too, was a master. She just didn't know. She didn't care. Some people brought misery upon themselves through the choices they'd made, and he was one of them. She grabbed his gun off the ground and put it in her pocket.

"You set that trap, Atticus?"

"What? No."

"You're lying. I confiscated a few others around here. They had your logo on them."

"If they did, that's not on me," he said, and Jodi realized it was pointless trying to get a man like this to tell the truth, even on what was probably his deathbed.

"So, Atticus," she said. "Here's what's going to happen. I am going to walk down off this mountain. When I get to the trailhead, close to it anyway, I am going to wait for the sun to go down. Then I'm going to use this last bullet of yours to shoot myself even worse, only nobody is going to know that. They're going to think you did it. Nothing fatal. But just enough to where me leaving you behind in this state, in order to get myself to safety, would make perfect sense to anyone looking at it from the outside."

"You'll send someone to help me after that, though?" he asked.

Jodi got up and went to him and handed him her flask of whiskey. "Maybe," she said. "But it is quite possible that in the trauma of my injuries, I am not going to be able to remember where you are. People might come out here looking for you once the sun comes up tomorrow."

"What's this?" he asked of the flask.

"Best whiskey a cop's salary can buy," Jodi said.

"Why?"

"You're going to need it. More than I will."

Almost as if on cue, the mother wolf let out a howl, calling her older offspring to join her in the evening's hunt. Jodi watched with a pleasure she was not entirely proud of as Atticus widened his eyes at the eerie sound of the pack howling to locate one another.

Jodi turned toward the plateau now and began moving, with no shortage of pain, away from him, back toward the trail that would lead her, in a couple of hours, to the campsite where she had interviewed the van life couple.

"Hey!" screamed Atticus Everett. "Where are you going? You can't just leave me here!"

Jodi did not reply, because he knew very well that she could, and she had.

39

After meeting Becky and her wife at the entrance to the regional trauma hospital in Santa Fe to give them the keys to Jodi's truck, with the understanding that they would retrieve it and the horses and keep them at their property until Jodi got back home safely, Ashley was distracting herself from worrying about the missing game warden by eating entire fistfuls of potato chips in a waiting room. Her radio crackled to life at 9:34 p.m., and dispatcher Karina's voice came grating through with the following horrifying information—officer down, a game warden, waiting for help, in the care of an older couple with an RV at the campgrounds near the Lower Fresita Hot Springs trailhead. Ashley's blood ran cold.

Ashley felt responsible for Jodi being out there alone against the worst sort of monsters and wanted to answer the call herself, but she did not want to leave Mila here alone. She also knew that Jodi had not wanted to upset her brother, Oscar, with the news about Mila's kidnapping. The only person she could think of who might be happy to come and wait for Mila, and whom Ashley would trust implicitly, was Lyle Daggett. She called the main number to the ranch and was surprised when the ranch owner, rather than the manager, answered. This person, Jonas Sauer, told her that he didn't know "where the hell my ranch manager got off to," but he said he'd told Sauer he was helping a friend in town. Ashley asked for Daggett's cell number and, when Sauer said he wasn't comfortable giving out that information, pulled the cop card. He gave it to her.

Lyle picked up after one ring. "Yell-oh," he said. Ashley told him everything she knew and asked him if he would mind coming to the hospital to wait for Mila. She assured him that, from what she had seen, none of the members of the Zebulon Boys' camp in the San Isidro National Forest would be posing much of a problem. Three of the four men were dead; one, the ringleader, was injured, on the run somewhere in the forest; and the woman was in a pit in the ground at the camp and would be detained in the morning. Lyle agreed to lock up Jodi's house and come right away. Ashley shared this information with the nurses on duty and, full of chips and vinegar, sprinted to the parking lot, got into her cruiser, and sped off to help her new friend and distant colleague.

By the time she got to the campground, however, she realized she was far from the first one there. Gurule's cruiser was already there, as were three television news crews. Jodi, however, was gone, taken, a reporter told her, to the very same hospital she herself had just left. To her disgust and dismay, Gurule was grandstanding in the spotlight of a news camera. As she got closer, she heard him say, "This is an ongoing investigation, but what I can tell you is that the Rio Truchas County Sheriff's Department has been instrumental in bringing down this terrorist ring, and we will keep the public informed as more information comes to light."

Of course, she thought.

He had actively hampered the investigation, but now that the public knew enough about it to be horrified on behalf of the injured officer, he was going to step in to play the hero.

She hated him.

Ashley got back into her cruiser and called Lyle from the road. He told her that Mila had been released, with crutches, that there would likely be no lasting damage to her leg, and that he was taking her home. Ashley asked him to check to see if Jodi had arrived yet, and after a moment in which he seemed to mute the call by putting his hand over the mouthpiece, the way they did in the olden days, rather than pressing the mute button, he came back on the line with her to tell her what she had already overheard a hospital employee tell him.

"She's almost here and might need surgery."

"Crap," said Ashley. "Okay. You take Mila home, and I'll head back to the hospital to watch her."

"You might not need to do that," said Lyle. "Her brother just got here."

"How did he know she was there?" she asked.

"It's all over the news, Deputy," said Lyle.

"Well, how about the other women?"

"Ana Luz is apparently in labor as we speak, and Altagracia is in the intensive care unit. They don't know if she's going to make it. Mila said there's a woman in the hole in the ground still at the camp but that she's one of the bad guys."

"Thanks, Lyle," she said, and they ended the call. She'd call for a search and rescue crew to look for the camp in the morning. The woman would be fine until then, most likely.

Ashley drove aimlessly for a bit longer, not officially on the clock— in fact, officially on her day off. Then, realizing her dad was probably having some issues all alone at home, even though he had gamely assured her he was just fine multiple times over the past two days, she took a deep breath and headed back to the little house where she had been raised, on a lot of land on the outskirts of Hispaniola.

40

Jodi woke up the next morning in a pretty yet unfamiliar room, in a
very soft bed with far too many pillows. Spare, with dark wooden floors
and just a bed, dresser, and small writing desk next to a woodstove.
Cozy, homey, smelling of pine smoke. It took her a minute to remember
where she was, and how she'd gotten there. The abbey. Right. She was
in one of the small guest cottages at Oscar's abbey. It all came back to
her then. How she had not needed to shoot herself after all, because by
the time she got to the trailhead after walking so far with an injury in
her side (which was, it turned out, worse than she had initially realized),
she had passed out, for real, and been found by a sweet retired couple
from Las Cruces who were taking a weekend trip to the hot springs.
How she'd thought to toss the gun into the woods before she arrived
at the trailhead once she'd begun to suspect from her dizziness that she
might not make it back alive. How she had come to in the ambulance,
seeing the worried looks on the faces of the paramedics, who told her
to just hang on. How they'd given her something to help her with the
pain in the hospital, and it had knocked her out. How she had been
aware enough when she came to, again, to request to go home, after
she'd learned that she had been stitched up and would be fine after a
couple of weeks off. How it was Oscar holding her hand at her bedside,
how their parents were there, too, holding each other by the door. How
her mother even seemed able to drop her long-standing grudge, after all
these years, in the face of her only daughter's possible death in the line
of duty. The wheelchair her father had pushed to the exit, where Oscar

had pulled the Tipsy Monkmobile around to drive her away. How the media were there too. How funny it must have looked to see her leaving the hospital in that ridiculous vehicle. How her mother held her like she never wanted to let go, not quite willing to apologize in words, but how that embrace felt like the apology Jodi had been waiting for most of her life anyway.

She had fallen asleep again on the way to the abbey. It was her idea to go there instead of home, because she didn't want to wake Mila and cause more issues. Lyle had texted her, in a message with no fewer than six typos, that he would be staying one more night at her place, that she did not have to worry about Mila, that Mila was fine. Was going to be fine.

Jodi had difficulty sitting up. Her side hurt like fire. Oscar had left her phone charging on the nightstand, along with a glass of water, easily in reach, with a handwritten note to call him when she woke up so he could come check on her. This she did, and two minutes later, he had pulled the chair up from the writing table and, once again, held her hand at her bedside.

"What happened?" she asked.

"From what I understand of it, a neo-Nazi kidnapped my niece, and you didn't tell me. Then you and Deputy Romero went all vigilante and chased them down in the woods."

"Is Ashley okay? Is Mila okay?"

"Everyone's fine. Becky has your horses and your truck. Mila's here at the abbey, in another of the rooms. She asked for a beer for her efforts, and I said no. You'd be proud of me."

Jodi smiled.

Oscar continued, "The news said that Sheriff Gurule found three of the Zebulon Boys dead in the woods, two of them killed by law enforcement in a shoot-out, and the third with his throat cut by a hunting knife they traced to the leader of the terrorists. They think he turned on his own man for some reason. The fifth one, Eric Parker, is thought to be in hiding in Mexico, where local law enforcement say they're looking for him. There was a lady in the terrorist group. They found her alive at the camp; news says Mila put her in the hole in the ground where they'd kept the girls."

"And the leader?" Jodi asked, both eager and afraid of what she might find out.

"Missing," said Oscar. "They're still looking for him. News said you told the paramedics he was the guy who shot you."

"Did I?" she asked, wondering, with a shock of fear, what else she might have revealed under the influence of the very strong pain medications they'd given her.

"That's what they're saying. But I don't believe anything I hear on the news. But if he shot my sister, I hope you shot him back."

Jodi smiled awkwardly, not prepared to tell him or anyone the truth about what had happened out there, and he, knowing her well enough to probably have read her mind, let it be.

"What about my things?" she asked, thinking of Atticus's cell phone and knife.

"All your stuff is in a plastic bag in the top drawer of the dresser," said Oscar. If he had any idea some of those things did not belong to her, he did not let on. "Are you hungry at all?" he asked. She wasn't. She still felt a bit nauseated and exhausted from the ordeal. Oscar agreed that it was fine if she didn't want to eat, but he insisted that she drink the bottles of ice-blue Gatorade he had brought for her. It was her favorite flavor.

"You remembered," she said.

"I have been so worried," he told her. "I didn't sleep all night."

"I'm okay. You need to rest."

"I will. Brother Gary said I could take the day off, and I think that as long as you're okay and don't need anything, I might take a nap for a while."

"That's fine," she said. "I think I need to get back home today, though. Lyle is very much doing more than his fair share out at my place right now."

"Yeah, I'll take you back after lunch, okay?"

"Okay." She noticed that he looked like he had something else to tell her. "What?" she asked. "What is it?"

"I mean, I have some news. I just don't know if this is the right time to tell you."

"Is it good news, or bad news?"

"Good."

"Then, yes. It is the right time to tell me," said Jodi.

"Okay." Oscar took a deep breath and grinned. "Are you sitting down?"

"Shut up. Say it."

"I can't shut up and say it. You'll have to pick one."

"Talk, jackass," she said, playfully slapping his arm.

"Ya, ya, okay, okay. I talked to my friend at Saint Gianna's."

Jodi perked up at this. "And?"

"They gave me the name and address of the family that adopted your son," he told her.

"Who are they? Where are they?"

"Weird enough, they live right here in Rio Truchas County. A Mr. and Mrs. Jorge Gabaldon, address in Hispaniola."

"Well, shit," she said.

"Yeah."

"Did you call them?"

He shook his head. "I thought that was something for you to do. I'll text you their information."

"Thank you, Oscar. For everything."

"No hay de qué. Just please, if you can, stop giving me heart attacks now. I can't take much more of this."

41

One week later, Jodi went back to work, against her doctor's orders to take exactly two weeks off. She left Mila at home with Oscar, with orders not to attempt to rappel down the side of the barn with one bad leg. Jodi felt fine, and the work needed to get done.

What she did not expect was to walk into the Fish and Wildlife district headquarters to check on the overnight calls, collect her mail, and indulge in another one of Catalina's famous breakfast burritos to find Becky, Catalina, Henley, Atencio, Ashley, and Vince Coteen, all waiting for her with balloons and a cake to welcome her back. Conspicuously absent, in spite of their invitation, according to Becky, were Sheriff Gurule and his wife, the dispatcher.

"Lyle said to tell you he's sorry he couldn't be here," Becky said. "But he had lots of catching up to do after so much time away from the ranch."

"It's seven in the morning," Jodi said, deflecting all the attention with self-deprecation. "Who eats cake at seven in the morning?"

"Her idea," said Catalina, poking Becky in the ribs.

"Baked it myself," said Becky.

"No, she didn't," said Catalina.

Everyone hugged her, and she hugged them back, and then they all had cake and coffee. Jodi noticed a large bouquet of white tulips, her favorite flower, on her desk and asked, "Which one of you did this?" No one there took credit, so she rummaged around in the arrangement until she found the card. As she read it, she could feel everyone watching her, just as eager as she was to know who it was from.

"Nobody you know," said Jodi as she stashed the card in one of her pockets. The flowers were from Kurt Chinana, of all people, who said he was sorry he couldn't be there for her welcome-back party, adding that he would be eternally grateful to her for saving his daughter's life. He had put his cell number in the note and asked her to call him.

She noticed that Henley, in particular, looked uncomfortable, and so she smiled to seem friendly.

"Um, Jodi?" he asked. "Can I talk to you for a second?"

"Sure," she said. "What's up?"

"In private," he said.

They went to the conference room at the end of the hall, and she closed the door behind them. "He's just a friend," she said, but the young wildlife veterinarian seemed surprised by this.

"I'm sorry. Who is?" He looked genuinely perplexed.

Jodi realized her mistake. "Oh God," she said. "Sorry. Is this about the—the flowers?"

"Your welcome-back flowers? No. Not at all."

"I'm an idiot."

"But now that you mention them, safe to say they're from Lyle?"

"Yeah."

"Cool. I mean, I was wondering. Because, you know. I thought— when we went to the wolf den, it just seemed like, I don't know."

"Like we had a little spark?" she asked.

"Something like that. So I was surprised to see him kiss you, because you told me, you know."

"That I wasn't seeing anyone."

"That."

"Well, I wasn't. Then. We just started."

"That same day."

"I mean, yeah."

"Okay, so I should say I'm happy for you, because that's what people do."

"But not because you are?"

"I don't honestly know how I feel about it. But that's not what I wanted to talk to you about."

"Okay." Jodi sat down, wincing only a little bit from the pain in her side.

"You all right?" Henley asked.

"Fine. It's just a little stitch. Go on. Tell me."

Henley sat too. "I went out to the wolf den yesterday, and the day before," he said. "And I only saw Virginia. I'm thinking something happened to Amadeus."

Jodi felt trapped. She wanted to tell him, so badly. She wanted to tell someone. Anyone. But she didn't want to put Henley in the crosshairs of the very powerful, very unethical people who were apparently running the state at the moment.

"Maybe he'll come back?" she offered, weakly.

"I don't think so. Because here's the thing. I think Virginia—now, stay with me here, because I know this sounds a little crazy, but—I think she might have known who did it and took revenge or something."

"What do you mean?"

"Well, I found some—what looked like bloody scraps of clothing. By the den."

Jodi looked at his eyes, and it seemed, at least to her, that Henley might have put two and two together, not about the poaching of Amadeus, but about Atticus being left to be eaten by wolves and, apparently, having had exactly that fate meet him.

"I'll head up and take a look around," she said.

"Stop by my place, if you have time. I collected what I could find. The scraps. Looked camo. And what might have been bullet casings."

Jodi let his eyes search hers, but only for a moment. She felt like he could read her mind. But if he knew, he was protecting her.

"I'll stop by. When would be a good time?"

"I'm headed there now. I'll be there all day. And evening."

"Okay. Thanks for the tips," she said.

"Be careful out there," he said, ominously.

"I mean, always," she said.

From there, the day was mercifully calm and very, very normal. Just checking fishing licenses, a couple of calls about raccoons getting in people's trash, a complaint about some elk getting over a fence and eating somebody's garden. It felt good to be working again, but she had a nagging fear that Atticus was still out there somewhere.

It was this fear that drove Jodi, at the end of the day, to make her way back up to Lower Fresita Hot Springs and, with Juana fully recovered by her side, to make the slow, painful hike back up to the spot where she had left the white supremacist terrorist. She did not know where he was, only that he wasn't there. And though Juana could sense that something had happened in this place, sniffing everything in sight, there was nothing a normal human could notice that was off.

From there, she found herself making a detour before going home, down to the town of Hispaniola, where she was now greeted as something of a hero everywhere she went. The news had reported about the plans, found by the sheriff's department at the terrorist group's base camp, to blow up several buildings in the town in just a few days' time. Gurule was basking in his undeserved glory, but Ashley had assured Jodi that she would be coming out with a statement of what had really happened, and of her joint announcement to run against her boss, and soon.

Jodi pulled up the address Oscar had sent her for the Gabaldon family and plugged it into her GPS. Off the clock now, but still in uniform and in her cruiser, she pulled up to the small adobe house. There was a truck in the driveway, and her heart beat faster as she thought that someone might actually be home.

Sure enough, after she'd rung the doorbell and knocked a few times, an older man, probably in his eighties, answered the door, seeming a bit confused.

"Hello?" he asked, narrowing his eyes against the light. "Is that the police?"

"Yes, hi, I'm Officer Jodi Luna, from New Mexico Fish and Wildlife. I'm looking for Mr. or Mrs. Gabaldon. Do they live here?"

"I'm Mr. Gabaldon," he said. "But my wife, bless her soul, is no longer with us."

"I'm sorry to hear that," said Jodi.

"What can I help you with? Would you like to come in?"

Jodi accepted the offer and soon found herself in a tidy living room, sitting on a chair across from Mr. Gabaldon, who shuffled to the sofa and took a seat.

"I don't know how to ask this, exactly," she said.

"Direct is always best. That's my motto," he said. She was surprised by how cheerful and kind he was. How trusting.

"Well, I'm not here on official business. This is personal." He waited patiently for her to go on. "When I was young, fourteen, actually, I got pregnant. My parents sent me away to Saint Gianna's School for Troubled Girls, at the time. They've dropped the 'for Troubled Girls' part now."

"A wonderful institution," he said. "We owe them quite a lot of gratitude. My wife and I."

"Yes, well, my brother is a priest, and he was able to access my records there. And even though they aren't supposed to tell the birth mothers about whatever happened to their babies, I—I didn't ever want to give him away, you see. And this has been a source of great pain for me over the years. And I guess I'm just hoping for some closure. They told us that you and your wife might have been the ones to adopt my son."

The old man's forehead bunched up, and he shook his head. "Baby boy, you say?"

"Yes."

"Are you sure it wasn't a girl?"

"I'm sure."

"Because my wife and I did adopt a baby from Saint Gianna's. We were never blessed with babies of our own, and we were much older when we finally decided that we were at a place in our lives where we had so much love and happiness that we just wanted to share it with a child in need. And that's how we got our Ashley."

Jodi's breath caught in her throat. "Ashley?"

"Yes. As a matter of fact, she's about to make a big announcement down at the courthouse. I told her I would watch it if they put it on the news tonight. But you can see her in person if you want to head over there. She's a police officer, like you are. A detective."

"Ashley Romero?" asked Jodi.

"Yes, that's her married name. She divorced him, but she kept the name because that's how she's known professionally."

"I'm sorry for taking up so much of your time," said Jodi. "There must have been some kind of a mix-up then, at the school, when they told my brother about you."

"No," said the old man, wagging a finger in the air. "I have problems with my short-term memory these days, you know. That's why Ashley moved back, to help me remember things. But I can remember things just fine from a long time ago. And now that you mention it, I remember hearing once, I don't remember who said it, but they said something about how sometimes the school would put the wrong sex on the birth certificate, in their own files, because they wanted to make sure the birth parents never tried to take the children away."

"Is that right?" Jodi felt a strange rush of adrenaline. Not exactly fear, and not exactly excitement. Just something.

"I don't know if that's true or not."

"Did they change the birthdays?" she asked.

"I don't know. When was your baby born?"

"December twelfth."

"Well, that's our Ashley's birthday too. It could be her."

"Wow."

"Well, I'll be," he said. Smiling ear to ear. "Wouldn't that be a blessing? My wife and I never agreed with the church policy on this. We thought it would be good for Ashley to know her birth family, if for no other reason than health problems, you know."

"This is amazing," said Jodi. "Has Ashley ever said anything about wanting to know her birth mother?"

"Yes, starting when she was little. She always wanted to know you, if it's you."

"We could do a blood test, if she'd be willing."

"She will, I'm sure. But I don't even need that, now that I really look at you. I mean, you do look a bit alike. You even move the same. And you both have the same job. It's rather uncanny."

"You know," said Jodi. "Thank you, again. I appreciate your time. I know your daughter, strangely enough. Quite well. And I actually would like to see the announcement. If you don't mind. And again, sorry for taking your time."

"It's going to start in ten minutes, so you better hurry. And don't be sorry. I like having visitors, and when you get to be my age, all your friends are in the ground."

Fifteen minutes later, Jodi stood off to one side of the front door to Hispaniola City Hall and watched as Deputy Ashley Romero took her place behind the podium before a small crowd consisting of four television news crews and a handful of other reporters or bloggers. Without getting into too much detail, she told them that she had new information about the current sheriff's possible involvement in aiding the Zebulon Boys and tampering with an ongoing investigation. She said she would be happy to share audio and video recordings to back this up, and she added that she was using this moment to announce her candidacy in the next sheriff's election.

"I had not considered running until I saw firsthand what kind of a corrupt leader we currently have," she said. "But now, I can no longer stay quiet."

Ashley produced a yard sign, with her smiling but still tough face on it and the slogan **A CLEAN SHERIFF FOR RIO TRUCHAS COUNTY**.

Jodi noticed as Ashley held the sign up for the cameras that she moved with similar fluidity and grace to Mila's, and she honestly couldn't believe she had not noticed this before. She noticed other commonalities too. Mila and Ashley both shared a sense of outrage at injustice but also a calm approach to it, a fearlessness in the face of danger. They were both also extremely capable and confident young women.

Jodi approached Ashley after all the questions had been asked and congratulated her. She felt extremely nervous, overjoyed, and scared and, to her surprise, began to cry. It was the first time she had cried in front of anyone other than Mila, for any reason other than Graham, in years.

"Hey, you okay?" Ashley asked. "It's been a terrible two weeks. I know how you feel. I mean, I don't. I don't want to say I know what it feels like to be shot. But I empathize."

"Wow, I do not know where that came from," said Jodi. "But yeah, I guess I'm just overwhelmed."

"You know, I have just the thing for that," said Ashley. "You got plans tomorrow morning?"

Jodi shook her head. "Taking the day off," she said.

"How about I swing by your place, just before dawn, and we go fishing, like we planned?"

Jodi nodded, thinking to herself that the river might be the best place in the world to break the news to the young deputy that she was her birth mother. But then Jodi realized that Ashley's adoptive father might break the news to her before Jodi did.

"We are definitely going fishing tomorrow," said Jodi. "In fact, I have a great stream right on my land. You'll love it. But I wonder, if you have a few minutes right now, whether maybe we could grab a beer and talk about a few things first?"

Ashley's face lit up. "Sure. Sounds good."

An hour later, Jodi sat across the same table by the fireplace at Goldie's where she and Ashley had sat to discuss work matters, each of them with a cold mug of beer. They also shared a basket of fresh-made tortilla chips and the "triple threat" sides of salsa, guacamole, and queso. The nice weather had brought everyone and their grandmother out to the restaurant, and Jodi felt self-conscious about being overheard. She leaned across the table and lowered her voice, though not so much that it couldn't still be heard over the din of patrons and the newest ranchera to blare from the jukebox.

"I don't know how to tell you this," said Jodi. "So I'm just going to say it."

Ashley looked concerned as she popped a chip into her mouth and, speaking past the food, said, "Just say it."

"I feel like Darth Vader," said Jodi.

Ashley's concern turned to confusion. "Sorry, what?"

"'Luke, I am your father,'" said Jodi, more to herself than to Ashley.

"You all right, Jodi?"

Jodi took a long, deep breath, and nodded. "Yes. I'm fine. I am also your biological mother."

Ashley was about to shovel another chip into her mouth but stopped short. The salsa fell off the chip onto the tabletop as her mouth hung open. "You're what?"

"I was fourteen, and I thought I was in love. What's even weirder is, you've met him."

"Hold on," said Ashley. "How did you know I was adopted?"

"Just hear me out," said Jodi. "The girl Paola, who you rescued? Her dad? Kurt Chinana? He was my boyfriend in middle school and freshman year of high school. Neither of us knew anything about anything. And we ended up making you. My parents are super-conservative Catholics, very old school, and they thought it would be best to send me to a place called Saint Gianna's School for Troubled Girls. They've dropped the 'for Troubled Girls' part now, and it's just Saint Gianna's School, but the basic goal of the school is the same—provide a safe place to live, and an education, for pregnant unwed teens and place their babies with adoptive families, all out of the public eye."

Ashley's face flamed red with the emotions she did not allow herself to show any other way.

"The school—they don't want the mothers to know anything about the babies. At least they didn't thirty years ago. I don't know how it is now. So I was unconscious when you were born. I didn't find out anything about you until my brother found out from the nun who used to run the show at Saint Gianna's. I went to see your dad earlier today. Your adoptive father, I mean. I had no idea it was you, though. They told us you were a boy."

"They did? Why?"

"I think they intentionally did that so the birth mothers would have a harder time tracking down their babies." Here, Jodi found her eyes filling with tears. "The thing is, I never wanted to give you up. They made me. My parents, the school. I told the school I wanted to keep you, but by then they said it was too late because we'd signed all the papers. I didn't know what I was signing back then. It has haunted me all my life. And I just wanted to tell you. I'm sorry. I have thought about you every day since you were born. You were wanted."

Ashley apologized, pushed herself away from the table, and stood up. "I need to get some air," she said. "This is—I didn't expect this. I'm sorry. I have to—I just . . ."

Jodi watched her long-lost biological daughter blink against the tears and push through the crowd to get to the front door. She considered chasing her, and begging for forgiveness, but figured that if Ashley wanted Jodi to be part of her life, she'd come back.

For the second time in her life, Jodi let her go.

42

Jodi had kept her first child a secret from her second child for a long time, and it was not as difficult as she worried it might be to just keep doing that.

After treating herself to one more beer, Jodi ordered take-out tacos, drove home, dismissed Oscar from babysitting Mila, and then settled in on the sofa with her youngest daughter to binge-watch the latest series Mila was enjoying. The drama of the past few weeks had made Mila act younger than her age. Jodi considered this a silver lining, because it had been at least three years since the girl had burrowed in to cuddle with her like this. Jodi wrapped Mila in her protective arms and relished the quietness of this normal moment. The terrible television show, the buttery microwave popcorn—all of it was just delicious and perfect and a blessing.

Somewhere around midnight, they agreed it was time for bed. Jodi turned off the TV and opted to leave the dishes until tomorrow. She offered to help Mila to her room and even to tuck her in, but the teen was getting around just fine with her crutches. They hugged for a long moment at the doorway to Mila's bedroom, and Jodi said, "I am so glad you're okay."

"Likewise," said Mila. "But it makes me nervous that guy is still out there."

Jodi nodded, but instinct told her there was nothing for either of them to worry about. She added the fate of Atticus to the list of secrets she was keeping from Mila and wished her a good night.

Jodi locked all the doors and windows, just in case, then took a shower, careful not to get the wound and its dressing too wet, before toweling off and shimmying carefully into a set of baggy blue pajamas. She crawled into bed, her head spinning with thoughts, and opted to calm her mind down in one of her favorite ways, by reading poetry, in this case a book by Marge Piercy. Jodi propped herself up with pillows, opened to a poem, and began to read by the soft lamplight. As she sometimes did, in her more woo-woo moments, she allowed the book to open itself, to the page it most wanted her to read. There it was, the poem "The Cat's Song." She read it aloud, to herself, softly, because poems often liked to inhabit not just the page but also the air.

> Mine, says the cat, putting out his paw of
>   darkness.
> My lover, my friend, my slave, my toy, says
> the cat making on your chest his gesture of
>   drawing
> milk from his mother's forgotten breasts.
>
> Let us walk in the woods, says the cat.
> I'll teach you to read the tabloid of scents,
> to fade into shadow, wait like a trap, to hunt.
> Now I lay this plump warm mouse on your mat.
>
> You feed me, I try to feed you, we are friends,
> says the cat, although I am more equal than you.
> Can you leap twenty times the height of your
>   body?
> Can you run up and down trees? Jump between
>   roofs?

Let us rub our bodies together and talk of touch.
My emotions are pure as salt crystals and as hard.
My lusts glow like my eyes. I sing to you in the
   mornings
walking round and round your bed and into your
   face.

Come I will teach you to dance as naturally
as falling asleep and waking and stretching long,
   long.
I speak greed with my paws and fear with my
   whiskers.
Envy lashes my tail. Love speaks me entire, a
   word

of fur. I will teach you to be still as an egg
and to slip like the ghost of wind through the
   grass.

When she finished reading, Jodi closed the book and turned off the light, to let what wanted to come to her next come. It did not take long. Absolute heartbreak. She had found her baby. She'd found her, and reached out to her, and the child, a woman, had run away. Jodi made no sound, but she allowed the tears to pulse from her eyes, down her cheeks, along her neck, and into the collar of her shirt.

In the next moments, their cries pierced the night. Wolves, on the hunt, ecstatic, for they'd found themselves a feast. This chorus of mournful wailing made her grateful for the safety of her home but also for the continued struggle to live, of everything that was still out there, in spite of humanity's best efforts to hate and hurt all that was beautiful and good. Jodi said a silent prayer of thanks—for the dark and wild spaces and the hungry, hunting, civilized beasts who still roamed this earth—and fell asleep.

Several hours later, just before six in the morning, Jodi was awakened by the sound of a fist rapping on the front door of her house. Outside, she heard Juana barking. It took her a moment to find her bearings and another moment to push from her mind any fear that it might be Atticus, returned to life, come to find her. Atticus would not knock, she told herself, as she pushed her legs off the side of the bed and stood. Her side still burned, but she ignored the pain and shrugged into her robe. She grabbed the small pistol from her nightstand and went to see who was making all that racket.

Jodi put her eye up to the fish-eye peephole in the front door and was surprised to find Ashley standing there wearing dark-gray fishing waders of the bib-overall variety, a Patagonia jacket, rubber wading boots, a pack vest, and a sun hat.

Jodi opened the door and said, "Ashley. Hi."

"Good morning," said Ashley. "Sorry if I woke you."

"No worries. What's up?"

"Sorry I didn't call first," said Ashley. "It felt—I didn't know what to say. It felt awkward, I guess."

"Come in," said Jodi. "Just, Mila's still asleep, so keep your voice down."

"Actually, I have doughnuts and coffee in my truck," said Ashley. "I thought we could just have those while I drove us to the river."

"You still want to fish?" asked Jodi.

"I mean . . . ," Ashley said, indicating her outfit.

"Okay. Did you park at the gate?"

Ashley nodded. "I don't know the combination to your lock, so."

"Okay. Give me five to get changed. You sure you don't want to come in?"

"I'm sure. I'll go wait for you by my car."

"It's your birthday," said Jodi.

"No, it's not," said Ashley, looking confused.

"The combination," said Jodi. "To my lock. It's your birthday. Open it, and come back in. Park alongside the house. I'll be right out. We don't have to drive anywhere, remember? I have a stream here."

"No, I know," said Ashley. "I just—I don't know. I didn't want to impose and take all your fish."

"That's ridiculous. My fish are your fish. Always have been. You just didn't know it."

Jodi saw tears sprout in the young deputy's eyes again and watched her palm them away.

"Be right back," said Jodi.

Ten minutes later, Jodi, dressed similarly to Ashley, walked by her oldest daughter's side, each of them with an almost identical tackle box and fishing rod, as the sun began to rise. It was cold enough that they could see the smoke of their breath.

"I didn't think you'd come," said Jodi.

"Likewise," said Ashley, and Jodi couldn't help herself. She laughed at the joke.

"You remind me of Mila," said Jodi. "I think smart-assery runs in this family."

They'd arrived at the creek, and the first rays of the sun ran themselves across the meadow, pouring golden light into the water. They could see several sleepy trout in the deeper water, waving like fat little submerged flags.

"Does she know about me?"

"Who, Mila?"

Ashley nodded as she bent down to wet the knot in her fly line before righting it.

"Not yet. I figure we can tell her over a trout dinner." Jodi began to prepare her rod too.

Ashley smiled, but she seemed sad and uncomfortable. Jodi didn't know what to say, so she didn't. She didn't say anything at all.

"Thirty years is a long time to keep a secret," said Ashley after a long silence.

"It is."

"I need to tell you something, Jodi."

"Sure. What's up?"

"When the sheriff's department did a search and rescue for that woman at the camp, some of us went to the meadow by Lower Fresita Springs. I was part of that group. Well, it was just me and one other guy, a volunteer firefighter. Looking for the General."

Jodi felt her blood run cold, but she tried not to show any emotion. "Oh?"

"I sent the other guy away when I found the man's boot," she said. "Told him we were done, then came back on my own, later, to look at the scene more carefully."

"What man's boot?" asked Jodi, trying to seem unconcerned as she cast out.

"The one that was still in the trap."

Jodi made eye contact with Ashley now, briefly, and, against her best efforts, flinched.

"I did that to protect . . ." Ashley paused here and looked away. "To protect whoever else might have known he was trapped. Literally."

"I see," said Jodi.

"There wasn't much left of him. The boot was empty. Wolves got inside it, I'd guess. I buried it anyway."

"I don't know why you're telling me all this," said Jodi.

"Because I also found this, nearby." Ashley reached into one of her vest pockets and produced the distinct, empty whiskey flask. "Dead Guy Whiskey? There's only one person I know of in the world who drinks this garbage. And there weren't any bottles of anything remotely like it at the camp."

"It's good whiskey," said Jodi. "I'm sure lots of people drink it."

"It is terrible whiskey," said Ashley.

"That's a matter of opinion."

"I sent that firefighter away because there are some secrets that are meant to be kept for a lifetime," said Ashley. "And some that are meant to be kept for only thirty years."

Jodi stood there, quiet, not sure what to do or say.

"I would have done the same thing," said Ashley. She stepped closer to Jodi and placed a comforting hand on her arm. "I mean, the guy tried to kill my half sister and my mother. Right?"

Jodi locked eyes with Ashley and realized she was safe with this woman. Her daughter. That she could trust her with anything. Even her life.

"Think maybe this spot is too narrow?" asked Jodi, changing the subject to the fishing. "Might have better luck if we head to that wider spot just up that way."

"I think you're right," said Ashley.

ABOUT THE AUTHOR

Alisa Lynn Valdés is an award-winning print and broadcast journalist and a former staff writer for both the *Los Angeles Times* and the *Boston Globe*. With more than one million books in print in eleven languages, she was included on *Time*'s list of the twenty-five most influential Hispanics and was a *Latina* woman of the year as well as an *Entertainment Weekly* breakout literary star. She is the author of many novels, including *Playing with Boys* and *The Husband Habit*. Alisa divides her time between New Mexico and Los Angeles.